Better To Have Loved

Emeline Rhys

Green Dragon Publishing

Table of Contents

Dedication
Prologue
Chapter One – The Grand House
Chapter Two – Dancing Partners
Chapter Three – Pints and Philosophy
Chapter Four – Sanctuary
Chapter Five – Psychedelia
Chapter Six – Another Beginning
Chapter Seven – Escape
Chapter Eight – A Star is Born
Chapter Nine – Origins
Chapter Ten – Full Circle
Epilogue
Past Storm and Fire - Preview
Thank You and Links
Other Books by This Author
Author's Note
About the Author

Dedication

I lovingly dedicate this book to my parents, without whom this story would never be written, indeed, I would never have happened. I love you both, dearly and forever. I also dedicate it to my husband and friends who have supported me throughout this journey.

Prologue

1974, Dearborn, Michigan

Kirsten knew she didn't have a father. She didn't think they were required.

Her best friend, Judy, didn't have one. Judy lived with her mother, brother, and grandmother, while Kirsten lived with her mother and grandparents. She didn't believe she lacked anything until she attended kindergarten. All her classmates had fathers. They might be more normal than she imagined.

She discovered fathers might be useful. They drove cars and worked jobs. Diane's father even built her a treehouse, something Kirsten always wanted. An apple tree grew in the backyard, perfect for a treehouse. Sometimes fathers yelled, but Kristen's grandfather already covered that. Still, she should get a father.

She wondered where she might get one.

CHAPTER ONE

The Grand House

February 16, 1967

Dear Katy,

It looks like fate has twisted my life's tail. I'm writing to you while on a flight to England. Yes, you read right, England! I'll be posting this from there, so you'll have seen it on the envelope. But why am I here, you ask? I shall tell you, sister dear.

The children I took care of moved here for the next several months, their mother transferred for specialized training in the Church. Now I'm taking care of Eileen's three children and Percy's two children. They're quite a passel—I feel like Maria Von Trapp on some days. And yes, I've taught them to sing My Favorite Things, at least passably well.

It felt like herding cats getting them all packed and settled into the plane. Can you believe all my belongings all fit into one enormous suitcase? I'm not much for gathering things anymore. Not after mom gave away all my baseball cards, anyhow. I don't know if I'll ever forgive her for that. I collected some valuable cards there, including a Roger Marin rookie card. Ah well, such is life!

I'll be in a town called East Grinstead, which is over an hour south of London. The name of the house is Saint Hill, a huge mansion built for some muckity-muck nobleman. Wish me luck! Perhaps I'll find myself a British boyfriend like you did. Have you two set a date yet? He sounds groovy. What sort of music does his band play? Does he have a day job, or is he all about the music?

You mentioned Larry got into trouble at school. Did you let him know I would beat him up if he dropped out? I should still be able to instill the fear of pain in our little brother.

Give Mom a hug for me and tell Dad I'm thinking of him.

Much love,
Julie

Juggling her large battered suitcase and her portfolio over her back, Julie trudged up the gravel driveway to the huge manor house. Her feet complained about the lengthy trip from the bus stop, and the portfolio kept catching the wind, threatening to make her into a kite's tail with each gust.

Saint Hill Manor certainly appeared palatial. Perhaps it qualified as a palace.

At least twenty windows showed on the façade. How many rooms did it have? Dozens of people shuffled in and out of the place, a beehive of activity.

"You! Girl! Have you checked in yet?" A gruff voice with a London accent called out above the din.

Julie turned around to find an older man with a fringe of white hair pointing a clipboard at her.

"I... no, I don't know where—"

"Over here, quickly now. What's your name?" He flipped through the pages, looking up when she didn't immediately supply him with information.

"Jensen. Julie Jensen. From Detroit." She put down her suitcase and portfolio while he searched for her name. The wind picked up, tossing her thick chestnut-brown curls into her face. With disgust, she pulled them out of her eyes and repaired the ponytail loosened by travel.

She glanced again at the grand house. Would he assign her to an upper room? Perhaps with a view across the extensive gardens? She beamed at the notion of waking up to such a view each morning.

"Aha! Found you. You're down in Hayward's Heath. Just a quarter mile down the path there. It used to be servants' quarters. Unit C. Next!" He dismissed her and looked to an Indian woman in a bright blue sari.

Blinking several times to hide her disillusionment, Julie grabbed her belongings and made her way to her new digs.

The disappointing row of attached cottages all looked the same. Sandy-colored stone with tin roofs, a depressingly small single window cut next to each door. She found the weathered 'C' plate on the third one and knocked.

After some shuffling inside and a muffled oath, the warped green door flung open. A small, round woman with brown hair looked her up and down.

"Yes? How can I help you?" Her clipped British accent sounded refined and not unkind.

"The guy at the table told me to report here. I mean, well—"

"Oh! You must be Julie! I'm Sheila. Come in, come in! Let me help you with your bag. Bloody hell! What have you got in here, rocks?" A swirl of activity with several grunts and shoves later, and Julie got her stuff into one of the small bedrooms.

The two bedrooms shared a tiny living area and kitchenette. Several paintings of the surrounding countryside and colorful rugs brightened the space. Sheila busied herself making tea and sandwiches while Julie plopped down on the overstuffed sofa.

Julie took a deep breath to calm her rising panic. She'd made it to her new place, her new job. Her travel, whether by plane, bus, or foot, had ended. Time to relax. Breathe in, breathe out. Repeat. Repeat.

Sheila came over with a perfectly English tea tray, complete with tiny sandwiches, lemon, cream, and scones. *How had she whipped all that up in just a few minutes?* It must be some strange English superpower.

"So, Julie, do tell me all about yourself. Where are you from?"

After taking a scone and slathering an indecent amount of butter on it, Julie took an appreciative bite and closed her eyes for a moment. Breakfast on the airplane had been hours ago, and not very tasty.

"I'm from Ohio, but my parents moved to Michigan after I turned fifteen, about eight years ago. Then I moved to Washington, D.C. about six months ago..." Trailing off, Julie fought against the memory of her ex-boyfriend, Jeffrey. She cleared her throat and continued. "I started taking care of some children for a woman who worked for the Church, and she got transferred. So, here I am, out of breath and grateful for these delicious treats." She grinned at Sheila, who smiled back, showing a gap in her front teeth.

"Well, that sounds like a great deal of exhausting travel, Julie! I'm Sheila, and I've been here for about a year. My son, Neil, is three. You'll meet him this afternoon, when he gets out of the crèche. His father stays over in the men's dorms. We're both teachers at the Church, giving seminars in advanced theology. The two of us met shortly after we joined. We're fortunate, as there's just the three of us here. David has to share with five other men!"

Looking around the small apartment—no, they call it a flat in England—she felt grateful for small mercies. Six adults in such small a space would have her running and screaming for the hills in no time.

"You can't get a place together? That must be very difficult."

"Oh, we might, but that costs more money than either of us make! We make do. There are hidden alcoves and paths in the woods if we want more privacy." Sheila winked and Julie's skin heated with embarrassment.

Julie scanned the room for a change of subject, and noticed no other doors. "Sheila, I need to use the... the powder room, but I don't see one. Where is it?"

"Powder room? Oh, dear, you mean the loo, don't you? The toilet is outside, three doors down to your right."

As much as she liked Sheila, Julie relished being out of the room. With two jobs, Julie kept busy. During the day, she took care of Eileen and Percy's five children. In the evenings, she worked on artwork for the Church brochures. They liked her work here, though being an American artist might have added foreign cachet.

Whenever someone discovered she came from America, they pummeled her with questions. Had she met Marilyn Monroe? Had she been to New York City? Did she know their cousin Bob, who lived somewhere in Indiana? Julie decided Brits didn't have a true grasp of how big America was, compared to their island country. People in Europe possessed more of a sense of community than Americans did, at least those Americans who lived in the city.

She must get used to certain things, like the tiny rooms, outdated plumbing, and the food. The food. Oh, yes, the food. They boiled everything for ten hours, which did not improve the flavor in the slightest, but Julie couldn't cook well enough to offer advice to the professionals. Not being close enough to walk to anything outside town and having no transportation meant she must accept the food offered.

The constant stream of people countered all those inconveniences. Some came for an hour, others came for a month. As the international headquarters for the Church, people came in from all over the world. Julie met people from Europe, Brazil, the USSR, Japan, Australia, even one man from Saudi Arabia. She couldn't imagine the tenets of this new religion gaining popularity in some of these countries, or in any country with a communist philosophy, but they must have influence.

She found no shortage of interesting men to talk or flirt with. The Church held frequent parties in the manor on the weekends. Some became large, formal events, sanctioned by the Church, with conferences, fundraisers, important guests, and strict rules. In addition, groups of friends met in one of the many large ballrooms for music, games, or chatting.

While not the bizarre world of Washington, D.C., this old palace had an interesting flavor to it. It combined old world charm and new world hope, as if changing this Regency building into a modern facility became a physical act of transformation for the community. It radiated out to spokes all over the world, drawing in the best and the brightest to this glowing center. *Well, "centre."* She needed to remember her British spelling.

Eileen and Percy took their kids on a trip to London. Julie wished them joy. She visited London just once and had no real wish to repeat the experience. The city seemed grimy, loud, and crowded. She wondered why her sister, Katy, harbored such a deep, abiding passion for the place. True, the shopping would be amazing, but Julie didn't crave accumulating things, so shopping became a chore. She often planned her shopping trips like a surgical strike. Go in, get what she needed, then escape. Julie much preferred the smaller, charming villages, with warm, cozy pubs for all to visit. She liked the picturesque country roads, with ivy-covered stone cottages and ruined castles to sketch. Julie preferred the rolling, gentle hills in the countryside, or the old growth forest, so lush and full of life. She imagined retiring in such a place.

Since she had the day off, Julie decided she'd do a little exploring. She'd had little time to wander around the rambling buildings.

The manor house itself warranted some attention. With thirty plus rooms, it would be a daunting prospect at first, but she stole time to wander.

Already familiar with the kitchen, the downstairs dorms, the teaching area, and the main ballrooms, Julie explored further. Rather than a hallway connecting all the rooms, the path rambled from room to room, with horribly tacky and ostentatious décor, to her simple, midwestern tastes. Cornices with gold gilt, huge oil paintings, and classical statuary in every corner. If she turned around too quickly, she would knock over thousands of pounds worth of intricate Rococo art.

Passing through the uncomfortable opulence, she began instead with the lower floors and underground areas, under even the servant's hall.

She brought a flashlight, or a "torch," using it to explore the dank storage rooms. After having read medieval fantasy novels as a child, she searched for hidden passages and false doors, but searched in vain. The house possessed a real dungeon, a hole used to store old files, but she'd been down there, retrieving records. No mystery remained.

Several hours later, with eyes tearing from the dust, Julie emerged from the lower caverns, as she deemed them. She decided she would have better luck on the opposite end of the spectrum, those rooms which had been the lord's chambers. No one lived there, but more of the church's documents lived in them. As those documents contained nothing confidential, they weren't locked up. She'd been in a couple times researching projects, finding old advertisements for inspiration.

She examined the geometric wooden carvings around the mantle of the immense fireplace, touching the edges of the mirror. The odd arabesque design seemed out of style with the other decorations. The art nouveau lines looked odd compared to the squared bits everywhere else, catching her attention. Vines with gigantic flowers lined the one edge of the mirror. She caressed them, perhaps harder than she intended to, and heard a click. Julie dropped her hand and glanced around, as if someone watched her. A cool breeze blew against her legs. She noticed a panel behind the fireplace swiveled out, revealing a dark passage.

I found one!

While breathing hard with both excitement and fear, she crouched, pushed past the empty fire grate and into the passage. She closed the panel most of the way. With sudden inspiration, she grabbed a book from a shelf and, apologizing to the book for using it in this abusive manner, wedged it to keep the panel from closing. With her escape route secured, she turned her flashlight into the passageway.

If the storage rooms seemed dank and dark, this passage felt even more so. Cobwebs and dust hung everywhere. The passage rose six feet tall and four feet wide. Shapes loomed along one wall, draped with a grimy white fabric. She peeked under one corner, finding several open grid crates with bottles inside.

A hidden stash of wine, perhaps? A rare vintage whisky?

The bottles looked gray with dust, but one crate had been left open and only half full. Julie lifted a bottle and wiped the label clean to read with the flashlight. It looked like whisky.

1934 Glen Grant. The year they bottled it? Julie knew next to nothing about whisky, except the Scots and Irish both produced it, and that it tasted better when aged, like wine. She peered at the crates, estimating they held about sixty bottles under the dust. A hidden treasure, of a sort. Did anyone even realize they existed?

After placing the bottle back in place, she arranged the cover to how she found it, but she couldn't hide her marks in the dust. She blew here and there, softening the marks, so it looked more random. She continued her explorations down the tunnel and around the bend.

Bits of old furniture lay here and there, many of them broken. A chair missing an arm, a table with three legs, a sideboard with one door on the casement. Someone must have moved them here, intended for future repairs, then forgotten. She dubbed it the Tunnel of Forgotten Furniture, grinning at her own silliness.

The tunnel floor angled down after Julie turned the corner, as the rough flagstones beneath her formed ledges, like shallow stairs. She stepped on each with care, aware a fall might render her immobile and alone. Yelling for help through the thick walls would be futile.

With this comforting idea, she heard a noise. A clattering, then several clatters and voices, filtered through the space. She stopped, straining hard to make sense of the words. Could it be noise from the kitchen? She reviewed a mental map of where she should be in the house. This must be above the kitchens.

Julie heard an unfamiliar noise, one which left a river of ice along her spine. A low, horrible moaning shook her bones, as if someone cried out in intense pain, pain which would not go away. The voice pitched too high for a man, or even a grown woman. It undulated; not loud, but in the tunnel. The stone wall didn't muffle the cry. She swept her flashlight to the right and left, keeping her back flat against the wall, searching for the girl.

The noise from the kitchen resumed and the moaning disappeared. Her skin felt ice cold. She saw nothing with her flashlight. There weren't even any pieces of abandoned furniture in this part of the tunnel, nor any abandoned crates of whisky. She'd had enough of adventure and exploration. Julie hurried back up the tunnel, through the entrance in the hearth, closed the door, and collapsed into the chair near the window once she felt safe. Breathing in the sunshine streaming into the bay window worked to calm her nerves, breath by breath. Her body tingled with the after-effects of adrenaline. She remained there a long time.

1974, Dearborn, Michigan

Kirsten felt her lack of father keenly today. She had a father figure. Her grandpa acted stern and strong, working as an engineer in Detroit. Her grandma was the nurturing type, "Oh, dear, did you skin your knee? Let me cook cinnamon toast and it will be all better."

But after fighting with her mother, she needed someone else to turn to, and grandpa didn't do that. Grandma would make cookies. She needed advice.

She curled up with her favorite stuffed animal, a dolphin she had gotten at Seaworld, and cried. The fight had been silly, about cleaning her room, but the argument made her mad and frustrated.

Her mom lived with her on the second floor, with their own bedrooms and bathroom, while her grandparents lived on the first floor. Her grandfather mostly built out the basement, and it became her playground. It sported a craft kitchen for her mom and grandma, a laundry room, even a workshop and retreat for her grandpa. This doubled as a guest room with a bed. Next to that, a storage room filled with wondrous things.

Kirsten didn't realize she'd been cosseted and spoiled at her house. Other than a few chores, like keeping her room clean, she had no responsibilities. She didn't even do this so well. Kirsten had lots of play time, the freedom of a safe, middle-class neighborhood. Her friends lived a block away, and a vast park with a playground lay across the street.

Making her clean her room wasn't fair. Wasn't it her room? Why should anyone else care about how messy she left it, or how many toys lay on the floor? The room had lots of places for toys. She simply hadn't finished playing with them, so she didn't put them away. But still her mother yelled.

1967, East Grinstead, England

Eileen and Percy took the kids out, so that evening, Julie dined with the main group of students in the dining hall. She asked Sheila if she knew of any local ghost stories. Her friend grew up nearby, so might know if something haunted the area.

"Oh, yes, there is indeed. A tragic tale, but it's the best sort, don't you think?"

Julie's voice rose with eagerness. "I suppose it depends on if you are part of the tale or not."

Sheila settled into her seat for the story, looking very much like a round bird, fluffing her nest and settling on her eggs. "Ah, true enough. Well, let me tell you this tragic tale. It took place about two hundred years ago, and isn't this always how such tales begin? We start with a girl, aged perhaps fifteen years old, the eldest daughter of the Lord. She fell madly in love with an unsuitable young man, the son of the cloth merchant in the village. Her father grew dead set against the match. He already arranged a match with the son of a wealthy banker in London."

"And did she elope with her lover?" Julie sat on the edge of her seat, her food forgotten. The icy shiver returned to her spine as Sheila told her tale.

"Well, she planned to. She packed up provisions, gathered as much coin as she could find in the house, and left to meet him. However, she never showed at the rendezvous, according to her intended. They never discovered what happened to her. However, it is said she may have gotten lost in the many hidden passages in the house, trying to find her way out to the servant's quarters. They'd been built for exactly that, to allow the servants to come in and out of the lord's rooms without being seen on the stairs. She haunts the passages to this very day, so they say." Sheila ended her story with the finality of an experienced bard, expecting praise for her skills.

Julie concentrated on practical matters rather than dwelling on the consequences of getting lost in those same passages. "How many passages are in the house?"

"Oh, no one knows. The old lord forbade the servants to use them any longer, so they've remained closed since ... so they say." Sheila gestured with a flourish.

Someone went into the passageway more recently, at least according to the dates on the whisky in the crates. Perhaps the crates' presence remained a secret to anyone else.

The conversation turned to more general subjects, to Julie's relief. She ate her stew and mopped it up with the homemade bread, trying to think of sunny days and spring breezes in the park.

Several people climbed on the stage, including two guitarists, a female singer, a man playing a recorder. Perhaps an Irish tin whistle? They played a series of tunes. One of the guitar players, an attractive, dark-haired man, sang a solo rendition of Harry Belafonte's *Day-o!* while playing the guitar.

Once the dinner dishes cleared and the tables put away, they played several tunes while Julie nursed her drink and sat in a corner. She'd never been a dedicated wallflower, but she preferred smaller parties where she knew most of the people. Julie also didn't care for the sweet, white wine much, but it tasted better than the punch in the ice swan. It had a fake coconut flavor she didn't like.

When the man with the tin whistle moved into a solo, the sound pierced straight through her skull. The party noise pounded her head like a drum. She needed to get away for a while. She'd met wonderful people, and more tonight, but she craved alone time. Drink in hand, she wandered with studied nonchalance into the next room.

A smaller group of people chatted near the hearth.

The group stopped talking when Julie entered. "Oh, I'm so sorry, I didn't mean to interrupt." She'd explored this room when she found the hidden passage last month, and avoided it since her adventure. *Ghosts, really?* Such an inane notion for a modern woman.

"No need for apologies. Do come join us." David, Sheila's husband, beckoned. He stood with four strangers.

"May I introduce Julie Jensen? She's one of our artists, staying near the house. Julie, this is Priya Bamji, from Bombay, Isabella de Santos, from Valencia, and Colum McKenzie from Perth. They have all come for one of my seminars next week."

"I'm pleased to meet you." Julie shook hands with each one. Priya looked at her with liquid black eyes, a short, dark-skinned thin woman with luxuriant black hair, perhaps in her mid-forties. Julie thought she'd been behind her in line that first day, but she couldn't be sure.

Priya wore a colorful sari of orange and pink, and wore a red dot on the middle of her forehead, which

Julie only ever saw in National Geographic magazines. Isabella stood tall, sturdy, with dark, curly hair, swept up into a mass on the back of her head, about her own age. Julie now understood what people meant by the term "flashing dark eyes." Colum, about thirty-ish, gave her a firm handshake, a medium-height, stout man with reddish-brown hair and a wealth of freckles.

David played the polite conversationalist, including everyone when he could. "We started discussing the global reach of the Church. Have you met many people from other places in your time here?"

As Julie settled herself into the remaining chair, she said, "Well, tonight I think I've met people from every continent except Antarctica. I've met people from Norway, South Africa, Uruguay, Japan, and Tasmania. I knew this would be a big production, but didn't realize how big. If I'd known, I might have dressed with more care." She made a show of looking down at her garb, a simple dark green dress with ruffles on the edges, with a single jade pendant. The elegant sari Priya wore made her self-conscious of her plainness.

Colum clapped a hand on her shoulder, almost pushing her over. "Don't be silly, lass, ye look lovely. The green sets off the reds in yer hair."

She flashed him a grateful grin. "Are you new arrived from Perth, then? I presume it is Perth, Scotland, rather than Perth, Australia, from your accent?"

He chuckled and flashed her a grin. "Aye, that's true. I've arrived this morning on the sleeper train from Edinburgh. Have ye been here long yerself, then?"

Julie shook her head. "Not so long, just a few months. I do artwork for the Church and childcare for two of our other teachers. I'm versatile." She couldn't help but grin at him. She loved the thick Scottish accent, with its rolled Rs.

"And how long have you worked for the Church?" Isabella inquired, with a touch of educated Spanish accent.

"Oh, less than a year. I began in Washington D.C. How about you?"

The Spanish woman gave a half-smile. "I have been an employee for two years now. I work at the Valencia office. We grow, though slowly. It is difficult to counteract the lassitude of Spanish momentum." Isabella pursed her lips.

The music resumed in the next room. Except for Julie, the group migrated toward the sound, where several couples already used the dance floor. A fresh set of musicians entered, and one carried an accordion. *Reason enough to vacate.*

Julie didn't want to be back in the noise. She felt less bombarded than in the other room, but the noise made her head ache. The swirl of strangers, combined with the harsh sounds and decorations, colors, and buzz overwhelmed her. She found an exit, escaping from the press of people.

She breathed in the freedom and strolled through the cool night air. The evening looked clear, but not as cold as it might be for March. Since she'd neglected to bring a jacket or wrap with her, this was a splendid thing. She took in deep breaths, sensing the night and reveling in the quiet and peace of the universe. The fresh, green scent of the nearby trees energized her. Faint hints of acrid wood smoke on the wind smelled like sandalwood incense. Peering up into the night sky, the moon looked almost full, shining its light upon the undulating lawn and formal gardens to the right. To the left, she noticed a light on in an outbuilding.

These structures had been, at one point, servants' quarters, stables, a blacksmithy, and the myriad other buildings required to run a large estate. Many of them still performed similar functions, housing materials for the gardeners, maintenance men, and the like.

She crept closer, noticing a cluttered and disorganized work bench through the open doorway.

The man who sang the Belafonte song stood hunched over an elaborate, electronic instrument. His thick, black hair kept falling over his square face. He glanced up as she crossed the threshold.

She cleared her throat. "Hello. I hope I haven't disturbed your work? We heard you sing earlier tonight. I quite enjoyed it, until I needed to escape the noise. Are you a professional musician?" Julie always nurtured a deep, abiding attraction to musicians, much to her father's chagrin.

The man straightened, wiped his hands on a rag, and walked toward her. He didn't seem tall, perhaps a few inches shorter than six feet, but taller than she, with a solid build. Not muscular, but not scrawny, either. She glanced at his soulful brown eyes, and her gaze traveled down to his jeans and white turtleneck sweater.

He held out his hand. "I'm Paul. I'm glad you enjoyed my performance. No, I'm not a professional, at least, not a professional musician. I guess I'm a professional electrician. And a teacher, and a traveler. I'm confusing you already, aren't I?" He flashed her a disarming grin.

She put out her hand to shake, but he took her fingers instead. After bowing low over them, he kissed her knuckles with a feather touch of his lips. "Your servant, madam."

She giggled, nervous. Who did such a thing this day and age?

"Pleased to meet you, Paul. I'm Julie. I'm an artist and a nanny, though I can't call either my profession. Are you new here? I don't recall having seen you before?" She rambled, but she didn't know why. A strange odor floated on the air, metallic and unpleasant. Did the smell come from the instrument on the workbench? Perhaps he'd been soldering something.

16

"I arrived a couple days ago, but I've been busy with coursework. I flew in from Minneapolis. They shipped me off for training. There's a new electronic mixology machine I'm supposed to be learning how to maintain. I got overwhelmed by the party myself, so I decided I'd escape and get work done while I found the chance."

"Am I disturbing you …?"

"Oh, not disturbed at all. Well, not bothered, at any rate. Most would agree I'm disturbed by nature." He flashed his disarming grin again. "Would you like to keep me company? It won't be too long, and I can finish this project. It's an oscilloscope."

"Pardon my ignorance, but what's an … osilly-whatsit?"

His chuckle came low, pleasant, and not in the least mocking. "It measures voltage, electrical signal changes. The Church uses them to help measure changes in your electrical impulses when you talk— sort of like a lie-detector test, though they prefer the term 'truth-detector.'"

It sounded Orwellian. "Do they interrogate people with them? Is that even legal?" She hadn't heard of such practices.

He shook his head as he returned to the worktable. "No, no, no, they use them on an entirely volunteer basis. It's part of a new technique they're testing out."

"Oh, that sounds more innocuous, then. I got concerned." She remembered the book, *1984*, having read it in school. The Church's practices sometimes seemed reminiscent of "Big Brother." She'd gotten qualms about the Church before, but she'd rationalized them.

"More innocuous than what the Catholic Church does, at any rate." He didn't seem to say this to Julie, though, more to himself. She sensed a bitter history there, but it didn't seem like the right time to delve into it.

"But this isn't the machine they sent you to learn about?"

"No, that's a mainframe computer, meant to analyze a color down to its basic components and hues. I'm an all-around repairman and mechanic extraordinaire, I suppose. I've been to specialized training in Chicago, Detroit, Omaha. Once I learn a thing, I teach it to others. A traveling trainer, if you will. I love teaching, no matter what the subject."

They devolved into a discussion about the different techniques used by the Church, which Julie encountered in her layout work.

He stopped to wipe his hands, and Julie asked, "And you are a musician as well? I heard you singing in the house."

He chuckled, making laugh lines crinkle at the corners of his eyes and his mouth. Did she detect a dimple there? "I love music. Folk music, but I'll dabble in anything. I'm not a fan of Rock 'n' Roll, though. I find it the sort of music that often leads to treble."

He paused, with a too-serious look on his face. Paul punned her. She groaned theatrically, then laughed.

He raised one eyebrow. "Don't tell me that fell flat? Don't I measure up?"

Julie laughed while she placed her hand to her forehead and rubbed. "Oh, please, stop! You're killing me here."

He grinned wide. "I'm addicted to puns, I'm afraid. Escape now while you can. This is merely a prelude."

By this time, Paul finished fiddling with his electronic mess, coming to sit next to her by the door. He dusted off two rickety wooden chairs with his no-longer-clean rag, offering her a seat.

They talked of their lives. He once studied as a priest in the Catholic Church, then decided to go to trade school to learn electronics. He loved puzzles as much as puns. She filled him in on the bare details of her journey to this point.

They talked about other things, such as the food offered in the local pub, the differences between American and British plumbing standards. A bizarre conversation for a first meeting, but she felt right at home.

Sometime later, they held hands, then kissed. She didn't have any memory of what had led to this, but every touch electrified her skin. Julie didn't notice the crick in her neck, or the cool of the March night coming in through the broken window. She didn't notice the flickering of the lamp above the workbench. All these details she would recall later, but now, everything was the kiss and nothing more.

1978, Dearborn, Michigan

Life is fun, Kirsten thought. She cleaned her room, and her mom wasn't yelling at her. Neither was Grandpa, and Grandma would teach her how to play Gin Rummy on Saturday.

Then, her world turned upside down.

Mom walked in the room and sat on her bed. "I've got some news, Hon. I'll be going down to Miami next month."

"Oh! Are we going to Disneyworld again?"

She pursed her lips. "Not exactly ... I'm going down to rent a house."

"Why?"

"Well, because we're moving down to Miami in a couple months. I need to set up the move for Aunt Sandy, you, and me. It will be an adventure! We'll live near Uncle George and Uncle Jack. You remember them, right? We stayed at their house the last time we went down."

A thousand ideas rushed through Kirsten's mind, but she couldn't focus on any of them. "But why do we have to move? I like my friends here."

She played with a lock of her hair. "Well, Hon, there are many reasons. Uncle Jack has a job for me down there. Also, it's much warmer. No more cold winters, which will help your bronchitis. Wouldn't it be nice to not be sick every winter?"

It would be nice to enjoy her winter break for once, but Kirsten didn't want to give in yet. "Can Judy come?"

"She might come visit, but no, you can't bring your best friend. I don't think her mom would like it."

Kirsten crossed her arms. "Then, I'm not going."

"Yes, you are. We have lots of plans. I'm hoping to have you down there in November."

"But I can stay here with Grandma and Grandpa."

"No, dear, you must come to Miami with me. Don't worry, you'll love it."

This wasn't happening. How could she leave her home? "I won't!"

"Give it a chance, okay? You might like it."

Kirsten pouted, while Mom left the room, reluctant. Kirsten knew pouting always gained her rewards with both Mom and Grandma. Grandpa seemed immune, though. He always required other tactics.

The next day, Kirsten complained about the plans to her friend, Troy, in their third-grade class. He seemed impressed.

"Can I take your place? I'll even put on a dress."

"Sure. Mom won't even notice, as I'm flying down on my own. She'll already be there. By the time she realizes it's not me, it'll be too late." They both giggled. It wouldn't work, but it helped to think about it.

"I might come down in your luggage?"

She shook her head. "That doesn't keep me here, though."

Troy scratched his head. "Yeah, I forgot. Why don't you want to go? There are beaches and palm trees."

"But all my friends are here!"

"You'll make new friends."

She let out a snort. "They're all rich kids, tanned and going to the beach all the time."

Her neighbor, Sharon, traveled on vacation to Fort Lauderdale every Christmas. She always came back tanned. A few years older than Kirsten, Sharon always acted snobby, looking down her nose at her. Part of that might be that Sharon stood four inches taller, but still.

Kirsten's friend, Darryl, came on board with the idea. He stood shorter than Troy, he said, so he'd fit into her luggage, while Troy carried it. Oh, how she wished that would work.

If she found a father, he'd fix this.

1978, Dearborn, Michigan

Kirsten sat cross-legged on the floor of her room, sorting her things. She wanted to take everything with her, but Mom gave her a limit. She got three gigantic cardboard boxes. Clothes didn't count towards the total, but her toys, books, and puzzles would have to fit into those three boxes. Kirsten owned *lots* of toys. Legos, puzzles, books, games, and stuffed animals.

The books must be first, though she did make a pile of the older ones to leave. She'd been reading before she attended school, to the dismay of her teachers. Kirsten wouldn't need the Golden Books or the Dr. Seuss anymore. She'd bring the Nancy Drew, the Little House on the Prairie books, Trixie Belden, Encyclopedia Brown, and definitely those old Fairy Tale books Grandma Jensen gave her.

She loved to read, her first love. Her mom said she loved reading because Kirsten had no siblings. Reading didn't require a friend.

Kirsten also loved showing off how well she read, because her teachers always seemed so impressed. In first grade, she blazed through the standard readers until she finished seven or eight books ahead of the rest of the class. Her teachers had talked about her skipping second grade, but Mom squashed the idea. Still, they made sure she got harder stuff to read in school, so she wouldn't get bored. They made her take a test, and said she read on an eighth-grade level, even in the second grade. Handwriting, though, that remained horrible.

She knew cursive, having taught herself in first grade with a book from the drug store, but it looked so messy. Her first-grade teacher said no first grader needed to learn cursive, but Kirsten said she had a children's book, written in cursive. Her teacher, the no-nonsense sort, insisted she must be lying. When Kirsten brought in the Babar the Elephant book her mother had brought from Europe, the teacher apologized. Kirsten understood then that she hated being accused of things she hadn't done.

After the books came the arts and crafts stuff. The Pentel markers her grandma's friend Uncle Richard gave her. He worked as a salesman for Pentel, bringing her fantastic big sets of markers. They were quality markers, with a pointy tip, but a soft side for larger lines. The inside cover of the tin container listed each color in English, French, Spanish, and German. The top cover always showed a painting, soft and drifty images, like water lilies or sunsets. All her construction paper, the glitter, pencils, drawing paper. Should she bring her Silly Putty? Would it be craft or toy? No matter, she wanted to bring it. Besides, it didn't take much room. She also kept drawings her Uncle Jeff made for her on their annual family trips to Canada. He always drew out cards for her and her cousin Kelly to color in.

Now for the games. Kirsten needed to bring her playing cards. Uncle Larry taught her how to play poker, and Grandma loved Gin Rummy. Great-grandpa Jackson played Concentration with her, but he used his own cards, with the big numbers on it so he could see. Puzzle books, Games Magazines, picture puzzles. *Wow, those take up a lot of space.* Okay, maybe she should leave those, at least the ones with missing pieces. Sorry, Monopoly, Life, she ran out of space. She hadn't even got to the toys yet.

Toys. What toys should she bring? Jump rope, that was easy. It took up no space. Roller skates? Too small for her now. She no longer cared about dolls, but she wanted to bring her stuffed dolphin. And her two stuffed bunnies. She didn't remember where she got them, but one had brown fur, and the other had gray. The gray one lost an eye. Both seemed the worse for wear, but she slept with them every night.

Leaving the dolls helped a lot. She had several Barbies, the Dreamhouse, van, and clothes. She'd leave all her Fisher Price toys. *My dollhouse!* Grandpa made it, and she loved it. She added wallpaper and carpet several times, remodeling. But it was so big, it wouldn't even fit in any of the boxes. Mom might make an exception for that. Troy and Darryl might have joked about coming in her luggage, but they just wouldn't fit.

She had a photograph she wanted to take, a black and white snapshot. It might be her father, but she never found the courage to ask her mother. Mom never wanted to talk about him. The man in the picture

23

looked handsome, with black hair and a mustache. He wore a black turtle-neck sweater. She packed it, hidden in a book.

Well, three boxes filled. She wanted more space. Could she fit things into her luggage without Mom knowing? She stuffed a couple minor things in the spaces in the boxes, putting aside another pile of things she might sneak in. Kirsten looked around the room, still seeing so many things she wanted to bring.

When her mom saw the results, she laughed.

"Those boxes are so stuffed, they're bulging at the sides, Kirsten."

"You didn't say they couldn't."

"I know, Hon, I know. Still, if we tape them well enough, they should ship safely."

Kirsten frowned, looking at the boxes which held all her treasures. "I'm not taking them on the plane?"

"No, dear, I am sending them in the mail. They'll take longer, but they'll get there okay."

Kirsten felt relieved she hadn't agreed to put Troy or Darryl in them. They wouldn't have enjoyed being stuck in the boxes for so long. Besides, she needed the room for her stuff.

"Oh. Mom, I have another question."

"What's that, dear?"

"Do we have to go to *your* Ami? Can't we go to *my* Ami? Do I even have an Ami?"

May 15, 1967, Valencia, Spain

Dear Katy:

My adventures continue, this time to Spain! Eileen and Percy are taking a seminar in Valencia. The city overlooks the Mediterranean Sea, and it's everything I ever dreamed Spain to be. And more! The food is amazing. I wish I could speak more than a few words of Spanish, but you know I never possessed much of a talent for languages.

After meeting so many exotic people at Saint Hill, I decided this would be almost provincial, but I am still amazed at all the differences I see. It's marvelous and broadening. The music is enchanting and makes me want to dance. Have you ever seen Flamenco? So much energy!

I met a sweet man back in England, named Paul. Remember, I wrote about him in my last letter? We shared a lovely evening and an even nicer kiss, but then I needed to travel with Eileen. He'll have gone back to Minneapolis by the time I return next month. Why do the good ones always have to go away?

How are Mom and Dad doing? I miss them. I miss you. I even miss Larry! It's lonely here in Spain, even though it's so beautiful. Perhaps because it's so beautiful, it's lonelier, since I have no one to share it with.

Love to you, little sister,
Julie

Julie walked out on the balcony and breathed deep of the warm, humid, salty air. She fancied she spied the island of Majorca in the misty distance, across the sea. She needed a respite, no matter how brief, from the screaming tantrums inside the apartment. All five children behaved as if she killed their favorite puppy, refusing to settle down, play nice, or even to stop crying. The heat got brutal, but the sun now set across the sparkling sea. She took one more deep breath and returned to her charges.

Both Eileen and Percy attended a sales seminar, taught at the convention center on a cruise ship owned by the Church, and docked in the harbor. Julie came aboard a few times, but she preferred land. She got seasick, even when the boat lounged in calm harbor waters. They gave her a bunk on the ship, but when Eileen realized how impossible it would have been for

25

her to care for the children when she couldn't even care for herself, Eileen found a place for her in town.

Julie didn't know anyone on land. Everyone she knew from the church stayed on the ship most of the day, so she remained isolated, despite the constant company of the five children. She'd taught history today, at least to the ones old enough to understand. Julie taught to Gary, Carrie, and Grace while bouncing either Chris or Angela on her knee. She loved teaching history and art to the kids. English and math, not so much. But she did her best.

After much coddling, cajoling, and silent cursing, Julie settled the children down. The two youngest cried themselves into a stupor, but now slept like angels. Julie told "The Little Mermaid" to the older kids, who now sat cross-legged, rapt in fascination at her story. She always loved the Hans Christian Andersen tales.

Grace fell asleep about halfway through the tale, one hand entangled in her baby-fine, straight hair. Carrie nodded off as well near the end, but Gary remained bright-eyed and bushy-tailed, not the least interested in sleep. She fixed him a snack, since they ate supper several hours before, opening her book to read while he ate. Julie didn't have much time to draw on this trip. Whenever she brought out her pad and pencil, the children turned into craft monsters, trying to scribble all over her expensive art paper. She kept them well hidden after the first time, and contented herself with reading in her precious spare moments.

Julie opened the book on her lap. The elementary mathematics text should help her teach, but she stared at the pages without comprehending the words. Why did Paul need to return so quickly? They got on well, even finishing each other's sentences. He charmed her, he was attractive, a musician, and interested in her. Ah, well. Perhaps having a partner wouldn't be so great. She'd seen enough of broken partnerships with

Eileen and Percy. Both married to others when they got together, they fought a lot, often in her hearing, about their ex-spouses. She didn't want to be part of that horrible mess.

Julie never considered herself to be righteous, but she grew up in a middle-class family in the Midwest. Her values hovered on the conservative side of today's mores, but she still didn't think it would be right to break up a marriage.

She applied herself to the book with determination, but it didn't last long. Mathematics eluded her. Her Geometry teacher made her promise not to take any higher math classes when he gave her a passing grade. She should have failed, but as long as she wouldn't use it again, he might reconcile himself in passing her. Here she sat, trying to teach young children the evils of math. Julie could puzzle out the easy stuff. She didn't know how she'd deal with teaching fractions and percentages.

The doorknob rattled with a key. Eileen must be here for her evening visit. They seemed to come by less and less. Julie often found her weekends free, while Eileen and Percy took the children to see the sights, but during the week she saw no adult but Eileen. They kept the pantry well-supplied with food for her and the children, so she didn't complain, but the constant conversations with toddlers and young children left her starved for intelligent conversation.

"I'm afraid only Gary is awake any longer, Eileen. The rest of the kids fell asleep about an hour ago." Julie kept her voice quiet, not getting up from her chair as Eileen came in, impeccably dressed as always in a robin's egg blue polyester pantsuit.

Gary wandered in from the kitchen at the sound, with jelly from his sandwich smeared on one cheek. Julie rose, wiping his face.

"Hello, my darling. Were you a good boy for Julie today?" Eileen picked up her eldest child at arms-

27

length, almost as if she picked up a puppy that peed on her shoe. Julie long since judged that Eileen didn't have a maternal instinct, an impression that hadn't improved with their trip to Spain.

"We learned about mermaids today." Gary said, sounding both interested and sulky at the same time.

Eileen arched her eyebrow at Julie, as if disapproving of such a frivolous subject.

"After supper, I told them the tale of 'The Little Mermaid.' It helped settle them all for the night." She didn't need to justify herself, but she felt defensive. As if Eileen ever told them bedtime stories.

"Well, it's fine. A small bit of mythology never hurt anyone, I suppose." Eileen smiled at Julie, but it didn't reach her eyes. "Are you coming down to the ship this Saturday, Julie? There is a sizable soiree planned. Percy and I will have the children there, as they have someone to run a nursery during the festivities."

"I'll try, Eileen, but can't promise anything. You know how I am on the water."

"I have a gift for you. It's one reason I came by. There's this new nasal spray my friend Charles swears by. Will you give it a chance? It would be nice for you to enjoy yourself."

"Thanks, Eileen, I'll try it." Julie thought she might have misjudged Eileen, being tired and cranky from the kids' behavior. "What time should we be there?" She didn't look forward to getting all five children ready and down to the ship by herself.

"Oh, we'll come and help get the kids, Julie, they are too much to transport across the harbor by yourself." Eileen fussed with Gary's hair, fixing strands here and there from their tousled state into relative order.

Julie felt a lot more charitable towards Eileen that moment than she had been for the last month.

That Saturday, when Julie arrived to the party, Eileen gave her the nose spray, and it helped.

The party started off slow, but picked up steam as dusk approached. Her stomach protested the ship's movement, despite Charles' nasal spray nostrum. She walked outside onto the deck, and breathed deeply of the salty ocean air. The breath and the spray mixed to make her nose itch.

Standing near the rail, Julie watched in wonder as the sun set low on the sparkling sea. It touched the water, sending sparks of crimson and orange across the glittering surface of the ocean.

She sensed someone standing next to her, and turned to see a tall, attractive black man with white-tipped sideburns. He gazed at the ocean beside her, enraptured by the beauty.

When the sun dipped below the water line, the sky alight with painted clouds, the man turned to her, inclined his head, and walked away, still silent.

She didn't know who her mystery man was, but she felt glad to have shared this moment of grace and beauty with him.

Two months later, Julie needed to deal with another ship. She swallowed again, hoping to settle her stomach. The waters seemed calm, but she still suffered. Almost as if the former ferry ship got lashed by a furious sea, tossed like a piece of flotsam before the storm.

Images like this did not help. She visualized a calm, sandy beach she visited in Michigan on Lake Erie. Gentle waves lapped at her feet in her mind's eye. Seagulls screeched and argued. The sweet, solid sand beneath her helped anchor her soul. She took several slow, deep breaths of the salty air, opening her eyes again.

It seemed to help.

They moved *en route* back to England. While glad to return to a place with more social freedom, she didn't care for the method of conveyance. However, fate tossed her about, not unlike the sea now. She had less control over her situation. Not that she couldn't leave. They didn't hold her prisoner. But where would she go? While Julie saved up a decent amount of money, she spoke little Spanish. Jumping ship now would be silly.

No, much better than to ride it out and return to England. Perhaps her sister, Katy, would have moved there by then to be with her fiancé. Julie hadn't heard from her, but she'd been in Spain for several months. Maybe a letter waited for her in England.

Wouldn't it be a blast, sharing a place with Katy in England? Well, with her and her husband. Hmm, perhaps not. She didn't relish being the odd woman out. She'd lived with Eileen and Percy. It created resentment all around. Lack of privacy, lack of social niceties, and all that mess. Julie disliked messes, particularly if she stood in the middle of it.

Julie's stomach rumbled and roiled again. She swallowed several times until she got her guts back under control, at least for the moment. *Calm, blue ocean. Safe, sandy beach.*

Would any of her friends still be in East Grinstead? Sheila, Paul, David, Priya, Colum? She hadn't inquired about their plans when she shipped out with Eileen. There'd been so much to do, helping to get five children ready for plane travel. It seemed like a blurred memory of chaos. She quailed at the thought of having to make a whole new set of friends. Not that she'd been bosom buddies with anyone yet, but at least she felt a baseline friendship with a few of them. Starting all over again would be too much chaos.

Chaos, no, let's not think of chaos. Calm, blue ocean. She considered painting the calm, blue ocean, with bits of cerulean and indigo, streaks of white and turquoise on her brush. Smooth, lovely, straight lines. A beach of sienna, cream, and white and a thin edge of foam between the two.

Julie spied land in the distance. Had they arrived at Portsmouth already? She sighed in relief that the voyage would be over soon.

Disembarking proved to be the chaos she feared. People and porters milled around both on the ship and on the dock, and no one seemed to know what went where. She glimpsed her erstwhile companion of the party, the man who shared the glory of the setting sun with her, but in a flash, he disappeared. Then Gary's plaintive wail cut into her whimsy, and she focused on the children.

CHAPTER TWO

Dancing Partners

1967, East Grinstead, England

Julie clasped hands with those on either side of her. The round table seemed tiny in the center of the echoing ballroom. The single candle in the center flickered, while the medium moaned low and tuneless, ululating in a slow, primal chant, to contact the ghost of the unfortunate girl Sheila told her about.

Imelda, a Church teacher, claimed to be a sensitive, so got this group together to hold a séance. Imelda dressed for the part, with a long, flowing gown and several shawls draped upon her ample frame. She wore heavy make-up and jangling jewelry, and a dot painted between her eyes, like Priya wore. Imelda gathered a group of ten people, including Julie, Sheila, and David. Paul, who hadn't left home after all, sat on her right, his hand warm in hers.

The room had always had its cold spots, but a strong frisson traveled up Julie's spine as Imelda's voice increased in intensity. Sound injected into her bones. The candle flickered again as Imelda chanted words in a language Julie didn't understand. She almost recognized a few words, but they danced outside understanding, as if they taunted her with meaning. Then the words morphed into English, accented with Imelda's exotic Caribbean lilt. "Are you here? Can you hear us? Give us a sign of your presence."

The candle went out. No breeze existed in the still room, but the light disappeared as if someone had snuffed the flame with invisible fingers. Doused in darkness, the frisson returning with a vengeance, Julie fancied the fingers which snuffed the candle now tickled her spine with the ice of the otherworld.

"How can we help you? How can we ease your suffering?"

Another moaning came, but not from Imelda, continuing as she spoke. Imelda fell silent, and someone gasped, perhaps Sheila next to her. Perhaps herself. The voice sounded higher, younger than Imelda's. The voice sobbed, keened, as if in unimaginable pain.

A breeze blew now. No, more than a breeze, more of a whirlwind. Icy tendrils tugged at her clothing. Julie wanted to let go of her hands and yank her clothes away from the questing touch of icy wind. However, her neighbors held her hands firm.

A loud bang, a flash of bright light, and the double doors to the hallway flung wide open. Eileen and Percy stood in the doorway, lights flooding in like the morning tide. "What in the nine levels of Hell is going on in here?" Eileen's no-nonsense voice cut sharp and commanding through the shroud of magic Imelda had created. Julie shrank into her seat so she wouldn't be noticed.

The glare blinded Julie after the darkness of the room. She blinked and dropped her hands from the iron grip of her neighbors. She felt foolish, but still had no way of explaining the things she had witnessed.

Percy crossed his arms. "Imelda, are you up to your old tricks again? You never get tired of scaring these poor children with your theatrics, do you?"

Startled, Julie stared at Imelda's face, seeing the truth in her eyes, as well as a sheepish smile, before the Caribbean woman got her features under control. With dignity, Imelda gathered her shawls about herself and flounced out of the room. The rest of the students milled about before shuffling through the door, chagrined at being fooled, unwilling to discuss the event among themselves. They retreated to their respective rooms.

At dinner, she glanced at Sheila and David as they ate. They returned her gaze with sheepish grins. Smiling back, Julie realized the tricks had fooled them all. How had Imelda fooled them? A recording, a fan, and a trick candle, all reasonable explanations. She wondered if Imelda had planted the tales she'd heard to give verisimilitude to her performances, sort of a hazing for recent members.

Paul sat on her other side, noticing the glances. He cleared his throat, stood, holding his cup of lemonade up in a toast. "When you toast to a ghost, you lift your spirits." This all seemed silly. A show, a circus, put on for fun, a hall of mirrors. The table erupted into nervous laughter and conversations resumed.

Imelda hadn't been in the tunnel when Julie first experienced the ghostly caress. Julie hadn't heard the tales at that point. The frisson returned, her steak and kidney pie turning into a congealed mass in the pit of her stomach.

A week later, Julie helped set up the same ballroom for a party. She stood on a tall ladder, securing bunting to the marble mantelpiece, when her balance shifted. Her perch became more precarious. She moved to get a better angle, to keep from toppling down onto the hardwood floor. The floor seemed far below when the ladder stopped wobbling.

She peered down and noticed Paul securing the ladder for her with a grin. "Would you like help? Unless you are planning on doing diving practice, that is."

"I would appreciate help, yes. If you could hold the ladder, I can finish this in a second," she replied primly, embarrassed he had witnessed her clumsiness. After she completed her task, she descended the metal ladder with great care.

"So, how do you organize a space party?" Julie glanced at Paul's face. He must be about to set her up for a horrible joke.

With a long-suffering sigh, she replied in the expected manner. "I don't know, Paul. How do you organize a space party?"

"You planet, of course."

"Ugh." Julie had perfected a look of long-suffering resignation for Paul's puns. "Did you really want to help me? We've got loads to do yet. An extra pair of hands wouldn't go amiss. You owe me for that pun, if nothing else." Without waiting for acquiescence, she handed him a bag of bunting. "These are to go all around the room, starting where I finished. If you can do this, I can remove the rugs and place chairs."

"Rescue a damsel in distress, get pressed into menial labor. I see how this works. I'll collect the reward for my gallantry later, then?" His smile seemed sweet, but sly.

"Perhaps, if you do a good enough job with the bunting. But I reserve the right to demand further payment." She wasn't about to let him extract a promise from her, but he intrigued her.

Julie didn't know what to make of Paul. He stayed longer than he first planned. Paul flirted with abandon ever since she returned from Valencia, and he excelled at it. He charmed on demand, full of laughter, puns, and exaggerated gallantry. Paul's sparkling brown eyes reflected his laughter, and he possessed an expressive singing voice.

In truth, he flirted with many of the young ladies, and not a few of the older ones. He loved flirting, though she glimpsed him stealing a kiss from

Isabella at one point. He demonstrated intelligence, with a keen sense of humor, though his penchant for puns sometimes got horrible.

But last week, she'd walked in on him in a deep embrace and kiss with a girl she didn't know. He touched people a lot, hands on shoulders, holding hands, pats on the head, but this had been more than a friendly pat. Julie then realized how much attention she paid to his actions.

She rolled up the rugs, being careful to bend with her knees, as her ample backside, bent over, wasn't the sight she wished to present to Paul. She struggled to carry the heavy Persian rugs into the storage closet.

Julie liked Paul, but just as she wasn't the only one he flirted with, he wasn't the only man who entertained her.

Colum may be broody, but his freckles danced when she coaxed a grudging smile from him. Colum spent his evenings with a book and a tumbler of Scotch rather than socialize, dance, or even kiss. He seemed more an old school, old world man. They had enjoyed a couple evenings in quiet conversation. They discussed history and social issues, but he obsessed over a particular aspect of history which she knew nothing about, the Jacobite Wars. Julie felt out of her depth whenever he steered the conversation to this era. She didn't like feeling ignorant, but she didn't have any interest in battle history, so she would excuse herself after he broached the subject.

Terry Holker, a Londoner, had arrived a couple days ago. While he didn't have the deep affection for history Colum had, he also kept solemn most of the time. Terry loved art as she did, so they discussed several of the Impressionist and Surrealist artists. His slim frame stood not much taller than she, slight and bookish. His blond, wispy hair always seemed to have been blown into a mess by the wind, even while indoors. The poor thing had a terrible squint, despite his thick glasses. He seemed to lack, however, any vestige of a sense of humor. He met any attempt at a joke or silliness with a slow, owl-like blink of incomprehension, followed by a literal, staid response. While Paul's puns made her groan in pain, she had difficulty enjoying the company of someone who didn't laugh.

She couldn't forget her mystery man, the one she glimpsed at Portsmouth. Had he come to Saint Hill? She hadn't seen him since then, but perhaps he lived off-campus.

Paul fluctuated between gallant, silly, fun, intelligent, and handsome. He played wonderful music, which had always been her weakness. However, he didn't seem to be the sort to settle down. Did she need someone who would settle down? Or would she settle for a fling?

Julie never believed herself prudish. She lived in a generation which ignored, shattered, even redefined sexual and societal roles, the sexual revolution. Julie also dared to move halfway across the world, away from her comfortable home and family in Michigan.

She'd never been someone who jumped without looking before. The move to England had been scary enough. How could she risk her heart as well? Paul seemed a little too rootless to comfort her.

But Paul made her laugh.

1967, East Grinstead, England

Julie stood in The Monkey room, the party booming around her. Several rooms of the Saint Hill mansion filled with people talking, drinking, or circulating. The Monkey Room had been named for the enormous mural on one wall, showing monkeys in various occupations. Monkeys on a carousel, monkeys cavorting as part of a circus with feathers in their hats, monkeys swinging from a giant maypole or dangling on various ribbons in a wide circle. The big monkey above the doorway presided over two enormous cornucopias filled with fruit, a huge feather sprouting out of his conical hat. While the decor had no resemblance to taste or elegance, one could use the designs as an excellent conversation piece.

Julie used the outrageous bits for that purpose now, in a somber discussion with Terry about the various activities of the simian subjects.

"From what I understand, the artist, John Spencer-Churchill, had been commissioned to paint this ... piece ... by Mrs. Drexel Biddle. Spencer-Churchill, a nephew of Sir Winston Churchill, no less. I would think such an illustrious ancestry would have given him a penchant for dignity, but this evidently hadn't been the case." He took a moment to take a sip from his whisky tumbler, pushing his glasses back up his nose.

"One's ancestry doesn't define one's taste?" Julie teased Terry, knowing her attempt would be in vain.

"One's pride in ancestry should inspire one to bridle their unseemly passions, at least in public." Terry said primly, though the edge of his mouth quirked up. Julie fancied his pleasure must be more in his own pride at bridling any unseemly passions than in Mr. Spencer-Churchill. She tried hard to imagine what those passions might be, but her imagination failed.

"And what of your own ancestry, have you anything to inspire you?" She regretted the question. The English, and indeed, Scottish, and Irish, would recount their entire genealogy, given half a chance.

As she sipped her wine, she listened with only part of her attention as Terry listed several of those ancestors he considered notable. She would have preferred to hear of the notorious ones, perhaps a woman burned for witchcraft, or the proverbial horse thief in everyone's family tree. The constant stream of Ministers, Civil Servants, and Permanent Under-Secretaries threatened to put her to sleep. She glanced about the room, and spied Sheila. She concocted an escape from the tedium of her own creation.

"Terry, I see Sheila, and I need to ask her about an upcoming project. Would you be so kind as to excuse me?" Severe politeness became the best tool to stop an Englishman's drone.

He rose as she did. "Certainly, of course, please. We can resume again later."

Not if I can help it, buddy.

She withdrew to the cluster of people around Sheila. Priya, Imelda, and two tall men, whom Julie didn't know. *Wait a moment, isn't that Sunset Man?* She didn't want to appear too keen, so nodded politely to both.

Priya adjusted the sleeve of her vibrant sari, this one in a deep, emerald green with silver details. Imelda had eschewed her theatrical trappings of the seance for a riotous colorful kaftan with a tribal design, reminiscent of African prints. Sheila wore a classic short black dress and pearls, so conservative next to the colorful plumage of her companions.

The two men, introduced as Jimmy Cranston and Roger Hubble, looked to be in their forties. Both wore casual office garb. Jimmy, from Las Vegas, had dirty blond hair, pulled back into a long, straight ponytail. His long, saturnine face cracked into an enormous smile, with twinkling blue eyes. Roger, her Sunset Man, black of eye, skin, and hair, grinned even wider. He had a hint of white at the sideburns, and hailed from Atlanta. His eyes registered no recognition of her, so perhaps she'd mistaken him.

Other than Paul, Eileen, and the kids, few Americans lived at Saint Hill, so Julie felt glad of a chance to discuss her home country with those who didn't think the country spanned a mere three hundred miles. The group bantered small talk for a while, though Julie snuck glances back at Terry, still sitting with his glass of whisky.

Julie looked up at strange sounds nearby, and noticed someone clearing the stage for music. Would Paul be one of them? His lack of roots didn't mean she couldn't enjoy his music, right?

Roger had asked her a question. The group watched her, waiting for a response.

"I'm sorry, Roger, I floated miles away. What did you ask?" Julie hoped her smile would take away any sting from her apparent disinterest.

He had a deep, lovely voice. "I asked how long you'd been here in England."

"I arrived in March, so about three months. But I stayed in Valencia for several weeks, while Eileen and her family took courses in the city." She swallowed to keep the memory of the ship from affecting her stomach.

Roger clapped his hands, the staccato sound making Terry glance up. "Aha! That's where I've seen you! On the ship. We watched the sunset together." A dreamy look crept across his face.

She grinned like a loon. "Yes, guilty! I didn't get much time to explore Spain. I had the charge of their five kids most days. A tiny center of chaos in the universe. When I got to the beach, though, the warmth and surf transported me to paradise."

"I can imagine. As the oldest of seven, I had to take care of the whole mob. It taught me a lot about control and the value of instilling fear in others." His bright smile took away the hint of literal interpretation.

"A genuine terror? Daily beatings and weekly lashings?" She arched her eyebrows in inquiry.

"Absolutely! I had the cat o' nine tails on my belt at all times." He mimicked a whipping motion with his hand, clicking his tongue. He grinned, showing brilliant straight, white teeth.

His eyes bored into her, liquid, and dark. They echoed his smile with laugh lines. He may have been older, but he possessed a young heart with brilliant eyes.

The musicians played an energetic tune. Julie spun around to see if Paul played, but she didn't see him. Sheepish, she turned back around.

Jimmy raised his eyebrows, his voice teasing. "So, who did you hope to see?"

"I thought my friend, Paul, might be on set tonight." She tried to emphasize the word "friend" without being obvious about it.

Jimmy jabbed his friend in the ribs with his elbow. "Oh, your *friend*, is he? I'd like to have more *friends* like that. You got a soft spot for musicians? Roger, here, plays the saxophone, you know."

She looked at Roger with renewed interest. "Do you? What sort of music do you play?"

He raised his eyebrows at her obvious interest. "Jazz, mostly. I love the smooth sound. I play with a band a few nights back at home."

Julie crossed her arms, with a glare to Jimmy. "So, you beat young children and play radical music. A real rebel, you are."

He offered his hand with a flourish. "I am at that. Care to dance with a rebel?"

"I would be delighted." She took his hand and they headed out to the large dance floor, where several couples had already begun to dance.

Roger danced much better than she did. Though Julie loved music in most any form, enjoyed listening, and on occasion, singing, she had no talent for dancing. She enjoyed moving to the music, but she didn't have the talent or balance for complex choreographed movements. When the formal dance styles gave way to looser forms, she didn't have to memorize steps. Roger danced gently with her, leading her around but not pushing or shoving. He had nice, warm hands.

The song ended too soon, as the players went on to a slower tune, "A Summer Place." She began to walk back to the group, but Roger kept a firm hand on her waist, taking her hand in his. They pressed closer.

She enjoyed the slow rhythm of the dance, almost as if they danced in another time, another place. A memory of dancing with her ex-boyfriend, Jeffrey, at a club in D.C., flashed through her mind, and she pushed the pain away. Julie brought her mind back to the present. She didn't want to color her impression of Roger with what Jeffrey did to her. She danced in a British mansion at a Church-sponsored party, despite being odder than any other Church she had been part of.

"A Summer Place" ended. Roger stopped as she gazed into his dark eyes, locked for a moment before he led her back to the group.

"I can't monopolize you, but I'd like another dance later, if it's okay with you?" He adopted the attitude of a poor, starving orphan asking for more food.

"Of course. You're a dreamy dancer."

"Must be my musician's rhythm. I've always been at home on the dance floor. I can tap dance, too." He performed a shuffle-step-toe on the wooden floor, with a flourish of his arms when he finished.

"Multi-talented, you are. Is there anything you can't do?"

Jimmy jumped in with a resounding "No, he's Mr. Perfect." Julie couldn't tell if his tone stemmed from envy or loyalty for his friend.

Roger sent Jimmy a sour look for his praise. "I can't draw a straight line with a ruler. And I'm terrible at anything resembling math." He gave a rueful laugh. "I hear you're an artist, though?"

"I do artwork for our advertisements here, posters, flyers, things like that." Julie remembered she had a project she needed to finish the next day. She'd forgotten with all the fuss about decorating today. Instead, she had rushed back to her room and changed her outfit several times until she had found a look for the party. While she had nothing fancy or colorful, like Priya's costume, her outfit slimmed her hips. She had chosen an A-line dress with subtle vertical stripes in rust and burnt orange tones. She wore an orange coral necklace with a matching set of clip-on earrings. Those had been a gift from her mother.

Roger asked, "What about your own work? Can I see your paintings somewhere?"

Julie laughed, "Oh, no, you mean in a gallery? No, mostly I create for myself. I used to sell at craft fairs back in Michigan, while I was still in college, but I've no head for business. I'm sure I lost money."

With a poke to his ribs, Roger said, "Perhaps you need a good manager, then? Or an agent?"

"Wouldn't I need someone good at math? I thought you said math wasn't your strong point?" Julie asked, one eyebrow arched.

Jimmy piped up. "I'm good at math."

"Well, I wasn't applying for the job, if that's what you're asking." Roger said at the same time. "Though that might be a logical step if you wanted to pursue your art."

Julie shook her head. "I'm happy creating on the side, drawing for pleasure. Once you cater to your audience, you aren't creating art, you're creating product. The work loses some of its soul, in my opinion."

Roger didn't answer, but pursed his lips, silent.

"Did I ... I mean, I didn't ... do you write your own music?" She sounded like a blathering idiot.

His pursed lips shifted into a rueful grin. "I do. And most of my tunes are well-received when I play it. But I have to perform covers of well-known stuff to get my audience interested in new music. I've often considered where the 'selling out' point came, but I think I'm safe. If my music doesn't get a wonderful reaction, I don't change a thing. I composed the work for myself, but play them for others to share the joy. If they can't enjoy my creativity, too bad for them. I still have the joy of playing them."

Julie beamed. "That's exactly how I draw and paint. It's for me, to enjoy and share with others. If they don't appreciate my work, then that's a failing in them, not in my work."

He gripped her arms, his eye wide. "Yes, you understand, you really do. I think most genuine artists realize this, whether they show their work commercially or not."

Jimmy tried again. "Your music gets interest, Roger. Didn't you tell me you got a call from that record label before you left Atlanta?"

Roger waved off the suggestion. "He didn't have a real record label, Jimmy. He wanted me to finance his record label. He wanted me to help him buy the recording equipment and everything. He had serious balls."

"Come out to Vegas. I'm sure you could find endless venues to play. You should see the crap they've got at the supper clubs. I mean, a few of the joints are classy, like the ones the Rat Pack perform for, but the dives have terrible 'talent'. Most of them aren't acts like Wayne Newton or Siegfried and Roy. Most are sad sacks with an old guitar and broken pipes, playing for scraps."

"And you want me to perform my crap for scraps, then?" Roger inquired with sweet irony.

Jimmy had the grace to turn red. "No, no, you'd get more than scraps. You could have a career."

"I think I'll stick to Atlanta. It's my home. I know the people. I know the vibe."

Julie decided she liked Roger well enough to inquire about plans. "Are you here in England long, then?"

"Just a couple weeks, I'm afraid. I came for the missionary course."

"Oh, I see." Julie hid her disappointment. Why couldn't the attractive guys with intelligence and humor stay?

The conversation moved to other subjects, with Roger claiming his promised dance from Julie before the end of the evening. She collapsed on her bed by the time she reached the sanctuary of her room. Her mind whirled, thinking about Paul and Roger. If she could only combine the two. Meld the best of both and create one super-guy of her dreams. She sighed with yearning, drifting into oblivion.

Julie spent more time with Roger and the others the next evening. Jimmy, Priya, and Sheila joined them in the library.

Priya asked Roger about his family in Atlanta, while Jimmy tried to impress Sheila with magic tricks he had learned. Julie sipped her tea and watched all four in amusement.

"Have your brothers and sisters all got families of their own then, Roger?" Sheila interjected, dismissing Jimmy's poor attempts at prestidigitation.

"Most of them, yes. But the two youngest are still single. I guess I'm a disappointment to our mother, as I never married. I'm the wastrel of the family, the bad example."

Priya frowned. "Just because you haven't married yet doesn't mean you never will, Roger. My brother, Tariq, got engaged last month, and he's forty-five. You never know when true love will step into your life. Everything comes in its own time."

"You're assuming I want to get married, though. Why buy the cow when the milk is free?"

Julie almost choked on her tea. She spluttered and coughed until Jimmy pounded her on the back. She waved him off. While she had heard the phrase before, never in mixed company like this. Her conservative upbringing must be showing.

Roger wore a smug smile. "You object, Oh Artistic One? Didn't you live in D.C. before you came here? Surely, you saw unconventional pairings?"

"I did, but you caught me by surprise with the, um … phrasing." Her face grew warm, radiating her own chagrin and embarrassment. She busied herself with mopping up the tea from her slacks.

Jimmy teased. "So, mere words can make you choke? I didn't realize you were such a delicate flower."

She straightened her spine to appear tough and street-smart, but knew she failed. "'Delicate', right. I grew up in Detroit. Few things remain delicate in Detroit, my friend."

Roger raised his eyebrows. "Tough girl, sure, I can see that."

Julie looked down at her brown corduroy slacks and deep brown button-down shirt with a beige scarf, and realized she didn't fit the image of a street girl. She shrugged with one shoulder, ceding her defeat in the battle. Why had she attempted the image in the first place? Roger excelled in needling her. Did she always have to rise to the bait?

Jimmy's question brought her back to the conversation. "Do you want to move back sometime?"

"Me? Someday, sure. I miss my parents, my sister, my friends, even my little brother. But Detroit is a stark place. Not supportive of the arts, you know. It's kind of depressing."

Roger settled back into his chair. "That's the best place for art."

Sheila cocked her head. "How so?"

"Not only do such places need art the most, they evoke the best art. Art should comfort the disturbed and disturb the comfortable. I don't remember where I heard it, but I believe it to be true. A depressed area, like an inner city, or a depression-style farm, needs art to have hope, see beauty."

"Things which are crumbling have the most beauty." Julie said, repeating a phrase she'd heard in college.

He gripped her forearm, his hand warm and strong. "Exactly! The new stuff, they all look the same, no character. They might be pretty, but pretty isn't art. I prefer the wrinkled, lined faces of the elderly, those who show true character, the crumbling blocks of ruined buildings which shows how time has defaced them. In music, the pain of experience is shown through the words."

Julie grinned. "I like that! I once read about a Japanese tradition called Kintsugi. They repair broken objects so the break looked obvious, part of the structure. Like broken pottery repaired with gold in the cracks, so the repair showed." She had seen pictures of this tradition somewhere, but couldn't remember the circumstances. Perhaps her Art Appreciation classes?

Priya nodded. "We believe this to be true in India. The older a statue or temple is, the more the stones crumble. We believe they crumble because they hold the beliefs and magic of many generations. Therefore, they are more beautiful."

"I like the concept," Julie said. "But most of the holy places in India I've seen pictures of are well-maintained."

"Yes, maintenance of such sites is a duty and an honor. However, a certain subsidence defies even the most exacting caretaker. This is when we say the stone has crumbled from the weight of magic."

"How beautifully poetic." Julie considered the abandoned buildings she had seen in England and

Spain with that idea. The notion inspired her, and her hands itched to draw. She brought a pad and pencil with her at all times, so she whipped those out and sketched what she remembered of a ruined Moorish palace she had seen in Spain.

Priya and Roger got into a further conversation about ancient religious beliefs, comparing Indian concepts with Mediterranean beliefs from his ancestor's history.

Jimmy's enthusiastic voice over her shoulder startled her. "Whatcha drawing?"

She didn't even glance up as she drew. "A palace I remembered from Spain."

She worked on the perspective lines of the rambling, squared blocks of Sagunto Castle, a ruin she had visited on one open weekend. The towers sprawled over the top of a hill, crumbling walls radiating out like clumsy spider legs. The main keep sat blocky and strong, like most of the Spanish castles, bits of crenelated wall peeking up here and there among the lush foliage. She added textures to corners, rough stone, and dressed masonry, a tease, a sketch, with economy of line. She stopped and surveyed her efforts. The group stood around her, peering at her page.

Sheila beamed, her eyes wide. "That is amazing, Julie. I've never watched you draw. Did you create this from your imagination?"

"Oh, no, this is a place I visited in Spain. A castle on a hill there, all ruined and crumbling. The discussion brought the place to mind. I guess the image needed to escape."

Priya moved to pick up the pad of paper to turn it around so she could see it better. "You captured the essence of the place. Is this Sagunto? I've visited before, a dry, dusty place, but beautiful all the same. May I?"

Julie grew self-conscious whenever others critiqued her work. Professional critique, a process she'd never gotten comfortable with in art school. She wondered whether any artist did. Perhaps that's why she never wanted to become a professional fine artist, as critique would be constant. With layout work, her efforts merely needed to fit particular parameters.

Even Jimmy looked impressed, with raised eyebrows. "This really looks great. And you drew so fast. Simply fantastic."

"Thank you. It's only a sketch. I might use the sketch to create a painting, though I'd much rather have painted *in situ*. That way I could see the place for reference."

Priya handed the drawing back. "Can you use photographs as reference?"

"Sure, but only if they are in a similar angle or perspective."

"I have several from my visit. You are welcome to use them if they will help." Julie closed the pad over the drawing. Why couldn't she take compliments on her artwork? Her mother praised her work all the time, never critical, offering honest critiques to improve. Perhaps her father's disinterest in her efforts made them forever inadequate. Or her sister Katy's skill, which outshone her own.

Julie jumped on the opportunity to shift attention from her work. "Thank you, Priya. That's kind of you. When did you visit Spain?"

Roger admired her efforts. This bit of affirmation made her prouder, and perhaps gave her more confidence in her own talents.

Julie and Roger made the most of the little time they had to get to know each other. Her schedule grew busy, and she chaffed at the wasted opportunities. Still, they carved out time each evening to walk through the village, have a meal together, or gaze up at the stars.

Roger burst with interesting facts about history and archeology. Not dull dates and battles, like Colum, but fascinating trivia which brought the past to life. "Ancient man believed the stars to be the hearth fires of those who had died before them. Their ancestors lit the fires to welcome the new dead to the heavens."

"What a delightful concept. More romantic than flaming balls of gas dancing around each other in the void of infinite space."

"That depends on what you consider romantic, doesn't it? Yours is at least poetic." His hand felt soft against her cheek, and she closed her eyes at the tender caress. Their relationship had, out of necessity, moved quickly for her Midwestern tastes, but she didn't mind. Whirlwind and steamy, with built-in tragedy. Everything a romantic tale needed.

He turned to kiss her then, under the twinkling velvet sky. He gave her a slow, sweet, savoring kiss, full of promise and a hint of desperation.

The next day, the sun shone bright, while fluffy white clouds scudded across the sky. Julie and Roger escaped for a picnic. He didn't have his saxophone with him in England, but he could sing, so he serenaded her with soft folk songs. Julie sketched him as he sang. She worked to capture the soulful eyes, and the very soft, kissable lips.

"Can I see?"

She handed it over to him for inspection. Such a quick sketch wasn't her best work. She preferred working in paints, with full color, but the sketch might be passable. The eyes worked well, at least, and she caught his hint of smile. The smile promised so much.

She felt relieved they'd chosen a secluded spot.

When Roger finally had to leave, they stole a few moments in which to say goodbye in private. She had only known him a few days, but an intense few days. She felt comfortable around him, as if she could talk about anything. Their parting didn't have much talking, though. They spent it in silence, holding hands, gazing at each other. They bent their heads so their foreheads touched.

"I could be back this way again, Julie. Or you could come down to Atlanta sometime." He touched the line of her jaw with his finger, warm silk on her skin.

"Perhaps. I don't know when. Sometimes I'm just so much flotsam on the Jet Stream, being tossed around on the ocean." She teared up, thinking herself silly.

"Shh. Things'll be okay, sweetling. We'll always be friends. Will you write to me?"

"I'll do that. I promise."

Then they shared their last kiss. His lips felt soft and lush. He held her chin up with his fingers. Then he left.

1983, Miami, Florida

Julie watched her daughter writing an assignment at the kitchen table. *My girl is growing up. She's asking questions I'm not ready to answer.*

Kirsten had just turned thirteen, growing up tall and thin, but her curves popped out all over the place. While she had never been the most graceful of children, she grew even less sure of her movements with this strange, distorted body. Julie remembered the awkwardness from her own adolescence. Worse,

Kirsten grew curious about her father, thanks to a genealogy project assigned in her class.

"But Mom, I don't understand. You don't even know how old he was?"

Julie placed a plate with Rice Krispies treats on the table. "No, dear, we didn't discuss it much. We sort of avoided many subjects of his life."

Kirsten grabbed the biggest one. "But you know astrology. Wouldn't you have asked at least his sign?"

Shaking her head, she bit into her own piece. "I hadn't gotten into such things until later."

"Oh. Do you at least know what he did for a living?"

Julie shrugged. "Well, he taught classes at the Church."

"The Church?"

"The Church I worked for then. We both worked there."

Kirsten made some notes. "Well, that's something, I suppose. Did he teach other things, perhaps? Is that why I'm good in math?"

Julie let out a laugh and took a sip of her coffee. "That must be. You didn't get a talent for math from me."

"Don't you like math, Mom?"

"No, my Geometry teacher made me promise never to take math again."

Kirsten chuckled. "Seriously? I love math. Well, maybe not Geometry as much, my teacher is a total airhead. She told us when she first got her microwave, she would turn the thing on with nothing inside to see what happened. But I love solving math puzzles. That's why I like Games Magazine."

She's definitely growing up and learning her own place in the world, already heading down a different path than Julie at this age. All she'd wanted to do at that point was watch baseball and paint. And hang out with boys.

"Do you remember how to spell his name? I can hunt him down."

Julie felt horrified at the idea of the child calling her father, and announcing herself as his bastard daughter. "You can't hunt anyone down, young lady. Remember your actions have consequences. Do you want to disrupt someone else's life to satisfy your curiosity?"

"I didn't think of that." She looked so crestfallen, Julie relented, standing to give her a hug. Lord, she's almost as tall as I am already.

"At least I have plenty of information on your side to put into the project. I got the packet from Meema. Look, it goes back hundreds of years. Did you see? All the way back to the Firestones in Germany in the 1700s. Does that mean we're all German?"

"Not entirely, no. Grandma's maiden name is Firestone, so that's the direct line Meema sent you. Grandpa is English and Scots, I believe. I know there's a McKenzie and a Sutcliffe somewhere in there. And Meema herself is Welsh. Her maiden name is Rees."

"How do you know it's Welsh?"

"Rees was originally spelled R-H-Y-S, I saw it somewhere once. Maybe on some paperwork? Did you ever meet my cousin, Peggy? She does a lot of this research, and has boxes and boxes of stuff."

"I want to write to her, too, so I can get more stuff. This is cool."

Julie grinned, happy to feed her daughter's passion, at least on her own family line. Better that than she delve into the other side.

CHAPTER THREE

Pints and Philosophy

1967, East Grinstead, England

Sheila threw up her hands. "Oh, do stop moping around, Julie. It won't help matters if you don't get out and do things."

Julie barely left the room they shared in the days after Roger left, except for taking care of the kids and meals. She took care of the children in the mornings until about two in the afternoon, when Percy finished his seminar. Then she had free time, and could take classes, explore, or socialize. Her weekends remained free, and most evenings. But she didn't want to do any of those things.

She still did artwork for the Church, but did less and less. She didn't ask for more work.

"I'm not interested in going out, Sheila."

"And that's a load of bollocks. Get thee up, woman, go enjoy yourself. That's an order, that is." And with this, Sheila yanked at the blanket upon which Julie lay, forcing her to scramble for balance on the single bed.

"Tonight, you're coming with me. There's a gathering in town. I shall not take no for an answer. Get your glad rags on by seven for half-seven." With this final decree, Sheila left.

Julie sighed, resigned to Sheila's efforts. Perhaps a night out would be good for her. She missed talking to Roger so much it ached. She still found it hard to credit they'd only known each other a few days.

While she pulled out several outfits, none appealed to her. Exasperated, she chose a frumpy, conservative one. The midnight blue button-down shirt sported a jabot ruffle at the neckline. The high collar screamed Victorian chic. A long, black, swirling skirt completed her mourning outfit. She pinned her hair back with barrettes, but then put it into a severe French braid. It would be out of her face, so she wouldn't have to bother with readjusting the barrettes every half hour.

Julie surveyed herself in the mirror, noting her grim expression, like the matron of a girls' school, out for a rollicking evening at the library, reading a Jane Austen novel. Fine, she'd change her shirt, at least. She chose a satiny, flowing blouse with orange and pink nouveau swirls. She tucked the edge into her skirt's waistband to cut down on the flow.

When Sheila showed up at seven, her friend looked her up and down, giving her a grudging nod. Sheila wore the manner of a sergeant inspecting his troops. "I was afraid I would have to make you change, but you'll do. Barely."

"I figured as much, so I spared you the effort." She stuck her tongue out at Sheila. They both laughed as they walked, arm in arm, from the dorms down to the village.

They met David, Paul, Colum, and Jimmy on the way down, and a townie named Victoria Riches. The prim British girl stood about Julie's height and about the same age. She pulled her ashy blond hair into a ponytail, revealing a round face with a buxom figure.

Victoria bid them all "hello" in a clipped tone. Brits sounded terse by nature compared to their American counterparts.

Julie dodged a potted plant on the pavement as they descended the hill. "Are you part of the Church here, Victoria?"

"Not in the slightest. I work at Ashdown House School, helping with their accounting. However, I've been up to Saint Hill many times, before all the moonbats moved in. No offense intended." She didn't seem as if she cared if Julie took offense or not, but her words held no malice.

Julie shrugged. "It's a church. They're in business of teaching and converting, not making friends."

Paul snorted at this, and even Victoria giggled.

As they walked down the street, with beautiful half-timbered buildings lining either side, they arrived at The Dorset Arms Pub. They walked in, found a big, round table, and ordered pints. Julie didn't care for beer, but she enjoyed the cider, a popular option at British pubs.

Paul turned to Victoria and held up his glass. "So, Victoria, tell us a bit about the history of this place."

"You mean the village? It's turned into a hotbed of religious focus, as just about every church in the world settled in the area. The hippies seem to believe it's a 'ley line' thing. The priests maintain it's a spiritual centre, so it attracts them all. It has always been a place people get drawn to. I suppose the credible attract the gullible."

Julie found it harder to ignore Victoria's jibes when she directed her vitriol at religious people in general. She also didn't want to get into an argument defending a religion she harbored her own doubts about.

Paul grinned at Victoria. "After what the damned Catholics put most of the Western World through, I'm surprised any one of them be attracted to the sacred."

Victoria stopped to sip her beer and glanced at Paul. "Well, the Catholics aren't the only idiots to embrace the inscrutable, not around here. A lot of heartache and money would be saved by burning the lot of them. You sound as if you've a bone to pick with the Catholic Church, Paul. What's the story there?"

He settled back into his story-teller posture, his hands crossed over his belly. "My parents raised me in the Catholic Church, and I attended seminary to become a priest myself. I once considered becoming a monk, but discovered I had cloisterphobia."

He paused, waiting for his audience to groan or laugh. They all groaned. "In all seriousness, as a younger son, priesthood seemed an acceptable option, if one follows the medieval tradition. Soon, I understood most of the church aristocracy got into it for the power. They didn't answer any of my questions about life. The church represented institutionalism at its worst, which I wanted no part of. Besides, as a priest, well, abstinence leaves a lot to be desired." He gave Julie a mock leer.

Paul took a long drink of his beer, downing most of it in one long swig.

Victoria raised her eyebrows. "And the blokes up on the hill there are any better?"

"At least some of them still value in having power over their own destinies, rather than over others. And there is something to be said for practical theology over other philosophies, such as communism or socialism."

Julie got nervous at the mention of communism. The McCarthyism craze had been strong thirteen ago, and she still remembered her parents' stories. Grim news reports on television and radio, about neighbors turning in their friends to escape punishment for themselves. The worst sort of witch hunt. She hid her shudder.

Paul still spoke. "It begs the basic questions of life. Are we, as humans, obliged to care for our fellow man to the exclusion of our own care? What is the purpose of our own happiness? And that begs even more questions. What is a soul? What is my relationship to my soul? What happens to me when my soul goes elsewhere? I don't *have* a soul, rather I *am* a soul. I *have* a body."

Julie quoted, "'We are not human beings having a spiritual experience. We are spiritual beings having a human experience'?"

His grin grew wider. "Have you read de Chardin's works, then?"

"No, I'm a dilettante. I must have picked the quote up somewhere random." Julie blushed and Victoria came to her rescue.

"I might get behind such a concept. I'm done with most organized churches, and I've been in several. I couldn't get past the hypocrisy of them, except perhaps Buddhism. They've got decent ideas, and their followers pay attention to them." Victoria took her last sip of beer, standing up to fetch another round. "Same all around?"

After they nodded and she left for the bar, Julie chuckled. "That's the angriest Buddhist I've ever seen."

Paul laughed. "Angry, but honest. I'd wish for more friends like her. Sometimes the double-dealing of societal 'manners' is maddening."

"Agreed!" They all toasted this, with the last swigs of their drinks.

When Victoria returned with refreshed pints, the conversation moved on to related topics, such as Sir Arthur Conan Doyle's firm belief in Spiritualism and the ghost stories of the local countryside. Julie avoided giving her account of the abandoned tunnels of Saint Hill but kept her ears open in case anyone mentioned anything akin to her experience.

After a while, she noticed Paul was no longer among the group. His pint glass had disappeared, but she didn't notice him leave.

Jimmy intruded on her thoughts. "I wouldn't say aliens are impossible. There have been so many rumors and sightings, are all the stories hoaxes?"

Sheila slapped her hand on the table. "They must be hoaxes. Where do you think they'd be coming from? What do they look like?"

Julie furrowed her brow, trying to recall the episodes of Twilight Zone she'd seen. "Aren't most of the recorded sightings of a thin, white body with enormous eyes and no hair? Sightings of actual creatures, not ships, I mean. It might be a Jungian archetype, I suppose. A thousand years ago, we would have termed them Gods rather than Aliens, setting up a shrine in their honor. The ancients begged them not to destroy our crops with furious vengeance and all that. Maybe they've been visiting for a long time, so the Gods of past civilizations are interpretations of those visitations."

Victoria returned with their pints, and Jimmy grabbed his. "But ancient Gods aren't tall, thin white creatures with enormous eyes. They resemble us, more or less."

Colum burst out laughing. "Tell that to those Egyptians jobbos, with their jackal-head and falcon-head Gods. Or the Aztecs, or even the Greeks, who's Gods changed shape whenever they bloody well liked. Even some of our Gods in Scotland aren't really human. Sure, and the Wee Folk might have been tiny aliens." He took a deep drink from his own

mug. "And Norse elves stood tall, thin, and bright, as Tolkien used as a model for his elves."

Julie heard a guitar being tuned. As she glanced up, she smiled to see Paul on stage, fiddling with his guitar strings. He glanced up, noticed her watching him, and waggled his eyebrows up and down. Eyes still on her, he launched into a Kingston Trio song, "I Am Henry the Eighth."

This song always annoyed her but seemed perfect for Paul. She gave him a long-suffering eye-roll, which made him smile as he sang the words, in a ridiculous, exaggerated Cockney accent.

He got most of the pub to join in on the chorus. A few sang the rest of the verses with him.

At long last, the song ended. He moved on to a more somber tune, "Last Night I Had the Strangest Dream," a sad anti-war song. Julie's eyes prickled with tears before it he finished.

World War II may have been over for many years, but she remembered not hearing from her father for a long time when they all feared him lost. He didn't return from the Japan Sea unscathed. Since he contracted malaria, he suffered from ringing in his ears and aching joints and back. However, he returned whole and sane, better than many of the soldiers and sailors. The Brits lost even more of their young men, as they'd been in the war for years before America joined the fight.

Paul followed this intense performance with another song designed to wring out the soul, "Turn! Turn! Turn!" by Pete Seeger. He then segued into a lighter mood with "Sunshine Superman" by Donovan, full of silly summer fun.

Paul got the entire pub singing, even if they didn't seem to remember the words. The crowd seemed strong, and he had them in the palm of his hand.

He followed in the maxim of leaving when on top, as he took a break then. He brought his guitar and half-pint of beer to their high-top table, making a show of swigging the rest of his glass. Another pint appeared, an homage from the appreciative audience. Paul seemed well-paid for his efforts in entertainment.

"Well? How did I do?" Paul breathed fast, hoarse from his singing. He didn't seem the least bit anxious about his performance.

"Wonderful. Well done."

"Bravo!"

"Brilliant!"

Julie gazed at him with love-sick eyes. She didn't care.

Paul came to Hayward Heath to pick her up for their date. She chose, rejected, and re-chose a dozen outfits, scarves, jewelry sets, and shoes in the two hours before the movie. This would be their first real date, the first time they stepped out as a couple alone. Now she wore a dark green knee-length flowing skirt, with a clingy sea-foam green blouse which she hoped showed off what assets she possessed to sufficient advantage. Julie chose a thin scarf to go around her neck, not wanting to block the bits the low-cut blouse showed off. The night might be chilly, so she added a cardigan sweater. She didn't care for green herself, but it set off the bits of red in her hair. Julie preferred to wear warmer colors—brown, red, gold, orange.

When she opened the door, he fidgeted and she noticed sweat on his brow. She'd never noticed him to be nervous before, but there he stood, fist clutching on a bouquet of pink and white wildflowers, a couple drooping down around the sides of his hand. He dressed in a white turtleneck shirt, a light brown suede sports jacket and matching pants. He'd done his best to tame his black hair, but light wisps defied his efforts when the evening breeze came.

"I hope *thistle* make you feel cherished." From the sheepishness of his grin, he realized how weak the pun was. Julie rolled her eyes and took the proffered nosegay. She invited him in as she searched for an appropriate vessel for the flowers.

She found a crystal vase in the kitchen, splashed water into it, making a show of arranging them on the sideboard. "What was the name of the movie? A foreign film?" She'd never been a tremendous fan of foreign films, as the effort of reading the subtitles while watching the images gave her a headache.

"Mondo Cane," he answered. "Which means 'A Dog's World' in Italian. Jimmy recommended it. It's been nominated for several awards."

They didn't speak much on the walk into town, but they held hands, which made her heart beat faster.

Julie didn't have many clear memories of the movie, as it chopped and flashed from scene to scene with no cohesive pattern. She remembered flashes of fishermen in Australia shoving sea urchins down the throats of sharks, dogs being skinned alive for a feast, make-up being put on corpses for a funeral. It seemed to be a documentary about strange rituals around the world, and the scenes seemed strange and graphic. About halfway through, Paul got up to go to the bathroom. She watched the movie alone for a while, but soon realized he'd been gone a long time.

She found the men's room. Several men walked out, so she got up the nerve to ask one of them if he remembered a man in there of Paul's description. The man said the bathroom was empty. Where did he go? She peeked in after the man left. No one.

Did he abandon her? It seemed rude and most unlike him. She headed home, her eyes glued to the ground. Her anger and indignation grew with each step. He'd ditched her. Julie's wrath never ignited quickly, but caught on well now, ready to burst into flames at a feather's touch.

She heard a car stop next to her. When she turned, she saw Paul's car, but no Paul. Jimmy sat in the front seat.

"Wait, why are you in Paul's car? What's going on?"

"Paul's in the hospital. Come on in, we'll go. He called me from there, so I walked down to pick up his car. I have a spare set of keys."

She got in, bewildered. Her anger shifted into worry. Jimmy careened through the narrow, winding streets of the medieval town, arriving at the rambling hospital on the edge of the community with a screech.

They made it through the endless maze of dim, antiseptic green corridors, lit by harsh fluorescent lights. *Did they build nothing straight in this country?* After several inquiries, they found Paul, hooked up to an IV, looking sheepish.

She could barely hear his whisper. "Julie, I am so sorry. The movie got too intense for me. I feel horrible at leaving you, but I walked outside for air, then passed out. Someone called an ambulance, so here I am. As soon as I came to, I made someone bring me a phone and I called Jimmy to find you. Please say you aren't mad?"

Her anger dissipated the instant she heard Jimmy say "hospital." They didn't have the most auspicious first date, but she wouldn't hold this against him.

"I don't blame you one bit. It got worse after you left. I can't understand how that horrible movie won any awards. Hey ..." Julie turned to Jimmy, her eyes narrowed. "Jimmy, you recommended this stinker. Why the hell would you do that?"

Jimmy shrugged. "I enjoyed it. Ground-breaking cinema, and all that. I didn't realize you were so squeamish, old man." He punched Paul in the arm in the time-honored male manner.

Paul managed a feeble half-smile. "Not the sort of movie for a first date, at any rate. Shall we try again in a few days? I might be strong enough then."

"I promise I'll be gentle with your frail self." She kissed him, gentle and chaste, on the cheek.

Julie threw another rock against the ancient stone wall and derived considerable satisfaction from watching it shatter into cream-colored bits. She threw another.

She had never been so outraged, so confused, and so hurt in her life. How dare Paul trifle with her heart in such a way? He'd been beyond cruel.

The night after that horrific first date, they all ate in the dining room of the big house. David sat next to Sheila at the communal dinner tables, his mass of unruly, curly black hair pulled back into a long ponytail. Their son, Neil, sat on a booster chair between them. He tried to decorate his own hair with half-eaten biscuits, while everyone laughed at his antics.

Sheila brandished a washcloth. "Neil, you are much too old to be wearing so much of your dinner. Let mummy clean your chin, dear."

David grabbed the cloth from her. "Here, Sheila, eat your own dinner. I'll handle this wee hellion."

With a grateful smile, Sheila dug into her own roast, mopping the meat juices with a chunk of Yorkshire pudding. She licked a stray drop from her thumb when Neil let out a screech of protest.

David intervened again. "Now, now, stop the sirens, young man. How about some soup?"

Paul chuckled and asked Sheila, "How long have you two been married?"

"Four years now, Paul. How about you?"

Julie stopped her fork halfway to her mouth, the baked beans dripping in a congealed glop onto her plate. She stared at him, waiting for his answer.

His eyes flicked from Sheila, who looked horrified, to hers. She saw the guilt and worry plain on his face. Her cheeks grew warm and the rage rose inside her. Married? Paul had a *wife?*

"Julie? Julie, I meant to tell you last night—"

She shoved away from the table and her chair clattered to the tile floor behind her. She escaped the now-hushed dining room, aware of so many eyes boring into her back.

After rushing out into the chilly evening air, she took a few deep breaths, her lungs burning with rage and shame. Twilight embraced the town in a brisk blanket of cerulean blue. She needed to walk. She needed to think.

Married. What in God's name was he doing flirting with every figure in a skirt? He took her on a date. How dare he trifle with her heart in this way? Julie stomped up the path, satisfied at the crunch her boots made on the gravel. The screaming pain of betrayal and confusion rushed through her blood.

When she halted and glanced up, she stood in front of the pub. With a shrug, she opened the heavy wooden door and stepped in. She'd never visited alone, but this would be a grand time to start.

Victoria worked behind the bar, and Julie closed her eyes in relief. Much easier to vent to a friend. She drank her cider and brooded, giving Victoria the facts. At first, her friend gave her shallow platitudes and advice. However, after several pints, Victoria started asking the tough questions. "Are you in love with him?"

Julie almost choked on her cider. "Love? I have no idea what love is, Victoria. I was in love with Jeffrey... but he..." She clamped her jaw shut.

"He what, Julie?"

Drumming her fingers on the mahogany bar, Julie didn't answer.

"Julie? What did he do to you? Did he hit you?"

"No, nothing like that, I mean. He, well, he left me for someone else, and it hurt. It hurt horribly. He abandoned me in a strange city, with no job, no friends, nothing."

"In Detroit? Isn't that where your parents lived?"

"No, no, I made the stellar move of following him to Washington, D.C. We both worked for the art department of a car company in Detroit who shifted offices to D.C., so we followed. We got this tiny, grimy apartment, but we had each other. Then he met Sandy."

"Sandy?"

Julie finished her pint. "Yeah, Sandy. One of my best friends from high school. She attended college in New York City, then came to visit. They got along together. Too well, it turned out."

"He slept with your friend? What a bloody bastard! Did you call him out?"

She stared at Victoria. "Call him out? What's that in American? No, he just left. He moved off to New York to be with Sandy and left me with an apartment I couldn't afford on my own and no friends." Talking about something other than Paul was what she needed. She wrapped the older betrayal around her like a shield. The ending had happened, and she made some peace with it. Paul became a fresher, rawer situation.

"What happened then?"

Julie shrugged. "A woman I worked with got me involved in the Church, and I started taking care of her kids. She quit the other job to work full time for the Church, and when she moved here, I came with her."

Victoria filled another pint and slid it across the bar to her. "So you ran away. And that was that?"

"Pretty much. Now I can't stay here."

"What options do you have?"

Another hard question. What options *did* she have? She might move back home. But her father never approved of her career in art, and she'd have to admit defeat. Julie might ask for a transfer to another location, but where? Or she'd have to stay and face Paul.

When Julie didn't answer, Victoria leaned on the bar and said, "I've got a notion for you."

Julie looked up. "I'm listening."

"I've a cousin in San Francisco, and another driving out there. You might transfer there. Your church has a branch there, don't they?"

They did.

Julie put in for a transfer that evening and got immediate approval. She avoided Paul for the three days it took to make arrangements, and so she ran away again.

Julie couldn't secure a flight all the way to San Francisco on such short notice. The closest she could get was Houston, unless she wanted to wait another week. She didn't want to wait.

Victoria once again stepped up to the plate and helped. She called her cousin, George, to have him pick her up at the Houston airport. Julie protested it as too much to ask, but Victoria would not be dissuaded.

"It's all I can do to help mend a broken heart, Julie. Besides, George loves lengthy road trips. Enjoy yourself. He's fun company. You've found precious little joy, and you need more. Have some fun in the Wild West."

The flight itself made Julie anxious. *Is this yet another horrible mistake? Or have I finally taken control of my situation?* More likely, she just ran away again.

Well, time to buck up and change your life, Julie! She hoped George would be pleasant company, at least.

The Houston airport looked huge and confusing, but she collected her luggage and found the arrivals lounge. She barely slept on the flight. Victoria gave her George's description, so she scanned the waiting crowds for a tall, thin man, about her own age, with a thick mustache and beard.

She spied someone of Victoria's description, carrying a sign that read "Julie." He wore a black turtleneck sweater (again with the turtlenecks?), dark slacks, and ankle boots. A beatnik? He sported a broad grin and his blue eyes seemed gleeful.

"Are you Julie?" He sounded hesitant.

"I am, and I'm pleased to meet you." She held out her hand to shake.

He took her hand, but instead of a handshake, he hugged her. Surprised at the intrusion, she realized he gave excellent hugs. She'd needed a wonderful hug. They held on tight for what seemed like a long time, then let go.

"Better? Cousin Vicky filled me in." He arched an eyebrow at her, as he held her at arms' length.

"Yes, okay, thank you." She turned flustered and shy, but he kept looking into her eyes, as if searching for the truth.

"No, sorry, I *am* better." She took a deep breath. "Okay, let's do this. Victoria told you I can't drive, right? That I can only keep you awake?" Julie hefted her suitcase and large purse, fighting back an unaccountable urge to cry.

"She did. Please, allow me." George grabbed the case, so she shrugged and grabbed the carpet bag of other stuff, the books and craft supplies which didn't fit into her suitcase. Traveling light had its advantages.

1985, Miami, Florida

Kirsten sprang awake, anxious, at a strange noise. A bang? A shout?

She heard voices in the living room, so craned her head to peek around the corner from her room. She saw her mom, her Aunt Sandy, and a man she didn't recognize, all sitting around the glass and rattan coffee table. Sounds echoed in the large white room with its tile floor, distorting them. The words sounded fuzzier than they should, though.

After hearing her Aunt Sandy slur in a sing-song voice, she rolled her eyes at their drunk antics. Her mom looked like she might fall out of the overstuffed chair, while the guy on the couch fell into Sandy's lap as she tried to keep her wineglass from spilling.

Kirsten shut the bedroom door to keep out most of the sounds. Many Friday nights found her mom and Aunt Sandy with a strange man or two after a night out on the town. They'd leave by the morning, but sometimes she woke up to find one asleep on the couch, stinking of alcohol. At age fifteen, she understood what they did, but whether they slept with her mom or her Aunt, both women stayed discreet enough to make them sleep on the couch afterwards, or leave.

Her mom never dated anyone, but Aunt Sandy kept a steady string of boyfriends, though none lasted long. Her cynicism and bitterness drove most of them off in short order. She always found more, though. Kirsten didn't know if her mom slept with any of them, as Sandy seemed more acquisitive.

As dawn approached, she dressed. Kirsten saw the latest acquisition still on the couch, but no one else sounded awake. She'd escape to the library, as she so often did after school. Kirsten still tried to research her genealogy, having requested information via an interlibrary loan. She didn't tell her mom about her research, after her initial horror at the idea.

Several hours later, Kirsten pushed herself away from the library table in frustration, heaving a huge sigh. She pulled back her long, dark brown, curly hair into a ponytail and twirled the point with her finger. She found no trace of her father.

Today, she'd searched through phone books from Minneapolis, looking for any similar name she might find. Unfortunately, she didn't know how he spelled his name, and her mother didn't remember.

She wrote a letter to the East Grinstead Branch of the Church a month ago, but got no answer yet. She used her best friend's address so her mother wouldn't see the reply.

Kirsten gathered her papers, handed the phone books back to the librarian with thanks, walking the mile home. She needed to consider things, and walking helped.

If she didn't find her father via this method, what's her next option? She wrote to the now-defunct branch of the Church in his hometown, but discovered, while one lady remembered him, no one else did. He hadn't been a member since 1971, and those old paper records had disappeared. The woman who remembered her father thought he'd moved to Dallas. Kirsten added the Dallas/Fort Worth phone books to her search. She already gathered twenty names and numbers from the previous phone books. These added another thirty names and numbers to her list.

Kirsten considered how she might make the phone calls without her mother seeing a huge long-distance phone bill next month. Both the Minneapolis and Dallas calls would elicit questions. She'd save money from her paycheck at Arby's, and offer to pay Tiff's mom for long-distance calls.

The calls shouldn't take long each, perhaps a minute to discover if she found the right man. If she did, the phone call would last longer. What would she say? How would he react? What would he be like? How much money would she need to save for phone calls?

Kirsten often thought about her first meeting with her father. Somehow, she imagined a face-to-face meeting in her mind, not on the phone, but she must consider the latter possibility. She didn't want to be disappointed in him, so convinced herself he might not be interested in acknowledging a bastard daughter. He would have a family of his own. He might be a jerk, an ignorant redneck in a rusted pickup truck, and missing teeth. If Kirsten convinced herself of the worst, and he turned out normal, she'd be pleasantly surprised. She excelled at this self-psychological warfare.

With a plan in mind, she walked back to her house, grateful to see last night's visitor gone, all trace of him vanished. She stuffed her papers away in her schoolbooks, beginning her list of chores for the day.

1967, On the road

As Julie and George got on the highway and headed southwest on Interstate 15, they explored each other's past. George talked about his father, a dentist set on a son who would follow in his footsteps. George's father flew as a pilot in the Air Force in World War II, until he got injured and discharged. However, George wanted a degree in music, which he pursued with his father's express disapproval. His mother worked as a nurse in the war, helping soldiers in Hawaii. He had a sister, born after the war, still in high school. His older brother, Fred, lived out in California.

"What instrument do you play?" Julie asked, though it gave her a twinge of pain, remembering Paul.

"Guitar, banjo, anything stringed and designed to strum." George answered. "I'd show you, but then my driving might suffer."

Julie assured him. "No, no, keep driving. I'd rather live to hear it another day."

"So, tell me about yourself, Miss Julie. What brought you to this point? What are you running from?"

She shook her head and then stared out at the passing landscape of suburbs. "I'm not running away from anything. I'm sort of lost, I guess."

"Mmm-hmm. Sure, and I'm not running away from anything either. Be honest, my dear. Everyone's running from something. Let's see if we can ferret it out. What's your dad like?"

Julie remembered her father, a big bear of a man. She shoved away the twinge of homesickness. "He was a sergeant in World War II, on a PT boat in the Japan Sea. A hurricane slammed his ship on the way to the Panama Canal. While he was shipwrecked at the naval station in Key West, Mom had me. Now he's an engineer for Chrysler, which is why we moved to Dearborn."

"Strong man? Yells a lot?"

She lifted her eyebrows. "Are there any sergeants who don't?"

"Fair enough. What about your mom?"

"Mom is the gentle sort. She's an art teacher in high school. A peacemaker."

He glanced over to her. "So there are a lot of wars for her to sort out, obviously. Have you got brothers or sisters?"

"Katy, she's two years younger than me, also an artist. Larry, he's sixteen. He's a brat."

73

"He's a younger brother, right? It's the law."

She giggled, covering up the sudden wave of homesickness for both her siblings.

George kept digging for the answers. "What was the last war about?"

"College. Both Mom and Dad approved of me being an artist, I'll give him that. But the math got too hard for me, so I quit. My father wanted to kick me out, since I didn't go to school anymore. My mother argued with him, and she never argues. To stop the shouting, I left. I lived with my sister in her place for a while. That's where I met Jeffrey."

She stopped then. She didn't want to talk about him, but George seemed to sense it. "And Jeffrey brought you to D.C.?"

"Yes. And when Jeffrey... left, I got a job with the Church, and taking care of a family of children. They moved to England, so I moved with them. Then things in England got complex."

"And Cousin Vicky called for the cavalry, so to speak."

Julie laughed. To hear the prim and proper Victoria called "Cousin Vicky" in a Midwest accent just seemed so surreal. The laugh got hysterical before she squelched her mirth with a sigh.

The conversation moved onto other things. They discussed the war in Vietnam, the US troops, all the demonstrations about the war, including one last month in San Francisco. Julie mentioned Muhammad Ali refusing to fight in the war. George brought up the first artificial heart in Texas. Julie brought up India's first female prime minister.

They discussed the tensions between the US and the USSR, and the Cambodian Civil War. Then they turned to lighter subjects, such as the marriage of Elvis Presley and Priscilla Ann Wagner. George imitated Mister Ed. They drove on in silence for a while after that, as if that exhausted the entirety of cultural discussion.

Julie must have dozed off for a sudden lurch woke her. She looked up, anxious, but George just avoided a tree branch on the road. She must have slept for a while, as the sun blazed high and bright. The car felt warm, sticky with humidity and trapped heat.

She'd never taken a road trip this long before, and they weren't even halfway through. She went up to Canada for summer vacations with her family, but just a four-hour drive from Detroit, to the lake where her family owned an island with several cabins. Her trip to D.C. was broken by stops in Ohio to visit both sets of grandparents, then Virginia to visit one of Jeffrey's cousins. She enjoyed this trip more, as George proved to be entertaining company, if on the goofy side. His capers almost reminded Julie of her little brother, the ultimate class clown. She refused to let herself compare him to Paul.

"Whew! It's getting warm. Can I turn down the window?" Julie mopped her forehead with her sleeve, finding nothing else on hand for the job.

"Sure, hold on," George cranked down his window, keeping his eyes on the road, as she did the same.

Above the roar of the wind, they resumed conversational tidbits. Julie told him about her time running the Rocky Colavito fan club. She talked of her little sister, also a wonderful artist. She spoke of her best friends, Gail, Helen, and Sandy. Gail married and had a baby, Ross. Gail's husband, Jan, worked as an auto mechanic.

Julie described the work she did in Dearborn at Greenfield Village. She spoke of Sandy and the apartment they shared in college.

George gave her a sidelong glance when she mentioned Sandy.

"What?"

"You screw your face up when you talk about Sandy. Did you have a fight with her?"

She swallowed. "No, not precisely. Well, she and Jeffrey... "

"Aha. Have you talked to her since?"

"No. I wrote her a letter when I arrived in England, but she never replied."

He laughed at her. "She doesn't seem like a staunch friend, if she isn't there for you when you need her."

Julie shrugged. "She helps me see past my rose-colored glasses. Sandy was my closest friend in college. When I first moved out of my parents' house, I moved in with her. We were close, but it's true, we don't see eye-to-eye on many things. Perhaps we complemented each other. Her pessimism modulated my optimism, and vice versa. We helped each other out."

"Alright, alright, no need to get in a huff." George raised his hand in defense, but he teased her. It made her warm inside.

They'd passed El Paso, but now her stomach rumbled. She couldn't imagine how George stayed up, considering he must have driven many hours

before he picked her up. Perhaps he slept before he came to the airport.

She yawned. "Hey, can we stop for some food? I'm starving."

"Sure. Let me find a place."

George pulled up to a dusty roadside diner, giving Julie a quizzical glance. She shrugged. This looked about as good as they were likely to find. Their fatigue and hunger made their decision for them.

When they walked in, all conversations faded out. Everyone watched them. Men filled the diner, dusty and dirty in work clothes, sitting at the counter. Julie stood out in her cream sweater and blue scarf, as if she committed a crime in wearing bright, clean clothes. She glanced at George, but it didn't seem to bother him at all. He took her hand, held his head high, walking over to one of the cracked red booths next to the dust-smeared window.

An older woman in a faded pink slack suit and an almost white apron came to their table. She'd piled her blonde hair high, with large plastic pineapple earrings swinging when she moved. She snapped her chewing gum. "What can I get you, folks?"

"Coffee. Lots of coffee. And a menu?" George grinned at her.

She grinned back. "Sure thing, Sugar. Be right back."

The line of workmen lost interest, or ate on a timed break, as they returned to their burgers and chatting to each other in muted tones. The muttering rose and fell like a strange wave of dust.

The waitress came back with mugs, a carafe of black coffee, and the menus. Burgers, sandwiches with egg salad, ham salad, chicken salad, or tomato soup. Milkshakes, pie, and ice cream sodas. Julie decided the burger would be the safest, well done, with French fries.

George told her he would cover the meals. She argued with him, but he insisted.

Julie sipped at the black coffee. She saw no sugar or cream, but she preferred it black and bitter. She took a couple bites of her burger, but the greasy mess made her stomach churn. The fries tasted good, though, and they filled her hunger. George attacked his egg salad sandwich with gusto. He poured the ketchup all over his fries, making a huge mound of mess.

Two sorts of people existed in this world. Those who poured the ketchup on the fries, and those who dipped the fries into the ketchup in a controlled manner. She sat firmly in the latter category.

She stared at his mess with her lip curled. "So, you never told me why you wanted to move to California. What's the story?"

He extracted one fry with way too much ketchup and lobbed it into his mouth. "Well, I finished my degree, so decided I'd see the world before settling into the humdrum life expected of me. My dad's a dentist, as I said, so he expected both Fred and I to follow in his footsteps. But I studied Music and Creative Writing instead. Well, let's just say he was less than pleased. A couple of my poems got published in Chelsea Magazine. Have you ever read it? It's a New York publication." Julie shook her head as he continued.

"Fred has a job out in San Francisco. He has his hands full with his wife and kids, so I asked if I could come out and help with expenses, as a roommate. He's got this snazzy Victorian house a block from Haight and two blocks from Ashbury. It's a fantastic spot for poets and other Bohemian types. There are coffee houses and places to share my work. That's about it."

George then had asked how she knew Victoria, so Julie explained how she had met her at the pub in East Grinstead.

"And she's your cousin? But you aren't British?"

"Ha! No, our branch of the family came over several generations ago. We keep in touch with our family across the pond, though. We've got a large family. Her brother moved over here about ten years ago and got his US citizenship. He lived near Fred in San Francisco."

"Lived? Did he move away?"

"Yeah. He's gone off on a hare-brained idea to Canada. He has this crazy notion he needs to leave the States because of Vietnam. Like they would come here and invade? Insanity."

Julie dunked one of her fries into the neat dollop of ketchup. "I don't know anything about the war. We heard bits on the news at my parents, but I haven't owned a radio or TV since I moved out. I don't read the newspapers much. Is it likely?"

"No way. C'mon, they don't even have a navy. The Pacific is huge, a lot of ocean to cross, and they're a tiny country. Sure, we've sent troops over there, but I'm sure it will all be over soon."

Julie's brother turned sixteen this year and would be of draft age soon. She shoved the idea out of her head, mopping up her remaining ketchup with the last few fries.

"Are you all done? We should get back on the road."

Julie swigged the last dregs of her now cold coffee and ate a few more bites of the soggy, greasy, burger. She wiped her mouth with the napkin, gathering her things. George left cash on the table for the bill. Once again, the few workers who still ate at the counter scrutinized them as they walked by. The food had been forgettable, but at least they got needed fuel.

☮ ☮ ☮

After eleven more hours on the road, their fatigue turned to loopiness. By the time they passed a sign that read "East Mojave Scenic Area," they felt strung out and totally beat.

The sunrise glowed with spectacular brilliance, painting the stark beauty of the desert mountains with vibrant tones of peach, gold, and crimson. With her artist's eye, Julie named all the colors she saw. Burnt orange, sienna, aqua, cyan, cinnamon, and many colors she possessed no name for, but remained beautiful to behold.

The spectacular sight revived her. She sat backwards in her seat, trying to see out the back window as the rising sun revealed the wonders of the desert. After a crick in her neck, she settled on seeing what happened to each side, watching the long shadows in front of her. She itched to paint, to record these unusual colors, this new, bizarre scenery. She pulled out her sketchpad, but nothing stayed in sight long enough for her to capture more than a quick sketch.

Despite the momentary high the celestial tableau afforded her, she still fought to keep her eyes open. Struck by a notion, Julie sang. Sing a song they both knew, and it might keep them alert. Besides, she'd done well enough in the high school Glee Club. Shy at first, she sang the first lines of a particular song, inspired by the sight of the rising sun.

"You are my sunshine, my only sunshine …"

George looked at her in surprise. Had he been dozing? Good God, she hoped not. A scary notion. But he joined in, their voices growing bolder.

"You make me happy, when skies are gray
You'll never know, dear, how much I love you.
Please don't take my sunshine away!"

They sang more verses, gaining volume and energy as they did so. Soon they belted the words out at the top of their lungs, beating on the dashboard and dancing in their seats as they sung out the chorus. Julie hoped the car would survive such abuse. When they finished, they laughed until they cried.

"Good idea, Julie. That got my juices flowing again. What's next?"

"How about a long song? We're still hours away. A song with endless verses. 'Ninety-Nine Bottles of Beer on the Wall?'"

"Oh, by the nine circles of hell, no! I'd find a beer bottle and knock you on the head before it's over. I detest that song."

"How about 'On Top of Old Smokey?'"

"Bingo! Much better, yes."

"On top of Old Smokey, all covered with snow …" Julie began.

80

At the same time, George sang a different line. "On top of Spaghetti, all covered with cheese …"

They both stopped singing, giggling and laughing until George snorted, unable to control the car. He pulled over to the side of the long, straight road. Luckily, they stopped in the middle of nowhere, with nothing around for miles. She grabbed a bag of potato chips from the back while they stopped, getting control over themselves, or as much control as they could.

George drove through the night as Julie cycled through her repertoire of songs. She mostly sang folk songs, such as "This Land is Your Land." She sang some Rock-and-Roll, like The Beatles or Fats Domino. She even sang a couple hymns she remembered from childhood.

Singing the hymns felt odd. Despite being Presbyterian, her parents rarely attended church. She felt less attuned to the religious beliefs they taught her. Julie believed in being kind to others. She didn't agree that Christians should have the monopoly. But she couldn't imagine a bearded man in heaven cared about people worshipping him. It made him sound as petty and petulant as the ancient Greek gods. She did intriguing research into other belief systems, chatting with George about them as another night faded into a bright, cloudless morning. The Church she worked for taught beliefs aligned with hers on this. They never defined the higher power, simply a spiritual presence.

"I don't give credence in an afterlife, or the devil, or any of that." George said, in response to her comments. "We have this one life to live, so we've got to do our best while we can. Anything more is superstitious claptrap, designed to keep us institutionalized under the church."

Julie had no idea how to define her concept of an afterlife, or what else she might feel about God. She just knew it didn't reflect with what she'd been taught in Bible class.

Their destination, San Francisco, had a reputation as a hotbed of their generation's revolution in religious indoctrination. A home of scandalous poets and wanton musicians. San Francisco fostered a huge subculture which questioned the status quo, the expected behavior of the "good family," along with all the appearances associated with it. It sounded so exciting, she looked forward to seeing it for herself.

They glanced around them and saw so much nothing, they began imagining things on the horizon. It looked flat, desolate, dry, deserted, and so lonely.

To pass the time, they made a game from their surroundings. She looked out to the right and swore she saw a shape on the distant horizon. When she pointed it out to George, they guessed what it might be, each guess becoming more and more outrageous.

"An outhouse," George guessed.

"Out here? For what? It's a stand of cactus."

He tried again. "A jackelope warren"

"What in the name of all that's holy is a jackelope??"

George flashed her a grin. "The creature who lives out there. Perhaps it's an alien homing beacon."

"We're in California, not Nevada!"

"It doesn't matter. Who said aliens only landed once?"

Julie narrowed her eyes. "Okay, why leave it out in plain sight, then?"

"It's cloaked to appear as a jackelope warren. Disguised."

She raised an eyebrow. "Perhaps as an outhouse?"

"Exactly."

A couple hours later, the heat of the day made Julie drowsy. She nodded off a couple times but kept jerking herself awake. About the fourth time, she looked at George, realizing he must be worse off.

"Shall we sing again?" She suggested.

"What about poetry, instead? We already sang all the songs."

"Hmm. Oh, wait!" Julie began reciting one of her favorite poems from childhood.

"Twinkle, twinkle, little bat!

How I wonder what you're at!"

He glared at her. "What the hell was that?"

"Have you never read Alice in Wonderland? The Mad Hatter recites it to Alice."

"No, I must have missed that one."

"Where are we, anyhow? Any clue?" Julie grabbed a package of crackers, handing him a couple to munch on.

"We crossed into California about an hour ago. At least, it's what I think the sign said. It had faded so much, I could barely read it. I didn't pay all that much attention. I hoped it wouldn't jump out into the road in front of me."

She giggled. "Did you imagine it would transform into a jackelope?"

"Perhaps. Or an alien. The froggy type."

"Not lizard types?"

He held his hand high in a dramatic gesture. "'There are more things in heaven and earth, Horatio, than are dreamt of in your philosophy'"

Julie placed her hands on her hips and gave him a mock glare. "Do I look like a 'Horatio'?"

This set them into another fit of hysterical giggles, which kept them going for much longer than it should have, had they not been sleep-deprived.

As they approached the famed city of San Francisco, home of the Beat Generation, the Golden Gate Bridge, and music festivals, they emerged from their sleep-deprived haze. Fred gave them directions from downtown, so they searched for a way to the skyscrapers. Julie felt so strung out and fatigued, the buildings tried to dance at the edge of her vision.

After making several wrong turns, they found Haight. A couple blocks down the road, they spied the Victorian house with the correct address.

Julie never saw so many Victorian houses before. A few looked ramshackle and long abandoned, while others sported bright, fresh paint. Some had horrible colors like lime green and day-glow pink, but most seemed more traditional, white, gray, or pale blue. They all possessed beautiful, huge porches with decorative railings, gingerbread detailing on the edges of the high-peaked roofs.

The yards looked small but fenced. The parking looked like a free-for-all on the street. They found a spot not too far from Fred's house, while George struggled to fit his car into it. Parallel parking didn't seem to be his strong suit. He might have performed better if he'd gotten any sleep for the last two days.

After dragging themselves like zombies from the car, they staggered, stiff from sitting much too long. Despite the bathroom breaks they took to stretch their legs, their bodies complained at the abuse. They didn't even bother grabbing their bags, but trudged up the wooden steps to the door and knocked. It took several minutes, but someone stirred inside.

The door creaked open. Fred looked much like his brother, George, though shorter and heavier. He seemed much older, though George mentioned Fred had five years on him. His brown hair looked darker, but his eyes held the same gleeful glint. He showed laugh and smile lines and laughed like Victoria.

"George? Is it you? You're hell warmed over! Come in, come in. Who's this?" His face changed once he recognized his brother, from cautious to welcome and warm. All of a sudden, Julie felt at home in this strange place.

Fred pulled them in, asking questions without giving them any chance to get a word in. While George liked to talk, he wasn't a machine gun with his words like Fred.

Julie didn't bother trying to say anything beyond "hello" when George introduced her. She was so tired. She only craved to lie down and sleep for a month. George must have been just as exhausted, as he asked Fred where they could crash, in his words, "like, immediately?"

Fred led them to a spare room with two single beds. Julie didn't bother undressing, though she rinsed her face in the bathroom down the hall. Dirt and grime from their trek through the desert embedded into her skin, and she wanted at least a part of herself to be clean before she slept. Then she pulled off her shoes and socks, crawling into the bed. George already snored in the other one. Never before had a bed offered such comfort, so welcoming, so... she fell asleep before she even completed the thought.

A blaring noise frightened Julie awake, a car honking outside. She didn't remember where she was. A snore cut through the darkness. Bit by bit, the pieces fell into place. George. Desert. California. They made it to California. They must be at Fred's house. She remembered Fred as a vague force of nature and welcomes. How long had she slept? She looked around for a clock but found none. It remained too dark to make much out of the surrounding shapes. She eased her way out of the toasty warm, comfortable bed. Her muscles protested with pain, so she crept out. She didn't want to wake George.

She made her way to the one window in the room, drawing the curtain to the side, so she could peer out into the street. The car stopped honking, but other sounds swept in. Rain made car tires swish as they rode down the street. The window grew blotchy with raindrops.

Julie turned back around to regard the sleeping, snoring form of George. She found him attractive, despite, or perhaps because of, his beatnik look. He seemed goofy and intelligent, two qualities she admired. Perhaps she would enjoy this adventure much more than she imagined. She already felt like she'd known him for ages. And a little fun might help take her mind off Paul.

She crawled back into bed, lulled by the rain, settling back into the blessed arms of Morpheus.

CHAPTER FOUR

Sanctuary

The next morning dawned hazy, with mist tumbling down from the mountains and through the sleepy streets. Julie woke, ready to wrestle saber-toothed tigers, or at least a contented house cat or two. She stretched and creaked, moaning with stiffness and pain as she did so. She washed her face and hands, did her best to brush her teeth with her fingers, and brush the wrinkles out of her disgusting clothes. First order of business would be to retrieve her bags and change into an outfit which didn't stink like a locker room.

The other bed looked rumpled and empty. Julie ventured into the hall, lost. She'd been in such a drunken daze last night, she had no clue where the front door might be, or where George and Fred had gone. Julie listened for a moment, catching male laughter to the right. She followed the sound. She took in a deep sniff of the wondrous, savory aroma of coffee. Her stomach decided just then to wake up and remind her with a shout it needed fuel. Yesterday's chips and crackers had been insufficient.

She opened a door near the end of the hall, finding the men in a large, bright kitchen with black and white tiles, white appliances, with a shiny diner-style table along one wall. The diner-style chairs sported red plastic cushions and chrome backs. The odor of burnt toast mingled with that of fresh coffee.

"Julie! Come in and meet Fred proper-like." George appeared miles better than the tired mess from the night before.

"Fred, this is my friend Julie. She kept me awake the entire drive. She serenaded me with sweet songs, recited poetry, and made me laugh."

Fred took her hand and brought it to his lips in an elaborate, gallant gesture. The gesture reminded her of Paul. She blushed and stammered a meek, "Thank you. Is that coffee? I would murder for a cup."

"Of course! Here, let me get you a clean mug." Fred scrambled in the cupboard above the sink and brought out a large black mug for her. He brought a carafe of coffee from the counter and poured. "See, no murder required! Would you like milk or sugar?"

"Oh, no, I prefer my jet fuel black, thank you!" Julie relished the hot, bitter drink on her tongue, sensed it caressing her throat. *Ah, nectar of the gods.*

"Would you care for breakfast? I finished making George eggs and toast. How do you like yours?"

"However you like them. I would eat boiled boot if cooked with enough salt."

Fred grinned. "One boiled boot, salted, coming right up!"

She studied him, since the coffee transformed her from a pre-caffeinated zombie. He still looked much older, but laugh lines creased in the corners of his deep, soulful brown eyes. He wore a comfortable, threadbare robe with purple paisley print all over it.

"George, can we get our stuff out of the car? My body has melded with these clothes. I want to change while I can still peel them off."

"Already done, Sleeping Beauty. The cases are in the hallway. I didn't want to bring them in the room while you slept."

"Ah, fantastic! I'm off to change. I'll be back in a flash."

Julie returned much refreshed. While she would have preferred to bathe, nay, to immerse herself in hot water and suds for a week, hunger remained a more pressing need.

After she ate, she stared at the empty plate, with no memory of the actual meal. "Fred, thank you so much. I'm almost human again." Julie couldn't believe she'd eaten those eggs so fast.

"My pleasure, my dear. George has told me much about you. Welcome to our home. You missed my family so far. The kids are at school and Karen's off at her mother's this week. You will miss me soon. I've got to go to work in about a half an hour. Is there anything I can get you before I go? You and George are, of course, welcome to stay here as long as you like, never fear." He still moved in a whirlwind, even after calming down from the night before. He exhausted with his energy.

"Thank you, thank you so much." He disappeared out the kitchen door, presumably to change into work clothing.

Julie took another sip of her coffee. "Whew, he's a bundle of energy."

"Yeah, he's more like a tap dance than a waltz. I prefer to stop and smell the flowers, rather than run them over with a sports car."

She shrugged. "It takes all kinds, I suppose."

"Indeed. So, what would you like to do now that you're here in the Wild West?"

"Wild? I don't consider Victorian houses all that much like wilderness."

"Ha! Wait until tonight. The nightlife here is a bit different." George looked at her with sly eyes. "Have you not heard stories of Haight Ashbury?"

"Sure, I've heard stories of San Francisco, but I put most of it down to exaggeration and second-hand stories."

He lifted his hands as if announcing an attraction at the circus. "Tonight we shall venture forth and find first-hand stories, then. Today, we settle in, find our place here, perhaps walk around the neighborhood."

"I should also check into the Church and find out when I start work." Julie's responsible nature took over. She made a mental tally of the money she had left, and what she would need to use it for.

George shook his head with a mock frown. "Not today. Today is for enjoyment. Tomorrow, maybe. Next week, better. Let's have a holiday."

"I think today is for relaxing and resting, after our marathon drive."

He brought his plate and cup to the sink, rinsing them off. "Right. You relax and rest. I'm going out to get the lay of the land. Need anything?"

"Something to read?"

"The library is this way, my dear." George led her into Fred's study.

Julie spent most of the day lazing about, exploring the rambling house, walking in the neighborhood until it rained again. With George away, she could take in her new surroundings. She perused Fred's extensive library, picking out a book on past lives and reincarnation. She found an enormous bay window with a comfy chair, and settled in for a lovely, relaxing read as the steady rhythm of the rain beat a soothing tattoo on the glass.

As the day faded, a great deal of banging and shouting came from out front. Before she roused herself from her comfortable nest, the house sprang into life again. Fred and George must have picked up the two children after work, as the hallway became a riot of noise and stomping.

She poked her head out of the library, almost colliding with a sturdy six-year-old boy, his dark, curly hair a mop above dark brown eyes, and a tiny red mouth, round in surprise. "Who are *you*?"

She knelt beside him. "I'm Julie. I'm a friend of your Uncle George's. And what's your name?"

He looked back to his father, uncertain how to proceed, but with a nod from Fred, he turned back and stuck out his hand.

"I'm Chris."

"Very pleased to meet you, Chris. And is that your sister?"

Fred held a toddler, perhaps about two, in his arm. She wore a pink frilly skirt. "Yeah, this's Carrie. But she doesn't talk much."

"Very pleased to meet you, too, Carrie."

The blond girl buried her face in her father's shoulder, eliciting a grin from Julie.

George ruffled his niece's hair. "Did you get good rest, Julie? Good. Well, let me help Fred get these two settled in. Then we'll go paint the town tonight."

Julie nodded as the parade passed by the library door and up the stairs.

Back in her room, Julie sifted through the clothes she had, picking out a colorful blouse and comfortable slacks. While they would be much more conservative than what others might wear, at least they seemed less stodgy than most of her clothes. She tied her hair back with a scarf so she wouldn't have to mess with it, putting on make-up. From her meager store of costume jewelry, she found the silver crescent moon pendant. She'd never had her ears pierced, and didn't like clip on earrings, so bracelets and necklaces made up the extent of her decoration. She always lost rings.

As she emerged from the tiny bathroom, she almost ran into George, on his way down the hall. They stood a little too close.

"Almost ready?"

"Sure, let me put my make-up bag back in my room, and I'll be all set. Where are we going?"

"Downtown Hippieland! Bring your rose-colored glasses."

George and Julie walked, arm in arm, down the three blocks to the corner of the infamous Haight Ashbury. As they approached, the setting sun washed everything in a brilliant orange glow, as if the buildings were about to burst into flame. Music and laughter swirled around them. People walked on the sidewalks, gathered in the street, and hung out in front of the storefronts.

The riot of images assaulted her. Bright colors, riotous patterns, and huge collars everywhere. Pinks and yellows, oranges and aquas. Paisley and tie-dye, psychedelic patterns which seemed like optical illusions from an Escher poster. Long hair on both men and women, with woven headbands. Flowers bloomed, painted on faces and woven in braids. She had walked into an alien world, so far from the Dearborn neighborhood of her parents' house. She stumbled as if drunk, trying to take in all the sights and sounds like Alice down the rabbit hole.

Julie sniffed the air. She detected an unusual odor, the pungent smoke of pot. She recognized the smell, as she'd smoked it with Sandy, but never right out in the street. The bravery of these people amazed her. Perhaps she wasn't drunk, but getting a contact high, right out here on the sidewalk, of all places. She slowed down, stumbling on the pavement.

George turned and gave her a quizzical glance, both eyebrows raised. "Are you okay, Julie? Did you trip?"

"No, no, simply overwhelmed, is all. I'll be fine, but give me a moment."

"Sure. No rush at all. Want to duck into this shop?"

Julie looked up at the sign overhead, which read, "The Psychedelic Shop" in curvy, oozing letters. The purple letters looked like they moved. The display window screamed with bright tie-dye t-shirts and skirts. She blinked and found the images burned on her retinas when she closed her lids. "Perhaps there's someplace to sit down? These are new boots, so I'm not used to walking in them yet."

"Come in. Let's see if they've a stool."

The shop was jam-packed with freaky stuff. A quick survey revealed bean-bag chairs in one corner. She made a bee-line for those, plopping herself down with a big sigh of relief. Her mind still spun.

George studied her with concern, but she nodded to him for reassurance. He gave her a half shrug, turning to explore the store.

Julie peered around from her vantage point near the floor, noticing glass cases along two walls. It held two shelves of glass pipes and strange contraptions which looked like they belonged in an alien's toolbox. She avoided looking at the wall with clothing on it. The mass of clashing colors assaulted her artist's eye, giving her a headache. Was she old and stuffy? She would have to loosen her straight-laced tendencies if she wanted to fit in this city. Would she be up to the task? Or would her Midwestern sensibilities be too strong?

She moved her gaze to the walls, with posters of musicians plastered at various angles. Big Brother and the Holding Company, The Who, The Mamas & the Papas, The Beatles, The Animals, The Jimi Hendrix Experience. She'd heard of most of these, but some Julie didn't recognize. Many in the same melting font the sign outside used. More Escher-like optical illusions decorated the backgrounds.

These artists didn't seem afraid to break the basic rules of color and composition. Julie felt both amazed and annoyed by their freedom.

She struggled to her feet, out of the grips of the amorphous mass of the beanbag chair, looking around for George. He stared into one of the glass cases of the alien torture devices.

"What are those?" She whispered to him.

"I think they're water pipes. You use them to smoke."

"Smoke ... pot?"

George grinned at her meek whisper. "Well, they aren't for smoking hams."

That did the trick. She giggled and hooked her arm back into his. Shaky at first, they ventured back into the busy street.

Once again, the noise and throngs of people assaulted her, but Julie kept a firm grip on George's arm. She used him as an anchor, but he didn't seem to mind.

They whirled through and around groups of people who talked, sung, played guitars and other instruments. She imagined a waltz in time with the ebb and flow of conversation and music. Snippets came through the cacophony.

"...but he said he was *already* sleeping with her, so ..."

"...the sound is really groovy, man, can you believe ..."

"...so the colors glowed with beauty ..."

"...like flying in the air above the clouds ..."

As they made their way down the street, louder music drowned out conversation, more organized than the little pockets of performers. Fred had mentioned a place called Freedom Garden. Perhaps they had a band set up on a stage. Despite standing on her tiptoes, the mass of people blocked her view.

Julie glanced at the shops they passed, seeing glimpses of music stores, bookshops, bars, and clothing stores. A couple places glowered dark or boarded over, but most burst with a riot of light and activity. One bar had a poster outside advertising poetry readings, another with a band list. Julie pointed out the former to George, who nodded and noted the location.

It grew difficult getting around the knots of people. Several times, others touched or brushed her, whether by accident or on purpose, she didn't know. Now, however, someone grabbed her arm. She whirled to see who assaulted her.

Intense blue eyes stared at her, topped with a long, matted mass of dirty blond, frizzy hair. The man peered into her eyes as if searching for the secret to life itself. He said nothing, but gawked into her.

George noticed she no longer walked next to him and came around to confront the man. "Hey, man, no need for that. Let the lady go." George tried to pull the man's hand from her forearm, but the intruder held on with a vice-like grip. He wore a kaftan of bright blues and greens, dirty jeans, and sandals.

"She's so beautiful, man! You can't keep such beauty all to yourself, man. Share the love, right?" The intruder snaked his other hand around Julie's waist, trying to extricate her from George's arm.

Julie gave him a sharp glare and said, in a resolute tone, "I prefer my escort. Let me go, now!" Still, he held tight, tugging on her. She tried to jerk her arm away from his grasp.

George let go of Julie's arm, and she panicked, but he only did so to use both hands to remove the blond man's grip.

"The lady asked you to leave. Do it now, or I'll make sure you do." George stayed firm with the man without turning belligerent. The blond stopped staring into Julie's eyes, swiveling his head, almost in slow motion, to George. As his eyes grew wider,

95

Julie noticed how glassy they seemed, how dilated his pupils grew. He must be on at least one mind-altering substance, perhaps several.

Just like that, he melted back into the crowd. Her arm still throbbed where he'd gripped her and wondered if it would bruise. She turned to George, a look of amazement on her face.

"Does this happen often, do you think?" Julie's voice shook, but she hoped it didn't sound as rattled as she felt.

George gave her one look, taking her into his arms. Her mood forbade argument, but she held in her sobs as the adrenaline drained out of her, leaving her arms and legs like jelly. Julie felt much safer there, inside his shell of protection. She wanted to remain there. After a few seconds, she took a deep breath. George sensed it, holding her out at arms-length.

"Better?"

"Better. C'mon. Let's move on in case he changes his mind and comes back."

"Madam?" He hooked out his arm for her to take with a quirk of his eyebrow. She took his arm with ceremony and aplomb, and a grin.

Much later, after many sights and sounds, both foreign and domestic, they made their way back to Fred's house, the sound of sitar music buzzing in their blood. Julie stumbled into the bathroom to change into her night clothes, a simple set of pajamas, light green and faded. As she entered the bedroom they shared, George stood by the window, gazing out into the moonlight.

Julie stopped in the doorway. He turned, walking the three steps to her. George took her hand into his, staring into her eyes, almost as intense as the drugged blond man had, but with much more care.

He grinned as she reached up to kiss that grin off his face.

She'd meant it to be a playful gesture, a peck. But he held her face in his hands, keeping it much longer than a friendly kiss. When they parted, she opened her eyes to find him staring into hers with question, invitation, and deep desire.

He kissed her forehead but not as a patronizing gesture. The feather touch of his lips came gentle and sweet. He moved to her cheek, then down her neck. Her spine shivered with the roughness of his chin against her tender skin.

"Are you okay, Julie? Would you like me to stop?"

Did she? Did she want this? He would stop if she asked. He wasn't the drugged, crazy man they'd encountered in the park. This was George, her pal, her chum. Her lover? He wasn't Paul, but that might be the best thing about him.

Julie didn't want to sleep alone. She put her hand up to his cheek, stroking it with her palm. It traveled down to his chest, then farther. She let him know, with her hands, that she didn't want him to stop.

George watched her hand travel down his chest. He cupped her chin in his hand. He closed his eyes as he touched his lips to hers, a butterfly touch. When he opened his eyes again, a smile played across his face. Not his normal, goofy grin, but a sweet one, which she ached to kiss again. So she did.

Together, they closed the drapes in the window, enjoying the intensity of the night.

Julie awoke, confused. She panicked before she remembered where she was, and why she couldn't move. She and George lay on the floor between the two single beds, wrapped up like a burrito in a tangle of blankets. Several pillows lay here and there, but not in any logical placement. George still slept, his warm, steady breath misting on her back. She remembered the night, smiling. She figured George would be a fun lover, but he proved to be a funny lover, too. They'd had comical moments as they figured out how to best use their space. Hysterical giggling ensued, hastily shushed, as to not wake the house. They did their best to keep everything quiet and discreet. At least the kids slept upstairs. This spare room worked infinitely nicer as a love nest than a Victorian bathtub.

She extricated her body, to get ready for the day. Julie had no idea what George planned, but she needed to check out her new job.

After she dressed and washed, she entered the kitchen with a sigh of relief. Fred must have already left for the day with the kids. She made coffee and toast. Being a thoughtful soul, Fred left the Yellow Pages on the table, open to "Churches." She wrote down the address of the local branch.

Julie wanted to get her art portfolio out, the one she used for job interviews, to show her previous projects. While the Church had transferred her, she wanted to make a positive impression on her new supervisors. They hadn't been able to assure a permanent transfer, but three months would be a decent start.

Julie rifled through a couple drawers in the kitchen, looking for a map of the city. Then with a mental smack on her forehead, she looked in the back of the Yellow Pages. It had a map of the metropolitan area.

Since she needed to bide until George woke to drive her, she played with the images she held in her mind. First, she pulled out a sketchpad, drawing her impressions from the night before. A girl dancing, flower behind her ear, with layers and layers of fringe dangling from her arms and torso, swirling in a dynamic circle. Her long, straight hair following the fringe in the swirl. A young man sitting, playing a strange instrument which George had called a sitar. He wore a macramé headband across his braided hair, and a ripped t-shirt, torn blue jeans, with leather sandals.

As she concentrated on the detailing in the sandals and the shadows on the ground underneath, she heard George cough in the other room. After putting her materials away, she headed back to the room. While peeking around the doorway, she admired his long, lean form, stretching luxuriously along the floor, still obscured in strategic places by the blankets.

"Up and at 'em, Sunshine!" She flung open the drapes, letting in the bright sunlight. It showed all the dust motes floating in the room. A long, low moan came from the floor.

"Ugh, I think it's illegal in the state of California to be so cheerful in the morning," he groaned and stretched.

Julie couldn't help smiling as she watched him. "Morning? It's almost afternoon. I'm glad you're up. I need to change into my professional togs and get in touch with the Church soon. May I beg your services as a chauffeur today? Or shall I surrender myself to the vagaries of public transportation?"

"Come back to bed. There's no hurry."

Julie remained strong despite the temptation. "Oh, no, mister, that's no bed. That's a hard, uncomfortable floor, and I've got things to see and people to do. Or something like that."

"Well, I suppose I'm open to bribery, then. A sweet kiss and a cup of coffee might purchase my services, at least for a time."

"Aren't you the epitome of gallantry?" Julie settled down to her knees, giving him a chaste peck on the cheek, but she figured this wouldn't be the end. Sure enough, he tackled her onto the floor, kissing her firmly and with purpose.

Several minutes later, she came up for breath. "George, I need to get on with this job thing. I can't live off of you and Fred forever. I don't think I'm cut out to be a kept woman."

"Who said anything about keeping you?" George grinned to reassure her he that he joked.

1998, Miami, Florida

Kirsten continued with her genealogical research over the years on her mother's line, turning the passion into a hobby. Once electronic sources became available, she extended the line, filling out places all over the tree. She subscribed to a magazine which catered to the obsession, Everton's Genealogical Helper, combing through each issue for clues. She searched for information on the several "brick walls" she had found.

While she still hadn't found where her Jensen line hailed from, she'd gotten a few hints. Scandinavian, yes, but there remained several options. Her birthplace in Denmark? Norway? Sweden? Perhaps even Iceland? She only knew the family arrived in the United States by 1760, but then the back trail went cold. She remained stuck on a common name, John Jensen. Too many people of that name popped up in the records to determine which one might be her ancestor.

As she flipped through the most recent issue of Everton's, she glanced at an ad which promised to find lost relatives. It gave a name, an address, and the offer. If they found nothing, she paid nothing. If they found information, she paid a hundred dollars.

A hundred dollars. Kirsten worked full time while trying to finish her graduate degree in accounting at night school. She shared an apartment with her boyfriend, struggling from paycheck to paycheck. The service seemed expensive, but it might be worth it.

She'd searched in lots of resources over the years for any clue to her father. But the information stayed so nebulous. The Church in East Grinstead had replied to her query, having at least verified how he spelled his name. However, they gave no other information due to privacy considerations. Her research into various phonebooks had come up with nothing. She'd discovered no other clues.

Kirsten wrote to the man in the advertisement and gave him all the details. Perhaps, just perhaps, this might bear some small fruit.

Several days later, she received a phone call from the researcher, letting her know it might take a while, as he did this part time. It involved a lot of writing and requesting records. She understood, having done research herself. Kirsten thanked him and wished him luck.

She waited on edge for several weeks but heard nothing. She moved on to other things in her life, and eventually forgot the matter. Just another rabbit hole with a dead end.

1967, San Francisco

Julie's visit to the Church had yielded mixed results.

The local branch sported a rather fancy façade, with glass windows and soaring architecture. A new-built place, the airy atmosphere reflected an eager spirit.

The receptionist, who couldn't have been older than seventeen, showed her to the art director's office.

Bradley Tibbets, so the name plate said, was the Director of Advertising and Marketing. He stood when she entered, and after looking her up and down, offered his hand. His palm felt clammy, and his handshake limp. She extracted her hand with difficulty as alarms clanged in her head. She'd met slimy men before, but he already seemed like the worst sort of the oily, used-car-salesman personalities.

"So, what brings you to San Francisco, *Miss* Jensen?" His over-bright grin didn't reach his pale green eyes.

With George's help, Julie had come up with an innocuous-sounding excuse. She didn't need to advertise her love life to a future employer. "I have a friend in town who has been ill. Transferring here to help her out worked out wonderfully."

Tibbets nodded, and he pushed his brown hair back a bit, raking her up and down with his gaze again. "I'm sure I can find some work for you, my darling. When can you start?"

Julie glanced down at the artwork portfolio she'd brought. She handed it to him, but he just stared at it. "What's this?"

"My portfolio, so you can see what sort of work I do?"

"Oh. Well, no need for all that. HQ wouldn't have transferred you if you were incompetent. Tomorrow morning at 8am?"

Julie swallowed and nodded. He escorted her out, one hand on the small of her back. She tried to walk faster than him, so he would stop touching her, but he maintained the contact. When she escaped, he got in a pat on her bottom. What a slime.

George tried to cheer her up by suggesting dinner out, but the sear of mooching guilt pained Julie. Her independent streak grew annoying. It made it almost impossible to accept gifts or generosity guilt-free. "How about cheap and cheerful instead of nice and expensive?"

He grinned. "Bingo! Your wish is my command, my lady. Cheap and cheerful it is. How about the pizza joint we saw, the one that looked like a diner?"

"That would work fine. Thanks, George."

The dirty, dusty diner they had eaten at on the way to California paled in comparison to this gleaming place. Black and white tiles covered the floor and ceiling, with bright red booths and silver tables, an echo of Fred's kitchen on a larger scale. The odors of garlic and baking bread wafted through the dining room, lifting Julie's spirits. She wanted to go change into one of her fifties-style skirts and neck scarves for the occasion. She just needed saddle shoes to complete the picture.

A large jukebox stood in the corner, flashing bright lights and playing "A Hard Day's Night" by The Beatles. About five other tables held groups or couples. No one paid them much attention as they made their way to an empty table near the window.

George had to catch the waitress' eye for her to come by with menus. She got them a couple glasses of Coke and George ordered a large pie with mushrooms and pepperoni for them to share. Julie protested they'd never eat it all, but he assured her they'd take the rest home.

He sipped on his straw and raised his eyebrows. "So, tell me how it went today."

She grimaced. "The boss is very handsy."

George frowned and clasped his hands. "Do you want to find a different job?"

Weariness made her shoulders slump. After the lengthy trip from England, and across half the country, she didn't even want to consider hitting the pavement at this point.

"No, no, I'll give this one a chance. Art jobs are hard to get, especially if you're new to the area. For art jobs, the best way I've found is to get your work noticed somewhere, by someone, maybe a write-up in a newspaper or magazine, create some reputation. It doesn't always work. If you're there in person with a printed recommendation, people find it more difficult to dismiss you out of hand, particularly if they can see you do quality work."

"That makes sense. I imagine it would be the same with musician jobs, too. Bring your instrument, play, and let them hear what you can do. Most of those jobs are found by the job-giver seeing you play at a concert or bar." George looked thoughtful. "Perhaps I should play here and there."

"I thought you only planned to stay a month?"

His grin turned wolfish, a caricature of a leer. "I might be convinced to stay longer. There are new attractions to this place, after all." He stroked her arm as it lay on the table, a feather touch. The hairs on her arm stood up and she got goosebumps.

Julie blushed and ducked her head. She rarely felt coy or shy. It's not as if George had been her first. She steeled herself to glance up, right into the large pizza pie which descended to the table in front of them, steaming and aromatic.

The next morning, to Julie's surprise, Fred stood in the kitchen when Julie made her way in, having left George sound asleep. He glanced up from his coffee and paper when he heard the door squeak, looking her up and down. "Well, you look ready to kill. Off to your new job today?"

Julie gave him a rueful grin. "Did George tell you of my delightful prospect yesterday?"

"He did, and if you decide it's not worth it, I might have a solution. We could use someone at my company to do layout work. It's what George said you do. Are you interested?"

"Well, sure. But, where do you work?"

"An electronics company based in Minnesota, but we have branches all over the world. I'm starting up the branch out here."

Julie never worked for a large company other than the Church. "What sort of work would it be?"

Fred walked to the sink and rinsed out his now empty coffee cup. "Flyers and posters we'll be giving out and mailings. Internal promotional materials for our members. It's not full-time, perhaps twenty hours a week, for $2.60 an hour, but it could change as we get going. We're slated to open doors next year. Right now it's a messy office, I'm afraid, but we'd find space for you. I work there as sort of an ambassador to the other groups."

"Don't you want to see my portfolio? To see if I can do the work?"

Fred gave a careless shrug. "George said you had talent. I trust his judgment."

Julie had poured her own cup of coffee, blowing on it to cool it down before she sipped. George hadn't seen her work, just a few pieces from her professional portfolio. Both brothers put a lot of faith into her, sight unseen. "If this turns out to be a dud, I appreciate the option."

"Great, just let me know."

"Fred, thank you. This is truly kind of you. Now I'm even more in your debt, though."

"Yeah, I know my brother mentioned you felt moochy. You aren't, of course. Hell, you've only been here a couple days. Official mooching begins after a month, you know."

Julie gazed at him over her coffee cup. "I didn't, but I'll keep it in mind."

As she arrived at that glittering office, Julie thought it might not be so bad. Perhaps she wouldn't have much contact with Tibbets. Alas, he waited for her as she arrived, and showed her into the marketing department.

In contrast to the sleek reception area, the marketing offices swam in dust and clutter. Piles of boxes, files, and papers covered each wall. Underneath them all, glimpses of desks and chairs creaked with complaint from the weight.

A tall woman tapped a pencil on the pad of paper she held, slim and elegant in a smart pink business suit. She shook her head as she spoke, making her immaculate bouffant of blond hair wiggle.

Tibbets cleared his throat as they turned to him. "This is Julie. She's transferred over from East Grinstead. She's an artist, and ready to tackle our layout work. Julie, this is Tamara Lange. She's one of our promotion experts."

Tamara gave her a chilly glance from head to toe, then nodded to her in grudging acceptance.

"Tony is our advertising sales manager." The slightly hunched man Tamara had been speaking to nodded with a thoughtful expression, his wavy brown hair bobbing as he looked up to her. He wore a typical office uniform with a button-down shirt and slacks.

Julie made the round of handshakes, welcomes, and assessments and Tibbets left. Grateful she'd dressed smart, Tamara's elegance still made her frowsy in comparison. Julie stood taller and straighter in reaction, although she possessed decent posture. She lifted her chin, smiling ruefully to herself at her defensive response.

Tony showed her to a cluttered desk in one corner, doing his best to shift the boxes and files off it. He made sure she had supplies, such as pencils, paper, ruler, and a stapler. He recommended she list what artistic supplies she might need for her layout work.

"May I see what I'd be working on? Perhaps an example of your finished products so I can get an idea of the standard? I don't want to waste too much of your time," Julie asked in a meek voice.

Tony gave her a grin. "Nonsense. My job comes in bits and spurts. I've nothing I need to be doing right now. I can help you settle in all you like, never fear."

As Julie sifted through the brochures, pamphlets, posters, and flyers Tony had dug up, she noted they had a sleek, slick style. The Church possessed money and power and wasn't afraid to show it. The stuff at the British branch had been paler, calmer, and less aggressive. They produced sober, simple flyers, not this glossy, professional stuff. Lots of photographs of beautiful people enjoying their life, possessing smiles with dazzling white teeth, all around them text written with loaded words, designed to attract and entrap the reader with sensuality and allure.

Julie sensed rather than saw someone coming up behind her. She turned to see Tony.

"How are you getting on? Need anything? Perhaps a cup of coffee to clear the dust?"

That brought a genuine grin to her face. "Oh, coffee would be precisely the thing. Where is it?"

"Come on, I'll show you"

Julie followed him down a hallway and around a corner into the unfinished room which served as a canteen. A silver coffee maker sat on the counter, perking merrily, music to her ears. As it finished, Tony poured them both a full cup, rinsing out the maker before started a fresh batch.

"It's a rule. If you take the last bit, you brew another batch. This is a never-ending need here, trust me!"

"I can well understand it. Coffee is one of my few vices."

He winked at her. "There are worse things to be addicted to, I suppose."

"I'm sure there are, here in the City of Sin. However, I think I'll stick to the coffee for now."

"Sugar? Cream?" Tony pulled out dry Coffee-Mate non-dairy creamer. She had tried the stuff exactly once, and had almost gagged.

"Oh, no, thanks. I prefer mine black. Thank you for showing me where to get it, though. That information will be invaluable." She blew on her cup before she sipped it. She turned to return to her desk.

"We get a break around lunchtime. May I take you out for a sandwich? There's a cheerful place a couple doors down."

"That would be delightful, thank you. Noon?"

"Sure, see you then."

The café, called Hofbrauhaus, had bright lights and clean tables. And, despite his penchant for disgusting non-dairy creamer products, Tony seemed nice. They talked, discovering a common interest in art and science fiction. They talked about Salvador Dali and Robert Heinlein before their food arrived. He seemed quieter and shier than George, but they had a few things in common, enough to base a friendship on.

She enjoyed her Rueben sandwich while he had tomato soup and a grilled cheese. About halfway through the meal, Tamara approached, asking to join them.

After she sat and ordered food, Tamara raised her eyebrows. "Have you been in the Church long?" Julie puzzled at the odd inflection in her question.

"No, I got involved in Washington D.C., less than a year ago. I worked doing art for them, and taking care of a member's children. When she moved to England, I followed along. Then my assignment ended, and I got a transfer here." Julie really didn't want to reveal her issues with lovers, so she made up a story about her reasons, despite her conscience twinging. "I've a friend who's ill, and I took the opportunity to help her out."

Tamara took a sip of her ice water and made a face, putting it down again. "I see. How do you like San Francisco so far? Have you been able to see much of the sights?"

"Not really. My friend, George, took me around the first night after we arrived, but the next day I saw some of downtown. I haven't even visited the Golden Gate Bridge yet." She gave them a shrug.

Tony held up a finger. "Be sure to climb up Coit Tower. It's a fantastic view from up there. And there are lots of places outside the city to visit, too. We've a beautiful city. Might as well enjoy it." Tony sounded like he belonged on a tourism commercial. "Are you from D.C., then?"

"No, I'm from Ohio, but my parents moved us to Michigan before high school. I moved to D.C. with a friend." Julie hoped glossing over the reasons would discourage further probing into the matter. She felt like a leaf floating on rapids in a river these last couple of months, but she might be able to settle roots down here, at least for a while.

The group ate their lunch with idle chatter. The locals shared stories about the area, the problems of opening up a new office, and funny stories about Tibbets. Julie felt awkward discussing her new boss, but she nodded.

Julie finished her day by searching for art supplies, making a list of things she wanted to have.

She then made a shorter list of the basics she needed, asking Tamara to whom she should give the lists. "Tony does the supply shopping each week. You should go with him to pick out the specific tools you need."

When she asked Tony when his next trip would be, he suggested first thing in the morning.

Unfortunately, Tibbets insisted on accompanying them. Julie did her best to walk on the other side of Tony, and out of grabbing range.

Julie had been amazed at the number of things on offer at this specialized store. While she'd been to art stores in both Michigan and D.C., they'd been tiny places carved out of larger stores, or converted almost as an afterthought to offer art supplies. But this place echoed like a warehouse. They carried more than art, as a good portion of the store sold office supplies, shipping, and packaging. But the art department contained a section for calligraphy, and another for stenciling. So many canvas and paint options, her head swirled. Julie became a kid in a candy store. She had to restrain herself, reminding her inner child she shopped with someone else's money.

Julie gathered the items on her "needs" list, pricing them out. She asked Tony if he had enough in the budget, and he approved more. She explored the stenciling area next, knowing she'd be doing layout work.

Lost in thought, she didn't realize someone stood behind her until she turned and almost crashed into Tibbets. He'd been standing right next to her. It made her uncomfortable, but it didn't seem to rattle him at all. He grinned at her, and moved off to get his own purchases before they left.

CHAPTER FIVE
Psychedelia

August 2, 1967

Dear Katy:
Hello, sister mine! I've been out in the Wild West for three weeks now, and haven't yet found a gold mine, so our early retirement plans are still on hold. Maybe you should send me a canary! What I have found, though, is a job and a place to stay, at least for now. It's a different world out here, Katy. There are artists and poets, musicians and dancers everywhere, every night in the streets. It's bizarre, as if I'm living in a twisted nirvana.

How are your classes? Have you had to take Life Drawing yet? Watch out for the teacher, Mr. Settins, he's on the grabby side. I think it's why he teaches that class. He's a lecherous pig.

I'm doing layout work for the Church here, and it's interesting work. They've got a decent budget, so I can do a few creative things. They aren't so rigid in their thinking about options, either.

I've found a wonderful friend in George, but unfortunately, he's heading back home to Michigan soon. Luckily, I've found a few other friends here, including his brother Fred, the people I work with, like Tony, and the aforementioned artists and dancers. I'm attending 'art-ins' in a studio apartment. Each week, they whitewash the walls. Then, they invite anyone in to paint them however they like—pictures, abstract, whatever. They let people see it all week, then do it again the next week. Sort of a drive-by art gallery. I got the nerve up to take a section of one wall last week, and drew a wizard in an invisible cloak in an autumn forest, a very Tolkien-style scene. Long white beard, pointy hat, staff, etc. You can see the foliage through the cloak. I wish I had a camera to send you a photo.

I'd best sign off now. Give my love to Larry, Mom and Dad, Gail, and Helen. Perhaps when you have a school break you can come visit me in the New Bohemia.
Much love,
Julie

On the weekend, she and George escaped for a night. Julie liked the job well enough, and enjoyed the people she worked with. But the sense of this city still seemed so alien. Detroit and Washington D.C. had an industrial focus. They worked, and they worked hard, in those places, being both industrial and industrious. This city, while many people worked, had a much more relaxed vibration about it. Enjoyment seemed to be an essential ingredient in life, a new concept to her. Julie's father wouldn't have approved. For him, hard work brought its own reward. It didn't seem right, somehow, for a city to be so joyful with itself. She became dismayed at how much her own father's attitudes had infected her own.

Julie needed an escape from this unease, so asked George to take her outside the city to see the sights. He drove around to the rocky shores along the coast. They traveled up the Pacific Coast Highway to the Muir Woods. Walking through the forest calmed her. They found a quiet spot in the shade. George laid out a large blanket, so they ate a picnic of fruit, cheese, and bread among the trees, bees buzzing around them and the wind soughing through the leaves.

After they had sated themselves, in both food and body, they lay among the dappled sunlight for a long time, refreshing their souls as birds serenaded them.

Julie brought watercolor supplies, in case she got inspired. After a while, she got up and set up a station to capture the light and color among the trees. Golds and greens, sepia and umber, with the occasional dots of yellow and white wildflowers. Washes of pale blue sky and silver clouds. George came to watch, but she didn't get as self-conscious as usual when someone watched her work.

Satisfied with her painting, she laid the paper out to dry in the warm summer sun, turning to George.

"Well, I'm refreshed. Up for round two?"

Julie peered at the mirror, putting the last touches on her make-up and hair for their sojourn. They planned to enjoy Haight Ashbury again, for a Saturday evening of fun. George had friends he wanted to hook up with to watch a concert. She'd met them before last weekend and looked forward to fun. She even put flowers in her hair, purloined from a bush along the street.

The flowers reminded her of the gardens behind Saint Hill Manor in East Grinstead, which reminded her of Paul. She squashed the memory and blinked the tears away, clutching to George's arm with firm determination.

Julie expanded her wardrobe in her month in California. She purchased kaftans in tribal designs. While the colors seemed bright, they remained tasteful enough not to offend her sense of color. The outfit she wore tonight was in her favorite palette, browns and golds with bits of brighter yellow as an accent. She had a copper colored hairband and wore her thick hair long in the back. *I'm a proper hippie now.* And she giggled at the idea of a "proper hippie," a true oxymoron.

They walked arm in arm down the street towards the park. George dressed in a jacket with fringe coming down all along the arms, in strategic places on the front and back, in a V pattern. Others drifted towards the park, like moths drawn toward a flame.

Julie didn't get as overwhelmed, having visited almost every evening since the first night. She learned how to ride the wave of frenzy and peace, another contradiction. She enjoyed all the new, bizarre music, tried the interesting drinks and smokes offered. Fantastic new art, and some not so fantastic, and colorful people, in all aspects of the word, surrounded them.

A new musical group played tonight, called Jefferson Airplane. Last week, Julie noticed them listed on a poster for the big festival coming up at Monterey. George promised to take her, but she loved the chance to preview the artists.

They ambled through the park, because people packed in tight, over-welcoming to strangers. One man with long brown hair and glassy blue eyes came up to her, placing a daisy behind her ear with gentle hands. Julie tensed, as did George, remembering the previous assault, but the drifter offered no worry. He wandered off, with stars in his eyes and a bunch of other daisies in his hand, perhaps for other random women. A large blond woman with heart-shaped glasses came to them, kissed George on the mouth, then Julie, and spun off to someone else.

When at last they found the tree where they would meet their friends, they waited and people-watched the seething crowds.

George pointed to the left. "Look at how long that guy's hair is! He must have been growing it for years."

Julie craned her neck until she saw his subject. "Wow! It's longer than mine ever got. I didn't realize the hippie thing had been around so long."

"He must have been a beatnik before. That began in the fifties, didn't it?"

She shrugged and gave him a half-smile. "You tell me. You're the one who loves those black turtlenecks."

George did his best to appear haughty. "Turtlenecks do not a beatnik make. I like the way they look on me."

"Sure, sure. You're the epitome of fashion. Oh, wow, see? She's belly-dancing. What are those on her fingers?"

"I think they're called castanets. She looks amazing. I didn't realize the back bent so far." George turned his head to one side as the dancer bent farther back. Julie didn't care for the interest he took in the dancer, so searched for a distraction from the limber young lady.

"Hey, isn't that Summer over there?" Julie raised her arm to wave.

"It is. And there's Jonas and Otter." He joined Julie in her gesticulations until the group saw them. They waved back.

As the friends converged and greetings exchanged, Otter pulled a bright red handkerchief out of his pocket and opened it with care, revealing a piece of paper, perforated into smaller bits. Each bit had a strange picture printed on them. He held six of them.

The man had a love of trying anything new. This must be his latest acquisition. Julie squinted at them. "What is it, Otter?"

"LSD. Acid. Everyone want a hit?"

Julie searched her memories for any side effects, but she only remembered that it caused hallucinations. From what the news said, it's what made Jimi Hendrix and Jim Morrison such famous poets and musicians. Would it do the same for her art? She'd tried other drugs, but this might be the strongest.

With sudden decision, she nodded. "Okay, I'm game. George? How about you?"

He narrowed his eyes for a moment, but then nodded. "Sure, but let's make a pact, first. The five of us watch out for each other. No wandering off on your own in this crowd. We'd never find ourselves if we got lost in this. Deal?"

Everyone agreed, taking one. Otter took two, explaining he'd had it before, so he understood how to deal with the effects. Besides, having one left meant he'd have to trip alone in the future, a lonely prospect.

Julie tensed herself after chewing the tiny scrap of paper and swallowing it. Other than her own tension, she experienced nothing strange.

Otter grinned at her, putting a hand on her shoulder. "It takes a while to set in, Julie. Relax. You'll feel groovy in a half hour."

They all sat under the enormous tree's canopy, as sitting would be safer than moving amongst the throng of people. The musicians should play nearby in an hour, so they had a perfect vantage spot.

George held her hand but dropped it to point to a man dressed in vibrant colors, leaping his way through the crowds. He reminded Julie of a mountain goat on an alpine peak, bouncing from rock to rock. After he passed, she examined her hand, an alien thing placed on her thigh.

Julie had done detailed study drawings of her hands in art class, but never understood how fascinating all the tendons and muscles under the skin could be. Julie flexed and relaxed it, studying the lines in her palms, and examining the texture of her skin.

The play of tendon and bone beneath grew intriguing and peculiar. When she clasped her hands together, it seemed bizarre, detached from the act, her skin numbed and separated from her body.

She turned to share this with George, but when she looked up, she forgot her intent. Julie sat back with her spine against the sturdy tree. The waves of color and people undulated like a heaving sea, the very mass comingling, breathing as one, in and out, in and out, like a giant alien creature of peace, joy, and eternal, universal love.

Julie ached to get up and dance, be part of this incredible journey, this one-ness of nature, but she grew heavy as an elephant, rooted to her spot. The tree held her there as though she melded into a part of its root system. Julie relished being part of the tree. She shut her eyes tight and reached down into the roots, into the loamy, thick, cool ground, down into the dirt, past the squirming worms and to the solid bedrock.

She pulled in a deep breath, relishing the coolness curling into her lungs, then let it out with a long, shuddering sigh. After opening her eyes, she rose again from the deep, into the bright, cool, thin air. She burst forth reborn, blossoming, new, and shiny.

Next to her, George breathed deep, staring into the crowd, transfixed by the sights. Otter also sat frozen, but Jonas and Summer entwined next to the tree, their hands exploring each other with reckless abandon.

Something shifted behind Julie's ear, a heavy thing which didn't belong. She put her hand up to her head and touched the daisy that stranger had tucked there, a thousand years ago.

Julie pulled the daisy out and caressed its petals, one by one, the silky smooth, fragrant petals. She placed them against her cheek to stroke their essence. As she caressed the soft fuzz along the stem, it reminded Julie of body hair, prickling with gooseflesh along her arms, as her own stem fuzz. In slow motion, Julie handed the flower to George for his examination, wanting to share her profound discoveries with him.

He turned, looking at her as if he'd never seen her. He put a hand against her hair, stroking it down to the ends. After fondling the tips between his fingers, he pulled them up to brush her nose. She chuckled at the tickling sensation, grinning. Her laugh echoed in her ears, as if from the end of a long hall. He leaned over and kissed her. The kiss took forever and no time at all.

An eternity of music intruded upon the kiss. The band played close by, deep tones vibrating through Julie's bones. The music grew strange and haunting, the heavy guitars whining up and down in a wave.

Julie wanted to get up and dance, but when she tried, George kept her down. "We have to keep together, remember? Let's all stay put. It's safer that way." His voice sounded slurred.

"But I must dance. I think if I don't dance, I'll break." So did hers.

George looked both worried and transcendent at the same time. "Well, okay, we'll get up and dance, but stay near the tree. The tree is our safe place. It's our home, it's our refuge. Don't leave the tree."

"I shall be like Buddha and be one with the tree." Julie agreed with solemnity and got up to dance. She danced gently, her feet in place, swaying her upper body in time to the slow guitar waves. The singer's strident voice rose above the noise of the crowd.

> *"One pill makes you larger,*
> *and one pill makes you small ... "*

Julie grew and shrunk with the waves of sound, as the crowd rose and fell with the rhythm. A physical wave rushed over her, the tide waxing and waning with the music. Despite his earlier admonishment, George got up and danced with her, his hands on her waist to anchor them both. Otter join them, dancing as one, swaying with the tangible sounds.

Much later, as they sat once again around the tree, they stumbled back into reality. The crowds had died out, and the music had long ago finished. Jonas and Summer had continued their own explorations. Had they made love right there? Julie thought so, but the specific memory eluded her. They didn't sleep, but clung to each other, hands caressing and touching.

Julie ached to have a pencil in her hand, or charcoal, or paint, or even mud, anything she might use to create, to draw, to paint the images. Flashes of inspiration cascaded through her mind. She resolved to have supplies the next time she did this, as the images flew so fast through her she couldn't grasp one to keep it in her memory. Flitting, fleeing, swift as doves, the visualizations screamed through her creative center.

Flashes of memory of the evening came to her as she became more grounded. She recalled others had joined her in the dancing, but George, sometimes Otter, had kept one hand on the tree as a physical anchor, keeping them from drifting into the chaos. The sounds remained a mélange of noise, but stripped of their three-dimensionality, no longer buffeting physical forces. At one point, she danced with Paul, but that couldn't be possible. Paul, Paul, a memory from a thousand years ago. She shoved it away.

Summer and Jonas stood up, languorous, stretching. It seemed like an excellent idea to Julie, so she gave a mighty, full body stretch, and it felt sumptuous. She kept stretching, moving, bending. Soon, Julie experienced an almost sexual pleasure in the stretch. She danced again, but with her own soul.

George took Julie's arms, lifting her to her feet. "I think we should head home, Otter. Will you folks be all right?"

But she didn't want to go yet. "We're still having fun. We're part of this amazing creature, this universal alien."

George looked at her askance. She imagined what she said would make no sense to someone who hadn't been in her head for the last several hours. She laughed at herself. "Sorry, I walked down strange paths, I guess."

"I guess so. But yes, I think we should finish this trip up in a more controlled area. Does that sound okay?" He stroked her cheek with a feather touch.

She put her hand on his and closed her eyes, savoring the sensation. "Yes. Yes, that sounds wonderful."

They thanked Otter for the trip, took their leave of Summer and Jonas, and wended their way back to Fred's house. The four-block trip seemed to last for miles, an entire adventure. Julie kept looking up to see the dancing stars, twinkling in the velvet-dark sky. When she did so, she would stumble and trip, so George had to remind her to watch her steps.

When they reached their room, they climbed into their beds. They had long since moved them together to form one larger bed, tying the legs to keep it from moving apart. The sheets slid so sensuous and cool on her bare skin, she wanted to abandon herself to the sensation. Julie kept squirming and moving around under the covers.

George chuckled as he caressed her hair. "Keep doing that, Julie, it will make my part much easier."

She teased him. "And is it a laborious job?"

"Not at all, but this way I won't have to move at all, just let you wiggle your way home, so to speak."

His skin brushed against hers and the hair on his chest rasped, scratchy and rough. She grew fascinated with the texture. Touching every inch with her hands, he finally took her wrists and moved them farther down.

"If you plan on getting stuck in a fascination loop, there are better subjects for your attentions."

"Indeed, there are."

They finished the trip in an intense study of each other's bodies, wrapped in a fog of isolation and sexual joy.

At work on Monday, Julie shifted the mockup photographs around, not pleased with their current layout. She offset and angled them. *Yes, that worked better.* A much more interesting visual this way. She tacked down the mockups in their spots, plotting out the text, using her ruler, stencils, and pencils.

"It's looking great, Julie. Is this for the new conference next month?"

Julie almost jumped out of her skin at Tamara's voice. She'd been concentrating on her project and didn't hear the older woman come up behind her.

"That's right. Tony asked me to put it together so we would have time to send it to the printers."

"What are you doing for lunch today? I've found a quaint little sandwich shop a couple blocks away. Would you like to join me?" An invitation from Tamara seemed more like a royal command from the Queen, so she had only one acceptable answer.

"Of course, I should be delighted."

Julie enjoyed her favorite sandwich, a Rueben, while she wondered what Tamara wanted. Though she always acted with perfect politeness to Julie, Tamara didn't waste time with idle chitchat. If she spoke to someone, she did so with a concrete purpose.

121

Tamara looked up from her club sandwich and asked her, without preamble, "I wondered, Julie, do you like children?"

Such an odd question, out of the blue, and related to nothing they'd ever discussed. Julie sat dumbstruck. She took a sip of her Coke to clear her mouth, giving her time to come up with an answer.

"I do like children. Are you asking if I want to have a family?" She put only enough quizzical into her response to sound curious but unconcerned.

Tamara's quick laugh burst out, clipped and loud. "Ha! No, nothing like that. Well, perhaps vicariously. I need someone to take care of my own children. You mentioned you'd worked as a nanny before. I've three young ones, aged two, four, and seven. Barbara, Janet, and Donald, in that order. My husband and I have, well, sought separate paths. Therefore, since I have no desire or means to quit working to take care of them, I need to hire someone to help. Would you be interested in that position?"

Julie enjoyed her work, but she also loved children. However, Tamara had such an abrupt manner, Julie might not be able to handle it in large doses.

Tamara must have seen her hesitation. "You'd continue to work at the Church. Artwork such as yours can often be completed at home, or on an evening shift, after I've come home for the day. The pay is $75 a week, and your own room, rent-free, in the apartments above the office. I've watched you work, and you have an admirable work ethic. I need someone to instill this in my children."

"It all sounds delightful, and I am tempted. I helped my mother take care of my little brother for many years. I do enjoy children." While Julie harbored concern about her relationship with George, she also remembered he'd leave for Michigan soon. That month-long mooching grace period at Fred's house stared her in the face.

"I'll even arrange for you to take classes at the art school for free, so you can further your career." Tamara made this offer like a royal bequest, an act of *noblesse oblige*.

Julie shifted her path. As George had to leave, she'd need a new apartment. This would not only be free lodging, it provided additional income. It put a serious dent in her social life, but without George, she doubted it would be as active.

With a broad grin, she nodded. "Tamara, I accept. When would you like me to start? When can I meet the children?"

Tamara pulled out a notepad from her clutch purse, writing a couple notes. "Today is Monday. Come home with me tomorrow evening, to meet them all. We can move you in this weekend." She flipped to another page and scribbled, ripping it out and handing it to Julie.

"This is my address and phone number in case you need it. Thank you, Julie. I look forward to having you in the household." Tamara held out her hand, formal, so Julie took it, wondering what she had gotten herself into.

July 1, 1967, San Francisco

Dear Katy,
Life has shifted again, but I think in a good way. I'm still working at the Church, but George went back to Michigan, as he'd planned. I cried, but we'll keep our friendship no matter what. I thought for a while we might have more, but he's great fun to be with. Anyhow, I think I need someone with more substance and purpose for a permanent partner.
I've an additional job now, taking care of three young children for Tamara Lange, one of my co-workers.

She's paying me and providing a room above the office to live in. She's even arranging for me to take art classes. The first one is next week, a specialized advertising class. I'll let you know how things turn out.

I told you to watch out for that teacher, didn't I? He's always been a pig to anything in a skirt. Don't let yourself get caught alone with him again, please. Since it takes a long time to gather all your art supplies, cheat, and start before the class is over. That way you're not the last one left.

So, tell me about your boyfriend. All you've told me so far is you met him in England. Is that where he's from? Details, sis!

Much love,

Julie

Julie pushed down her tears of frustration. Janet cried so hard, her little face grew a deep, angry red. She gave no clue to the reason for her rage, but Julie did her best to rock her into calm. She bounced Janet on her knee, stroking her straight, white-blond hair.

Donald hadn't gotten home yet from elementary school, but Barbara played in her room. While bouncing the baby on her hip, Julie checked in on Barbara, discovering she had taken every single toy in her box, a significant number, and strewn them around the room in a chaotic mess. Dolls, building blocks, stuffed animals, and books lay everywhere. Julie daren't walk in, for fear of stepping on a toy and dropping Janet.

"Barbara! What on earth are you doing?"

"Playing." Barbara excelled at pouting, setting her face into a determined expression. She'd messed up her reddish-blond hair, spiked out in all directions.

"You may play with one toy at a time, Barbara. Put the rest away, now. Start with the books, please." Julie emulated Tamara's manner when taking the children to task, so orders wouldn't be confusing.

The child argued, but received a level glare of determination from Julie. Barbara placed each book on the shelf, with sullen glances at the door after each one. Julie remained in the doorway, watching her, bouncing Janet on her hip, until the front door downstairs slammed.

"Good job so far. Keep at it, young lady. I'll come back and check your progress. The dolls are next." If she didn't give explicit instructions, Barbara would always find a way to wiggle out of them. A born lawyer, this one.

She climbed down the stairs, expecting to see Donald coming home from school. The bus dropped him at the corner, two houses down. However, Tamara stood there instead.

"Julie! Whatever is wrong with Janet?" The child still sobbed, her face blotchy, though the screeching had calmed down while they stood in Barbara's room.

"She's been horribly fussy but calmed down from earlier."

Tamara looked doubtful but accepted the explanation. While she acted business-like in all other things, she turned solicitous of her children. "Very well, as long as she's getting better. Is Donald home yet?"

"Not yet. Is anything wrong? You're home earlier than normal." Julie searched Tamara's face for clues.

"Oh, no, I started a project and realized I'd forgotten my notes. I'll be back out again in a moment." She strode into her library/office, grabbed a file from one of the mahogany cabinets in the desk, bustling out again.

Julie figured the office had first belonged to her husband, the absent Charles Lange she'd heard of but never seen. She wondered what he'd been like and why they'd broken up. Julie shrugged, realizing the reason was none of her business. She rocked the child on her hip, pleased Janet had fallen asleep in her arms.

That evening, Julie worked late in the office, finishing up a project for Tony. She finished at Tamara's by five, and done at the office by nine. It didn't leave her much time to socialize during the week, but she made up for the lack on the weekends. She fell deep in concentration when a door closed elsewhere in the warren of rooms.

Who would be here this late at night? She had a momentary twinge that it might be Tibbets, and shivered. He gave her the creeps. He'd done nothing she could call an incident since the art supply run, but she avoided him.

Julie stayed cautious, hiding herself in case of an intruder. She switched off the desk lamp, cringing at the loud click, and found a spot behind the filing cabinet, and waited.

A man's chuckle answered a woman's question. She glimpsed their shadows along the far wall, near the corridor. They must be embracing. Had a couple from the streets wandered in, looking for privacy? She almost emerged to ask them to leave when she recognized the voices. Tamara and… Tony? Tony had a wife! Well, Tamara had a husband, but she'd separated. Tony? Julie liked him, he'd become a friend. She felt betrayed by this action, as if loyalty was a prerequisite for affability.

As she crouched, still in shock, the couple moved past the doorway and into full view. Tony wrapped an arm around Tamara's shoulders, hers on his waist. She stared at him with simpering eyes. Tamara didn't simper.

They moved on to Tamara's office. As soon as the door closed, Julie gathered her purse in the dark and snuck out of her office. Julie tiptoed to the door, barking her shin on the receptionist's desk in the dim light. When she cried out in pain, she halted, waiting to discover if she'd alerted the lovebirds to her presence.

When nothing stirred, she crept to the door. She had just opened it to go out when Tamara cried her name. "Julie!"

A wealth of fear and anger dripped in Tamara's voice. She looked up to Tony and Tamara, both trying to button their shirts. Tony's face turned bright red, even in the low light. Tamara's brow furrowed with anger. "What are you still doing here, Julie? You should have been done hours ago."

"I had that project to finish for Tony. The brochure layout for the festival next week. It's due in the morning."

Tamara crossed her arms, glancing at Tony next to her. She rolled her eyes as he still fumbled with his buttons. "You're not to say a thing of this to anyone. Do you understand? Not a soul!"

Julie took a deep breath. "I won't tell anyone, I promise. But you shouldn't be here! Anyone might have been in the office! We all have keys!"

With five long steps, Tamara came right up to Julie's face. She tried to retreat, but her back hit up against the door. "Not. A. Word. And I think it would be safer if you found another job. Soon."

Julie fumbled with the door handle and escaped, her heart pounding in her chest. For a moment, she thought Tamara would slap her. Or worse.

Dammit, dammit, dammit. Now she'd have to find another job *and* another place to live. Why didn't she just keep her mouth shut? Her Midwestern morality didn't have a home here.

She wanted to cry and shout and scream in the street at all the unfairness. Instead, Julie headed down the street to the late-night café where she often ate dinner, ordered a chocolate milkshake and a Rueben sandwich, thinking.

What options did she have? She'd barely exchanged a few words with Frank since George left, or she'd hit him up for that job with his company. But after mooching off him a month already, she had no stomach for that shame.

Speaking of shame, her other option was to go home to Michigan. No, it would be a bitter day in Hell when she ran home to her father.

Could she get her old job in England back? Only if Paul had gone. Worth a phone call, at least.

1968, East Grinstead, England

Victoria had written to her, to assure her that Paul had transferred away. Back to Minnesota, or somewhere else, she didn't much care. As long as he'd left. A brief long-distance phone call to Sheila told her she still had a job in East Grinstead, and Eileen agreed to take her on again as a nanny. It seemed like a step backwards in time, a regression to a past life. She had enjoyed her months in San Francisco, and in some ways, it had changed her perspective on things.

For instance, the affair between Tamara and Tony had shown her that not all marriages are right, even if it had made her too uncomfortable to remain living there. Sometimes one must break a poor match to make a stronger one. However, Paul never hinted that he wanted to leave his wife. He never expressed interest in a change, just a fling.

After an uneventful journey back to England, Julie slid back into her old life with little fanfare or grief. Victoria became a closer friend and confidante, and Julie felt more at home than she had in years. For once in her life, perhaps, she'd made a wise choice.

Eileen, when angry, didn't shout. Instead, she got haughty. "I didn't hire you just to have you be unavailable. If I need you for the children, you must reset your priorities. I apologized for the short notice, but there's nothing I can do about it."

Julie tried to hold her frustration behind clenched fists. "Eileen, if I just had a social conflict, I'd cancel, no problem. But this is work. I'm on a deadline. They gave me more responsibilities, since they're ramping up the new membership drive. I've got to get this artwork done before tomorrow morning. I can't work on art with the kids around. There's no way to concentrate, much less keep my art supplies from being confiscated or destroyed by curious kids."

Yesterday, her boss informed Julie that he might consider her to run the East Grinstead art department. Doing this job well might be the deciding factor. She would have had plenty of time to work on it tonight, at the expense of sleep. But Eileen sprung the news on her. She and Percy had tickets to a London event. She needed Julie to watch the children until they returned, well after midnight. No other option, no advanced warning. Julie returned for this? She'd had about enough.

"I love these kids as if they were my own, but it isn't fair to expect me to have no plans during the evenings. I'm here for them during the day, but I must get fair warning. Did you not realize you needed me out tonight?"

Eileen drew herself up, tall and straight, looking down her nose. "I did not. Percy did. He bought tickets to this charity event as a surprise for me. It's an art exhibit." Eileen sounded like the height of nouveau riche snobbery, proud of her rise into the upper echelons of the social elite of London.

Julie snorted. "Then he should have told me. Eileen, I'll try to find someone to mind them, but I simply don't have the time tonight."

Eileen's gaze grew colder than a glacier on midwinter. "Do not trouble yourself, Julie. I shall find someone else. Permanently. Please come back tomorrow and we shall return your personal items."

Eileen then strode, quick and haughty, out of the room.

Lovely. Half of Julie's income came from Eileen and watching the kids. She'd been saving her extra money for a while, so had a stash, but not a big one. If the promotion didn't come in, she'd have to rein in her budget tight. At least her job covered her spartan lodging.

Julie still shook with adrenaline, so she retrieved a pad of paper and pastels from her room, making her way out into the town. She loved to sit and draw in the nearby serene park. Since Eileen had fired her, she wouldn't have to worry about having time for work tonight. Besides, she would be in no shape to do demanding creative work until she calmed. Julie recognized it for base escapism, accepting it.

She found her favorite bench and closed her eyes, centering herself as they had taught her to do in class. She took several more deep breaths, slow and steady, calming her jangled nerves, spiky anger, and ruffled feathers.

When she opened her eyes, trees rustled in the gentle May breeze, with pink wildflowers dotting the grass. The sweet trill of birds came from the soughing leaves. No one else came near.

Julie wanted to draw the more unusual-shaped trees near her. One had a thin, low-lying branch which looked like a Victorian swing, so that's what she drew. A young girl, in full swing, with a flowered hat and white, fluffy petticoats billowing around her outstretched feet, clad in white shoes with straps across the top. The girl should be smiling. Julie took her darker pinks and made a hint of a grin on the girl's face. Turning attention to the hair, Julie wanted sunshine, so she must be blond. Just as she contemplated making the lawn dappled with sunlight, a sound made her glance up.

Just the trees rustling in the breeze. Yet, it blew stronger than she expected. She glanced up at the sky, noting the gathering darkness. She gathered up her materials in haste. Bits of pastel lay scattered, as she got messy working with them. A few of them broke as she shoved them all into the cardboard box, with its individual spaces for each color. The first drop of rain would ruin her artwork.

Everything stashed, Julie grabbed her pad and pelted to the house. She stopped, ran back, picked up the box of pastels she had packed and forgotten, and ran even faster. She stayed hunched over her drawing, trying to both shield it from the incipient rain and keep it from brushing against her, as the pastels weren't fixed yet. As she reached the house, several large, wet drops plopped on her head. She made it to her room and surveyed the drawing, looking for the splotches. No, it looked fine. Julie had made it.

It would have been adding injury to insult to have had her art ruined within two hours of her being fired. At least now she might replace a horrible memory with a pleasant one.

Julie hoped she'd ruined Eileen's plans for the night, and the imperious woman had to stay with her own bloody kids.

As she turned down the hall, she ran right into Paul. He looked good, tanned, and beaming for miles.

Her heartbeat skipped and she backed up to the wall. "What! What are you doing here?"

He grinned, guileless and maddening. "Julie! I hoped I'd run into you. I'd heard you returned."

"You left. I made sure you left."

"You're right, I *did* leave. I transferred to Spain for a couple months. But I'm back now." He reached for her hands. "Look, I wanted to explain—"

She snatched her hands back from his questing fingers. "You have nothing to explain! You're married. That's the end of the story." The confusion bubbled within her head, making her foggy and sluggish. Why'd he come back? She'd moved halfway around the world to escape him, and now he came back?

"Julie, please, can't we talk about it? Not now, not here, perhaps lunch? Down at the pub? I'll be there tomorrow at noon. Come, please. Just give me a chance?"

His brown eyes pleaded with hers, and she blinked away the tears that threatened to burst forth. She spun around and walked out into the rain, heedless of the damage to her drawing.

The next morning, she paced back and forth in her small dorm, while Sheila watched her. "Settle down, Julie. He just asked you to lunch. He didn't ask you to elope with him."

She spun, fixing Sheila with an angry glare, her muscles tense. "He wouldn't be able to. He's married!"

"Yes, and that isn't a crime."

Julie stared at her friend. "Fornication is! Adultery is!"

Sheila raised her eyebrows. "And has he done any of these with you?"

"You know damn well he hasn't. That's not the point. He tried to."

"That's precisely the point, Julie. He's asking you to let him explain. Can you not at least give him that much of a chance?"

She crossed her arms and turned away, staring at the small window but seeing nothing. "I don't want to."

"I realize that. But it's only fair, isn't it? You've never struck me as an unjust person."

Julie let out a deep, angry breath. She didn't want to admit that Sheila had a point.

"I'll have the steak and kidney pie, please." Julie loved the savory gravy and flaky pastry of this British staple. "And a pint of cider, thank you."

"I think I'll have the fish and chips, and a lemonade, if you please."

They had the cozy restaurant almost to themselves. Later, as the pubs filled, the restaurant would get more business. Only one other couple dined in the dim room. Dark mahogany panels lined the walls, while what may have once been red velvet covered the booths. The walls had memorabilia from the World War I era, such as old photographs, recruitment notices, bits from planes, and many things Julie couldn't identify.

She raised an eyebrow. "You realize lemonade doesn't mean what it does in America, right?"

"Yes, but I like the carbonation. It's an improvement, in my mind."

"Fair enough."

An awkward silence lay over them. Paul reached for her hand on the table, but she snatched hers out of the way and into her lap, her jaw snapping shut over the imprecations she wanted to scream at him.

"Julie, my wife and I, well, we have an arrangement."

She narrowed her eyes. Her jaw ached from clenching it so hard. "What sort of arrangement?"

"She knows that when I travel, I'll be away from her for long months. She has sort of given me permission to sow my oats."

The heat rose in her cheeks. "Sow your oats? Am I a field ready to plow, then?" Her voice dripped with anger. She kept her tone low, but sound carried easily in the empty pub.

"Of course not. A poor choice of words. Annie appreciates I might meet people who I would like to get to know better when I'm traveling. Can you understand that?"

"I suppose I might grasp the theory. That doesn't mean I'm one of them."

He closed his eyes as if praying for patience. "No, it doesn't. It means you are someone I would like to enjoy lunch with. Will that do for now?"

Julie thought of Tamara and Tony, and their extra-marital affair. If Paul had a pre-arranged agreement, they wouldn't be hurting his wife. That wouldn't be so bad, would it? She supposed it wouldn't hurt to be friends.

To deflect the decision, she asked, "Have you eaten here before?"

"I have, but it's been a while. The food is good enough. Basic British fare, nothing fancy, but reliable."

"Fare enough." Julie emphasized the word "fare" so he could tell she made a pun. She didn't have his skill, if "skilled" was the right word to use.

He gave her a sidelong glance, screwing up his face.

That drew a chuckle from her. "Now you realize how we hurt when you do it."

Their drinks arrived, so he raised his in a toast. "Here's to second chances. May our second be more successful than the first."

"I'll drink to that." Julie took an obligatory sip.

Paul took her hand. "I am sorry I left you in the lurch last time. For future dates, I promise, no more gory movies."

"I appreciate the sentiment very much." Julie smiled at Paul as he took her hand. This time she let him. It tingled with pins and needles, so she shifted to relieve the pressure.

"Does the graphic stuff not bother you, then?"

She shrugged. "I guess not. I don't panic at blood in real life, though I prefer not to deal with it. Maybe I'm able to disassociate enough from movies and television to realize they aren't imminent danger."

"Perhaps I should work on disassociative techniques."

Julie shrugged, "Might be downright helpful. Like when you have children." She clamped her jaw again after referring to his marital state.

Paul heaved a sigh and squeezed her hand.

Julie retrieved her hand from his grip, despite his attempt to keep it. "This will take me some time to get used to, Paul. I don't like the idea of being... your bit on the side."

"Julie, Julie, that's not what you are at all. You are a friend. A friend I would like to keep. A friend I enjoy being with. If it moves on to being an affectionate friend, fantastic. If not, that's also fantastic. Let's play it by ear, okay?"

Julie didn't want to give in. She still smarted after her dustup with Eileen the day before. She had, at least, put Eileen's plans into disarray. They'd to cancel their trip to London. Her supervisor gladly moved her to daytime hours, with full time work. The promotion looked even more promising now. Julie held better control of her destiny than she had in a long time.

This new-found confidence seemed to make her more edgy. She had never considered herself the ladder-climbing career sort. She'd give it the old college try and see how it worked. Perhaps she should also do this with Paul's friendship.

She took a couple more breaths. "All right. Let's see how it goes. It still seems unfair to both me and your wife. What's her name, again?"

"Friendship should never be unfair, my dear. And my wife's name is Annie." How could she resist that grin? He grinned all the way, his mouth, his eyes, even his hair seemed to be joyful and entreating.

The waitress approached with a huge tray on her shoulder, setting up a tray stand. Her steak and kidney pie not only came with chips, but with a green mess of mushy peas. Julie hadn't yet worked up the courage to taste the green mushy mess. She pictured a new alien species which invaded dinner plates all over the island.

After she sampled a small, cautious spoonful of the glutinous mass, she blinked a couple times, testing the taste and texture out in her mouth, taking another, larger bite. It seemed like a thick split pea soup, with pepper and other spices in it.

Paul had avoided his but noted her pleasure in the dish. "Like the mushy peas, do you?"

"I'd never tried them, but they're delicious."

He wrinkled his nose. "Not my thing. I prefer my food with crunch and texture. The taste is fine, I love peas, but I like to bite my food, not slurp it."

"What about soups?"

"Stew and chili, fine. Cream or puréed soups? No thank you."

"Interesting. I wonder if you had issues dealing with moving to solid foods as a baby."

He shrugged. "Maybe. I've never been a fan of them."

"Perhaps now is when I should let you know I make a mean chili?"

"Already trying to impress me with your domestic skills? My, you do work fast." He raised his eyebrows in mock outrage.

Julie shot him a quelling glare. "Tease. Merely making conversation."

As they strolled towards Saint Hill, they held hands. The night remained bright, as the moon shone full and the sky looked clear. Stars sparkled above them in a glittering display of jewels on velvet. Julie breathed in deep of the cool air, smelling the leaves, flowers, the hint of smoke from nearby chimneys.

"Was that a sigh, or are you enjoying the night?" Paul sounded halfway between concern and teasing.

"Just enjoying the night air. It's so different here from where I grew up near Detroit. The light pollution is almost non-existent. You can see the stars and smell the trees."

"Minneapolis is the same way, but if you go north, into lake country, you have the universe laid out before you." Paul wore a dreamy expression, his eyes on the distant horizon. They stopped walking and faced each other. "My family always travels north in the summer, to vacation among the ten thousand lakes. We would get a cabin on the lake, go fishing or boating, and relax into the wonder of nature."

"We do something similar, but into Canada. Our family has an island, perhaps three acres long, with three cabins on it. We all go up on vacation each summer, doing about the same. There is a family on the mainland, they've been friends with our family for three generations. They have a massive farm, so we get to go pick fresh strawberries and peas, get fresh bread and butter from them. Pure heaven." Julie remembered the annual trips with great pleasure and wistfulness.

Paul stroked her cheek with a tender brush of his fingers. He bent down to her, ever so lightly brushing her lips with his. She caught her breath, and turned it into another deep, though ragged, sigh.

"That was nice." She beamed up at the silhouette his head made against the moon-bright darkness.

"Yes, it was ... nice." He bent again to kiss her with purpose.

1968, East Grinstead, England

They didn't have a lot of options for privacy. They both shared rooms with other people. The huge estate stayed busy with people going in and out, with no real rhyme or reason to their movements.

Over the course of the next several days, Julie and Paul found stolen moments to enjoy each other's company. They chatted, kissed, with not a small bit of physical exploration. However, to take it any further, they'd need true privacy.

They had discussions to figure out trysting spots. They decided the bathroom in the B&B where Paul stayed would be the most practical place. It had a lock, and some residents took long visits, so to speak. As unappetizing as this sounded to Julie, she had to agree. They might explain any sounds as a normal occupant's colonic struggles. She teased Paul about how he chose the most romantic places, and how she must, one day, tell their children about this swoon-worthy gallantry.

They planned their rendezvous several days later, when Paul assured her the B&B would be empty, at least long enough to ensconce themselves in their chosen sanctuary. If one of his roommates returned, at least they'd not be caught *in flagrante delicto*. They locked themselves in, standing in awkward silence.

"Isn't this the part where you're supposed to sweep me off my feet, despite our banal surroundings?" Julie asked him, raising one eyebrow.

"Shouldn't that be our *baño* surroundings?"

Julie recognized the Spanish word for bathroom and fell into a hysterical giggle. She covered her mouth to keep it from echoing.

"It isn't conducive for romance, is it?" He eyed the space on the floor. Like most bathrooms in the UK, it looked tiny compared to US bathrooms. The floor space might accommodate them both lying down, but only if they bent around the plumbing. At least it had been meticulously cleaned. His landlady would have brooked no speck of dirt or grime in her house, upon pain of court-martial.

Julie searched for further options, chagrined they'd considered nothing beyond privacy. She glanced at the bathtub, a cast iron Victorian job, complete with claw feet, painted blinding white. "Perhaps the bathtub would serve? We'll put down a couple towels, perhaps, on our knees? It'll be tight, but it might work. It'd be more comfortable than the floor."

"Very well. Milady?" Paul reached for her hand, turning it over, kissing her wrist. Julie closed her eyes, savoring the soft, barely-there sensation, surprised at how this tiny contact rushed to her toes. It added suspense and anticipation to their contact, realizing, for the first time, they had the freedom to do whatever they wanted.

She opened her eyes as he kissed further up her arm, to the crook. Even though he'd shaved, it tickled so much she flinched. He peered up, as if afraid he had somehow done something wrong, but then she closed her eyes again, enjoying the attention, trying hard not to move.

Up the kisses traveled, to her shoulder, her neck. She let escape a moan of pleasure at these incredible sensations of tickle and ecstasy. The hairs on her arms sprang up, as she suppressed the frisson which climbed up her spine.

She glanced at him, his brown eyes locked with hers, intent.

"Your eyes are like reflected, still pools on a stormy day, you know."

She closed them again.

By the time his lips reached her mouth, she opened hers, more than ready for his now insistent kisses. They held each other tight while kissing, hands fumbling to loosen clothing, caress, touch, and stroke.

They made their way to their narrow "bed," not noticing it wasn't the softest of king-sized feather beds.

Later, after awkward gymnastics and fits of giggles, they curled up together in a sitting position in the tub. Julie lay back on Paul, his arms around her.

His chest vibrated as he chuckled. "Well, I think this might be one for the record books."

"Oh?"

"How many times do you think such a setting has actually worked for such an act? I'm sure we're trailblazers. Perhaps I should call Guinness and have them create an entry for their World Record Book?"

"Perhaps you should not!" Julie widened her eyes, aghast until she understood he was joking.

"Don't worry, I'll keep this as our special secret. Besides, no one would believe us."

April 16, 1999, Miami, Florida

Dear Mr. Stein:

Let me open this letter to state that I am looking for nothing from you. I do not need money, nor acknowledgement, just closure, perhaps practical information, if that is all you can give. I have been researching my family for many years, hoping for at least medical background and genealogical data for my research.

I have reason to believe that you are my father. My mother is Julie Jensen, and she worked for the Church in the 1960s, in East Grinstead, England. She had met and became involved with a man named Paul Stein. As a result of this liaison, she became pregnant with me, and has raised me on her own.

I understand you likely have a family of your own. I have no wish to have this family upset by an intruder, so I would request at least information, if I can. Do I have any half-siblings? Is there any history of disease in your side of my family? Diabetes? Cancer? Heart disease? I would greatly appreciate it if you could share such details as you may.

If, however, you are able and willing to acknowledge me, I would be most appreciative. I've enclosed a picture of myself so you may judge for yourself if we might look alike.

Sincerely,
Your daughter,
Kirsten Jensen

Kirsten chewed the back of her pencil and looked at the letter. It read clinical and detached, but it must be. An emotional request would be blackmail, and she disliked such manipulations. This, however, should be enough for even the most hostile putative father to accept. She hoped.

She made a copy before she signed, sealed, and mailed it. The researcher from Everton's Genealogical

Helper had gotten back to her, a year later, with information on her father. He found an address in Missouri, a birth certificate, and a marriage certificate.

Next, she used the birth certificate to research his branch of the family. It listed her grandparents' names, so she wrote to the State of Minnesota to get their birth certificates. If he never replied to her letter, she might find out where they all came from.

After she posted all her record requests, she gave her mother a call.

"Hello, this is Julie."

"Hey, Mom. It's Kirsten."

"Who else would call me Mom? How are you, hon?"

"I'm doing okay, I guess. Stressed with the new job, but its interesting work. I'm at a CPA firm up in Jupiter. It's larger than the ones I've worked at before, about twenty accountants, five partners. They're all nice folk."

"That's good, I'm glad. Sandy is threatening to quit her job at the hospital again, but you know her. That's a constant." Julie and Kirsten shared a laugh at Sandy's never-ending complaints.

Kirsten didn't want to broach the subject yet. "What about your job? Are you still doing design work at the architect's office?"

"Well, secretarial work, but yes, Joe sometimes has me working on decorating the plans he creates. I fill in the plants and external pretty bits before he presents it. He sticks to the building parts."

"At least you're doing artwork again. You said you missed it when you worked property management."

"I still get little time for artwork I *enjoy*, but at least this is something. And this place is much closer to home. I don't have to take the Metrorail to work. I can ride my bike again."

Kirsten couldn't figure out a good segue, so she dived right in. "Oh, I wanted to let you know. I may have made progress in finding my dad."

There was a moment of silence on the line.

Kirsten pressed on. "I haven't found him yet, or anything, but I've gotten a birth certificate and marriage certificate. I can at least find out about his family."

Her mother sounded guarded and hesitant. "I suppose that's fine but be careful."

"Mom, if I find him, I mean, we're all adults now, even any children he might have. I don't want anything from him, and I'll tell him so. I just want to learn who he is, you know? Fill the hole in my psyche. Discover his half of my roots." Mom always knew her parents, what they were like. She didn't understand, deep inside, a part of Kirsten would never be complete without this knowledge.

May 20, 1968, East Grinstead, England

Dear Katy:

I'm so sorry I haven't written to you in a while. Things have been hectic around here, now that I got promoted to Art Department Manager. I no longer take care of Eileen's children, as we had a "difference of opinion"' on what my priorities should be. I miss the kids a lot but having the freedom to set my own hours helped me advance here. It also allows me my own free time to pursue my art. I've even had paintings on display at one of the local pubs, getting several compliments on my work. My friend, Victoria, helped me out there.

I'm sure you won't be surprised to learn I got involved with Paul, after all. I think you'd like him, despite his silliness and his tendency to pun through everything. He is sweet, musical, and intelligent, not to mention dashingly handsome. He's got dark eyes and hair and plays guitar.

143

I'm sure that would be enough for you to fall for him. He's a true flirt, and while I'm not the only female whose company he enjoys, I'm happy to have my part of him. He joked the other day that each of his harem had a part to play in the world. My part? To bear him children. Can you imagine that? If he wasn't so silly, I'd accuse him of the height of arrogance, but there isn't much he can't make light of.

How are your plans coming with the move to England? Are you still slated to come up this winter to meet with your fiancé? I'd love to be there to meet you when you arrive, so please write to me as plans solidify.

How are Mom and Dad doing? Any news on Larry? Is he doing any better in school?

Give my love to everyone, and please tell Gail I might have missed her last letter. It's been a long time since I've gotten a letter from her. I got Helen's yesterday.

Love always, your sister,
Julie

Julie needed more burnt sienna. She used more of the warmer colors than the cooler ones, so she always ran out of her favorite palette. Would mixing regular sienna with black work? Not the same but adding a bit of green brought it closer. The green reminded her of Paul's eyes.

Taking a deep sigh, she concentrated on her work. She painted a pastoral scene. The landlord at the pub had commissioned her for this. He wanted the view from the back of the pub, across the village park, with the hills in the distance. Craggy trees grew here and there, though she moved one closer to the edge of the canvas to improve the composition. She wanted to give the sky a sunny cast, but with clouds for character. Today seemed like a good day for it, with clouds scudding across the sky, dark with horded moisture, looking both ominous and atmospheric.

One of them grew larger. Julie should finish painting for the day, before the cloud grew more than ominous, dropping its horded rain upon her and her painting supplies. She'd gotten quick about gathering up her things, since the weather had mercurial moods.

As she climbed the hill to the house, she ran into Sheila and David, walking with Victoria and their son, Neil. They stopped under an awning as the rain dripped around them.

"Were you out painting again today, Julie?" David inquired, polite as all Brits when on their game.

"Nigel at the pub asked me to paint a scene for him. My first international commission piece!"

Sheila grimaced. "Surely you've had commissions before? You're a wonderful painter. I adore the fantasy works you've done." Sheila loved anything whimsical, be it fairy tales, Tolkien books, or science fiction movies. She read them all to young Neil.

"Oh, I've done commissions before, but all back in the States. This is the first time I've gotten one since I came over here. I wish he wanted a fantasy piece. While I love the countryside, I've never been a tremendous fan of vanilla landscape painting. I'm itching to put an intriguing element in the scene, like a stray cat, looking at the viewer, or a cloud shaped like a dragon."

Victoria chuckled, shaking her coat to dislodge the stray drops. "I'm sure you could sneak a cloud dragon in without Nigel getting into an uproar. He's a most accommodating gentleman. You have to be to run a successful pub, you know. The customer is always right, and all that rubbish."

Julie mused on this. Wrestling her creativity into someone else's idea of perfection often became a painful process. "I think I could come up with something. Thanks for the notion."

David glanced up at the sky and got a drop in his eye. He shook his head, his shaggy dark hair looking like a dog's. "Oh, did you hear about the hidden treasure up at the house?"

"Hidden treasure?" Victoria asked, but the question piqued Julie's interest.

"Someone explored the hidden passages in the house and found several crates of ancient whisky in a tunnel. They plan on selling it off at Christie's, making a bundle. It might help fund the Edinburgh expansion."

Julie remembered her own quiet explorations several months before. "How long have they been there? Did they find anything else?"

"Since the late thirties, at least. Thick dust covered the bottles, from what I heard. I wouldn't mind sampling the wares. Must ensure the quality is good, right? What else would they find?" David mimed taking a drink.

Julie gave him a half-smile. "Oh, perhaps a ghost or two." The rain eased, the sound of drip, drip, drip slowing. "I'm off, folks. Enjoy what's left of your walk." She dashed out, shielding her portfolio from stray drops, despite it being well-protected by the water-resistant sides.

1968, East Grinstead, England

Julie moped in her room. She didn't normally mope, but she gave in to the urge. Today had been a mopey kind of day.

Paul and Julie escaped for a quick stroll in the park, hand in hand, before she had to get back to work in the office. He broke the news to her with compassion, but she hadn't taken it with grace. Somewhere within her, she realized he must return to Minneapolis, to his life there, and to his wife. Her emotions turned into a roller coaster of morose fatalism. First, Roger had to leave, then George had to leave, and she had done well in getting over both of them. Now, Paul abandoned her.

Julie hadn't admitted such an inevitable conclusion to their affair. Now, she had no choice. While she took pride in her practical nature, this time she resisted practicality to wallow in her own misery, her own painful heart. She grew weary of being the practical one, the accommodating one, the one who bent over backwards so everyone else got their way.

She found a man who made her laugh and cry. A man to whom she could talk about anything, cherished her, and awakened in her a passion she didn't think she possessed. Sure, she'd enjoyed lovers before, but they paled in comparison to the sizzling passion with Paul. She mused on how much of this might be the forbidden nature of their love, but that was only part of the overall strength of their partnership.

Their love affair lasted several months after the halting, not-so-auspicious beginning. It grew into a warm and comforting relationship, spicy and daring. It became a part of her very being. When he left, so would a piece of her soul. What would she do without him? This notion sent her into another black hole of despair.

Sometime later, when her tears had become hiccups and sobs, the door rattled.

She'd locked herself in, not wanting anyone to disturb her misery, but Sheila's voice intruded. "Julie? Julie, are you okay? Is this about Paul leaving?" She sounded so sympathetic, so understanding, it made Julie cry again, in full force. Sheila unlocked the door and rushed in.

"Oh, my dear, sweet girl. It'll be okay, it will be fine. Shh, shh." Sheila held her tight, rocking her as she would her child. "It hurts, it hurts terribly. I might tell you it will get better, and it will, but you won't believe me yet. Shh, shh."

Julie had cried herself out and into a fitful sleep. Sheila laid her down, tucked the blankets around her, leaving her to slumber.

Several hours later, Sheila returned. Julie still slept, so she felt loath to wake her. However, corporate had summoned everyone to a huge meeting. She placed a gentle hand on Julie's shoulder and shook.

"Julie? Julie, wake up, dear. Julie?"

She moaned and rubbed the dried bits of sleep and tears from her eyes. She blinked, bleary-eyed, at Sheila.

"Julie, Sharplin has called a general meeting. He wants everyone out on the lawn in about fifteen minutes."

"What … what's going on? This's strange."

"I'm not sure, though the rumors are flying fast and furious. Why don't you freshen up, while I wait outside for you, and we'll go down together? David's already there with Neil. I brought you water." She handed Julie the glass, tepid and without ice, giving her a sympathetic look, then left the room.

Julie roused herself and stumbled into the bathroom. She scrubbed at her face with soap and hot water, brushed out her sleep-tangled hair, and tied it back in a sloppy ponytail. She surveyed her face in the mirror. The redness had receded, and she looked almost presentable. Her clothes had rumpled but would straighten out as she moved. Delaying would do no good. After taking a deep breath, she drank the water in one swig.

Fifty people already stood on the lawn, milling about in groups and cliques, the murmurs and conversations rising and falling like waves. Everyone had their own theory for the cause of this unprecedented meeting. Snippets of conversation floated by as they passed.

"…think Sharplin is dead …"

"…shutting us down, I'm sure…"

"…government denied our charter …"

Julie and Sheila passed several groups as they met David, Priya, Colum, and Jimmy. Julie sighed in relief when she didn't see Paul. David held Neil in his arms but surrendered the wriggling boy to Sheila as she approached. Julie made a silly face, since trying to cheer someone else up might make her happier.

Julie touched Colum's arm to get his attention. "Any believable theories?"

"Not with any teeth, no," the Scotsman said, with a half-smile. "There is no shortage of theories, but most are gae crazy."

The head of the Church, Jasper Sharplin, climbed the dais to a microphone, a stand of trees at his back. He often stayed at Saint Hill, but Julie only glimpsed him in passing, having no personal encounters with him. Sharplin seemed a larger-than-life figure, with his thick, square glasses and fancy tailored suit.

He stepped up to the microphone, speaking with no preamble. "Strong rumors have circulated about actions which the UK government plan to take against us. Therefore, we are moving our World Headquarters to Spain. We will accomplish this move with the least amount of disruption. We shall move our essential functions into new offices in Valencia. However, room is still at a premium there. The rest of the administrative functions will move to the Edinburgh and Paris branches. Please coordinate with your supervisors for your assignment. Thank you."

He left with no further information. Was the announcement so short because he was worried, stressed, or because he had a curt style?

The crowd buzzed, almost a frenzied reaction to this shocking news.

David glanced at Sheila. "Sharplin always had a tendency towards paranoia about government interference with his Church, but if the rumors have grown substantial enough to force him to move his operations, something big must be in the works. Fancy a move to Scotland, my dear?"

Sheila shrugged and said, "Wherever the wind blows us, sweetie."

Once again, time to float along on the flimsy raft she called destiny.

CHAPTER SIX

Another Beginning

1968, East Grinstead, England

A week later, Julie packed her clothing and the few belongings she'd gathered in her months in England. A miniature Big Ben Victoria gave her. Next, a watercolor of the Thames by a local artist in London. A faux Wedgewood tea set. She did her best to protect these with packing to ship to Michigan. She didn't know what her quarters would be like in Edinburgh. Julie wanted her things safe at her sister's place. Katy wouldn't mind holding them for her.

Her throat contracted as she packed the crystal pendant Paul gave her on a shopping trip to London. After swallowing, she lifted her head, finished her packing, and shut all memories of him out of her mind. He would leave today. The best thing would be to put him out of her mind, remove the barbs he stuck in her heart, and live on.

She must be strong.

Julie wasn't so strong, though. Even completing everyday tasks felt like pushing through an invisible, viscous sludge. Movements came slow, halting, her decisions all weighted, her satisfaction in such decisions, nonexistent.

Eileen apologized to her the day before, after barely acknowledging her existence for several weeks.

After the apology, her former employer invited Julie to be her nanny again, but this time in Valencia.

Eileen knew about Julie's miserable time in Spain, but either forgot or didn't care. *She only apologized to me, so I'd take care of the kids again. She is only nice when she needs help.* Well, this decision she didn't have to second-guess.

Julie gathered her cases, three medium-sized bags and the two boxes to send to America. She hefted the large purse for the train journey. Her portfolio-sized flat bag held a decent-sized sketch pad, pencils, a book, even toiletries. The train would be a long, overnight journey, so she brought plenty of things to keep her mind occupied, and off other things.

Sheila already headed up to the new office, along with her family. Julie would be one of the last to leave the Saint Hill Manor, with its outrageous murals and manicured grounds. She'd miss the space, the trees, the charming village. She'd miss Victoria, whose honest sarcasm made a refreshing change from the supercilious gushing of other employees. Julie would miss the fresh air and laid-back vibe. They'd be staying in the city, so it would be like London, loud, crowded, grimy, dense with people and stories.

A bus would take them to the train station. She hauled her bags in two trips. Victoria offered to post the packages for her and met her on her second trip. They hugged and promised to keep in touch, despite being too insular a personality to keep long-distance friends.

Julie took a long, last look at the manor and surrounding countryside, turned to the bus, only to walk straight into Paul.

Great. The one person I hoped not to see before I left. And now, she'd have to say goodbye in front of everyone, exactly what she dreaded.

Julie struggled to keep the emotions bubbling inside her from showing on her face. Betrayal, rejection, anger, pride, despair, all fought for dominance. Paul held still, staring into her eyes, waiting for her to get herself under a vestige of control. "I hoped I might bid you farewell, my dear."

Julie clenched her jaw so hard it ached. "And *I* hoped we might avoid such a scene." For the first time, Julie appreciated Eileen's frigid inscrutability and wished she possessed it.

"Julie, Julie, please don't be mad with me. I *do* love you, but you know we can't stay together. We must move on, we must part. I will always remember you, with love in my heart and a smile on my lips, my sweet queen of hearts." He took her hand, despite her stiff resistance, and brought it to his lips in a chaste, medieval-style kiss. She yanked it back, glaring at him.

Julie didn't want to forgive him. She wanted to punch his smiling face, cry, and fling herself into his arms, and he'd take her away forever.

Instead, after several moments of angry glaring, and with a deep, shuddering breath, she relented. "I will remember you with fondness, Paul. I must go now." Her answer came clipped and stiff. If she let any soft words out, a flood of tears would follow. She pulled her hand from his, turning away. She controlled her stride to the bus door, careful not to run, steeling herself from looking back.

Later, alone in a compartment on the train, she gave in once again to the tears she'd held in check. She sobbed in time to the clickity-clack of the train along the rails.

August 20, 1968, Edinburgh, Scotland

Dear Katy:
I know you love London, Katy, but you should come visit me in Edinburgh if you get a chance. It's a

beautiful city. I imagined it would be dusty and grimy with centuries of coal dust and Victorian chimneys, but it seems surprisingly clean, and the architecture alone is enough to take your breath away. Even more than London! The streets are a labyrinthine mess in most places, but they're fun to wander around. And all these men with sexy accents.

The food is different from what I'm used to. They deep fry everything, but at least they've discovered the magic of sauces. The English haven't yet embraced this innovation, other than the ever-present Brown Sauce and salad crème (mayonnaise!). The drinks are heartier up here, too.

I'm enjoying my time. The work is hard, and they've given me accounting work. Which, as you know my lack of ability at math, is sure to make you laugh. I'm doing my best. The office is short-staffed, as they've divided their upper echelon between this office and Valencia. Sharplin seems to think the UK government is about to shut him down, so they have the true leaders in Spain, while this place in Edinburgh works as the nominal headquarters to the outside world. Sort of a bait-and-switch operation. It's such a flattering sensation to be disposable bait.

Since you're coming to London in November, I'll take a trip down to meet you. Give me a call when you leave. I can't wait to see you again.

More later, I must get back to work. They're keeping me busy here.

Much love,
Julie

Julie massaged her forehead and stared at the numbers again. They just made no sense. She'd never liked math, and she lamented volunteering to help when the official accountant transferred to Spain. She'd only promised to help, but her boss put her in charge of payroll. People's livelihoods now depended on her ability to do math.

She worked with last month's payroll paperwork, mimicking what the previous accountant, Corey, had done. She presumed he'd known his job. Only a few things changed with the payroll, like addition of people from Saint Hill. The rest didn't seem so hard, though trying to read his handwriting proved a challenge. Julie classified them as artistic symbols rather than numbers. These now danced in her head in a Dali-inspired animation.

She closed her aching eyes. She'd need far more coffee if she wanted to get these figures done tonight. The sun set hours ago.

Several hours later, dead tired and eyes blinking with grit and sleep, she pushed herself back from the old, wooden desk, and gathered the papers. Julie couldn't tell if it looked right, but it was as right as she could make it, with so little sleep. She glanced at the wall clock. Three in the morning. At least she only had a block to walk to her flat.

Julie shared the flat with two other women, Charmaine and Holly, but they'd gone to the Perth office for a couple days, so the place echoed with emptiness. She rattled the iron key in the flimsy door, stepping in. Even with the bedroom lamp on, the room looked dim, dust glowing from the outside lights. The city never went dark, like Detroit or D.C. Light always shone in the streets, if not the corners and alleyways. When mist hung in the air, it glowed like fairy dust, sparkling motes dancing among the breezes, sprinkling her hair and face with fairy kisses.

Julie could do with fewer fairy kisses and more sleep. She didn't even bother undressing. After kicking off her shoes, sturdy to deal with the ankle-turning cobblestone streets, she flopped on top of her covers. She fell asleep in moments.

The raucous, metallic ring of her alarm woke her, four hours later. Cursing, she slammed her hand down and turned to go back to sleep. She'd left the paperwork and paychecks on the secretary's desk for the director to sign and distribute. Sleep beckoned her back into his warm embrace.

Several hours later, noise from the street and the pervasive odor of the nearby Drambuie factory roused her from her stupor. The smell always made her stomach roil, the sick sweet aroma wafting into her flat, tendrils finding every nook and cranny. She stumbled towards the bathroom and retched into the toilet.

Julie knelt, miserable, reamed out, and disgusted. Despair dug its claws into her guts and her mind. Yes, Edinburgh possessed enormous beauty, but she worked too much to enjoy it. She sat in that office day and night, trying to catch up. She'd made no friends with scarce time to socialize. Even Sheila and David provided no company as they moved on to Perth.

Julie rose, washed her face, and studied her reflection in the mottled mirror. Despite seven hours of sleep, she had bags under her eyes and her skin looked sallow. It would be noon by the time she showered and got to work, but she didn't care. She needed a change and would ask her boss to move her from the accounting work.

Julie dressed to suit her mood, in black corduroy slacks and a navy blue blouse. She plaited her hair into a severe braid. She pictured a no-nonsense woman and dressed to show others she meant business.

When she got to the office, she sought the director, Charles "Chas" Brenner. While he might be an over-meticulous twit, he ran the office well enough. His secretary, Barbara, scrambled as she came in. The stink of nail polish told Julie what she'd caught Barbara at.

"Did you get the payroll, Barbara? I left it on your desk before I left." Julie asked for forms' sake. How would Barbara miss it? She'd placed it front and center.

"Payroll? No, I don't think so. Chas bellowed about it earlier."

"I put it right here, Barbara. I swear I did." Confused, Julie glanced at the messy desk.

Barbara shuffled a few things around, then held up a manila folder. "Oh, here it is. Chas must have put these transfer orders on top, covering them up."

Julie's rapid heartbeat slowed. "Whew! I thought I was in trouble again."

"Well, I'll let Chas know we found them. It wouldn't do any good to let him know he hid them himself, would it?" Barbara winked at her with conspiracy.

Julie waited outside while Barbara faced the lion's den. After much shouting, arguing and paper shuffling, she emerged.

"All clear, though I wouldn't ask him for any favors. He's not in a pleasant mood."

"Ah, well, yes, I'll move on back to work." As determined as she'd been to confront Chas about changing jobs, the timing would be unwise.

While her workload eased over the next few days, it would increase again as payroll came due. However, tonight Julie was determined to enjoy herself. She'd treat herself to a pub dinner, a nice evening out, and perhaps a stroll along the Royal Mile.

Barbara recommended a restaurant, The World's End Pub, a historic place near the bottom of the cobblestoned Royal Mile. This pub sported several rooms for people to eat, drink, and socialize. Like most pubs she visited, odd memorabilia hung on dark wood walls and even from the ceilings. The atmosphere grew thick with smoke from cigarettes, pipes, and cigars, whether or not the current patrons partook. The odors overpowered her; smoke, whisky, beer, and stale sweat. She hesitated at the front door, not wanting to get sick again, but after a few moments, she walked in.

The dim interior seemed crowded, but she found a stool near the bar. A sign on the back wall bragged the pub had been open for several hundred years. It smelled like it.

She glanced at the stained menu and played it safe with fish and chips. It's hard to ruin such a thing in the World Capital of Fried Foods. Any pub worth its salt could cook fish and chips. She ordered that and a pint of cider, sitting back to enjoy people-watching.

Several groups of people sat at high-top tables, though the largest, the loudest, sat near the black and white television at the end of the bar. A soccer game played on television, though they called it football here. She discovered the fans acted just as rabid if not more. They cheered for a goal, then subsided.

Near the bar, a couple old men nursed their pints, while a younger man, already drunk, tried to talk them up. Perhaps to buy him another pint.

This place disheartened her. Her normal optimism faded into seeing everything in their worst possible light, rather than give the benefit of the doubt. She took a sip of the cider, trying to think of happier things.

As she made this resolution, a group or four shouting people entered the pub. Two men and two women, all about her age, all American, stumbled in, cheering at the television. She grinned at the assumption, but she had a feeling about them. Even before they spoke, their volume, their confidence, their disdain for everyone else's comfort or privacy declared them such. Though Julie tried to disabuse most people of the common "loud American" stereotype, she knew the reality when flung in her face.

Like a ship pushing through ice floes, this group shoved their way through the people to the bar, ordering drinks in voices loud enough to be heard in London. They snagged a table, where they laughed, told stories, made merry, oblivious to censorious stares around them. First, they asked for Budweiser, and the landlord laughed at the request. They settled instead on local ale, McEwan's Scotch Ale. The local offering must have been up to snuff, for no loud complaints erupted.

Watching them gave Julie more amusement than watching television. Julie gave a grudging smile watching this band of misfits among the quiet and somber Scots, oblivious to the ruckus they cause by their actions and reactions. She chuckled at the looks passed from person to person within the bar, and the not-so-quiet comments about rude Americans. Julie, ensconced at her table in the corner, watched the drama unfold.

She'd assimilated enough to be taken for, if not local, at least not foreign. No one pegged her for an American, she believed. Once she said anything, they knew her for a foreigner, but she spoke in a quiet, enunciated tone with no arrogance. Her American accent had softened with her time here. Most people she'd asked assumed her to be Canadian.

Julie finished her dinner, but didn't want to leave back to her empty, tiny flat. She didn't relish walking back in the rain, either. However, only a futile fool waited for the rain to stop in Scotland. If the sky didn't outright pour, the mist and fog grew pervasive. But Julie came prepared with a paperback, so she pulled it out, sat back against her chair, and proceeded to escape into the world of Horatio Hornblower.

Sometime later, she glanced up from the descriptions of a particularly vicious storm, realizing her own stomach churned with sympathy. Perhaps she should skip this section while digesting fried foods.

The Americans had quieted down, while the Scots got louder. *Interesting.* Drink greased the wheels of many social situations. Here, drink brought each group to a happy medium, a compromise of social grace. Julie grinned at how many world conflicts might be cured, if not avoided, if everyone drank together more.

A pretty young woman entered, long reddish-blond hair dripping with the rain. As she removed her cap, she glanced around the room and made a beeline for the loud Americans. They greeted her with cheers and claps on the back as she pulled up a stool, settling in. When she went to the bar to fetch a drink, she glanced Julie's way, halted, and came towards her.

"I'm so sorry to bother you, but haven't I seen you before? Perhaps at the Church?" Her voice came soft and light, difficult to discern in the din as the Scots cheered for another goal. Her accent marked her as American. Maybe Californian? She spoke with a west coast lilt.

Julie blinked a couple times herself, peering at the woman. She looked familiar but faces sometimes swam together in her memory. *Best be polite, though.* "Sure, I work there. I'm Julie."
She stood up and put her hand out for the girl to shake.

"Yes, that's right, Julie. I'm Barry. I came in a couple days ago from the States. I thought I'd seen you in passing, the other day. I'm pleased to meet another American. Won't you come join us?"

Julie looked at her erstwhile entertainment and shrugged. They'd be safer than reading about storm-tossed seas on a queasy stomach.

They approached the table while the group looked on with expectant eyes.

"This is Mark Johansen, he's from Minneapolis." Julie did her best to clamp down a gasp at the mention of Paul's city, shaking hands with the tall, Nordic man with blue eyes.

"Raymond Theroux is from Montreal." Julie noted the short, dark, round man seemed older than she'd guessed, perhaps around forty. The woman next to him had curly black hair and a round face. "Kimberly Berger is from Los Angeles, like me," Barry said. "And, last but not least, Tammy Rudell, from Cincinnati." Tammy's reddish hair flew up like a wavy aura in response to the humidity. While not as tall as Barry, she carried herself with aplomb. Her posture put Julie in mind of finishing schools, with scores of girls walking about with books balanced on their heads.

While shoving this image aside, Julie introduced herself. "I'm Julie. I'm from Detroit, but I've been in the UK for almost a year now."

"What do you do, Julie?" Kimberly asked, with a polite inquiry.

"I started out with artwork, but now I'm doing payroll and paperwork." Julie didn't know if they were all Church employees like Barry, or just friends, so she didn't elaborate. She kept her frustration and annoyance out of her tone at the mention of her current torture. "What do you all do?" She looked from person to person, eliciting their personal stories.

Barry sipped her pint. "I'm a musician and a free-spirit, but I don't 'do' anything. I 'am,' if it makes sense." She gave a sunny, bright smile, the grin of someone happy with life and content with themselves. "I grew up in LA, playing guitar and singing with friends. I made it up to San Francisco, hanging out with my friend Peter. About that time, he formed a group with other friends, so I moved here. If I stayed, we might be Peter, Paul and Barry." She paused for a reaction.

Julie knew the band Peter, Paul, and Mary. They'd been a colossal hit on the folk scene, and even the mainstream, performing on Jack Benny and getting gold records. And Barry claimed she might have been part of this phenomenon?

Almost without noticing, she hummed "Puff, the Magic Dragon" under her breath. She stopped before anyone else noticed.

Julie focused back on the group, where Tammy spoke about her life in Ohio, working for her parents' garage. She lived in Akron, one of the Church's larger hubs. *Oh, then they* are *all part of the Church.*

She'd missed the thread of the conversation, as they all laughed at Tammy's last statement. Julie laughed along, pretending she knew why.

Raymond spoke up next, plunking his pint glass on the wooden table. "I ran a hunting lodge in Ontario, but got injured, so I needed to retire from that life." He pointed to his leg. One thigh seemed much thinner than the other. "A moose decided my body would be a more comfortable carpet than the road. It broke my leg and left me stranded for two days before rescue came. Part of the flesh got corrupted, so the surgeons removed a sizeable chunk of muscle. But, I healed and headed to the city. And now I'm here, doing research." His slight French accent delighted her.

Kimberly worked as a nurse at a hospital in Los Angeles. "As low woman on the totem pole, whenever I requested *any* time off, one of the senior nurses would take the time herself. Since she had seniority, they denied my request. After three years of this, I quit, moving in with my friend, Barry." She poked her friend's ribs.

By this time, most of the pints stood empty, so Julie volunteered to stand another round. She understood the rules of rounds at a pub, and the party seldom got smaller, so paying for the round early proved more economic. She got everyone's orders and escaped to the bar.

Julie didn't feel isolated in the group, but she felt overwhelmed by the personalities. Perhaps she'd become so accustomed to the understated actions of the English, these brash Americans grated upon her. She damped down the urge to cover her ears when they laughed loud. She gathered the pints, determined not to be foolish.

Over the course of the next couple weeks, Julie hung out with Barry, Tammy, and Kimberly a lot. Raymond and Mark flew back to the States, their training over, but the girls made a habit of going out every few nights to blow off steam in well-deserved debauchery. They worked hard, all day and most evenings.

The work remained grueling, and Julie struggled with the numbers. She couldn't settle into this position. It didn't suit her, but she'd never liked confrontation. It seemed easier to plow on than to ask for a different duty, as her boss always seemed in a foul mood. Besides, her life remained in flux, so perhaps it would change on its own. She didn't want Chas to decide he didn't need her and fire her. Then where would she be? Stuck in Edinburgh with no job, no place to live, no options. No, better to put her head down and do her best. At least she occasionally got a "break" with artwork or other non-financial tasks.

Today, Julie worked on a new poster for colleges and hospitals. She finished her final mockup, after several tries and rejections, bringing it into Chas' office for approval. He'd gone to a meeting, so she left it with a note on his desk, escaping. She'd have time off this

evening, and she meant to spend it with the girls. Julie
didn't want to risk getting caught and assigned another
mind-numbing task today.

She escaped the office and to her flat without
incident, changing into evening togs. Any outing in
Edinburgh required layers, to combat the changing
weather, even if they didn't plan on staying outside.
Long skirts would get muddy, wet hems, so she found
a pair of corduroy brown pants with her favorite loose-
flowing gold satin shirt. She tied her hair up in a
matching gold scarf, grimaced at herself in the mirror,
and added a pendant. She didn't own any genuine
gold, but her teardrop goldstone pendant nestled in a
fake gold setting. It worked well enough.

They headed to Victoria Street, where Barry
knew of a club called The Place. Julie grew apprehensive
as they climbed down three flights of dank, concrete
stairs into the basement. The close, stifling air slapped
her with heat. The dampness on the walls might be the
building itself sweating in sympathy. Muted sounds
below hit her full force as they opened the thick fire
door at the bottom.

The place heaved with people and sound. In the
back, they spied an area where the band stood taller
than the throng of dancers. Behind them, an ornate
spiral staircase glowed with a red exit sign pulsing
above it.

She didn't recognize the song but recognized
the style as mod music. Tammy mentioned a band
from Glasgow called The Pathfinders. As the girls
threaded their way closer to the music, Julie moved to
the rhythm. She enjoyed it but would have liked to get
pints in her before she danced, something refreshing.

Julie craned her neck in the reddish, dim light,
but didn't spy a bar. No one carried anything looking
like a drink. This must be a music-only, no alcohol
venue. *Well, might as well enjoy it.* Barry flung up her
arms, tossing her head side to side, hair spiraling out,

eyes closed, and spinning to the beat. She attracted a considerable amount of male attention. Kimberly and Tammy danced with each other, so Julie moved to the beat alone. She closed her eyes, which eased the claustrophobia, experiencing the music thrum through her.

Julie danced with abandon, paying little attention to her surroundings, swaying to the music, the beat, the guitar. She moved and swung, bumping an unknown body now and then, but moving more, back and forth, around and around. Someone's hair brushed her face a hand caressed her waist. Then it disappeared and she felt a wall against her back.

After opening her eyes, she found herself on the edge of the frenzy, with no sign of the other girls. She searched for Barry's bright blond hair, a feature which stood on the tall girl, but found no sign. Shrugging, Julie closed her eyes again and danced.

The band moved through several tunes, from one to the other, not stopping in between, but now they took a break. While the crowd shuffled to a stop, a few still danced, moving to the silent drummers in their minds.

Julie spied Barry and Kimberly. Tammy had disappeared, so they searched and found her in a corner with a tall young Indian gentleman, in an intimate, intense conversation. They let her be and found a place to cool off.

Kimberly found stools near one wall, so they sat and fanned themselves. The heat increased when people stopped moving, as the air became stultifying and still. Julie took in a deep, labored breath, and then several more, until her lungs felt satisfied once again.

Barry tried to speak, but the noise level remained high, so Julie pointed to her ear, indicating she couldn't hear.

Barry shouted into her ear. "I said, 'are you having fun?'"

"I am, but it is sweltering in here. I might go out for fresh air."

Barry and Kimberly both nodded, resuming fanning themselves with their shirts.

Julie glanced at Tammy and her new friend, noting that their conversation moved from a verbal one to a much more physical one. She could only tell which limb belonged to which person by the color of the skin.

The music began again. As one, they all moved.

The beat grew stronger and faster. Sweat dripped down Julie's face, and she needed to escape. She found Kimberly, tapping her on the shoulder to get her attention, gesturing that she'd be outside. They waved to Barry, but Barry fell into a bliss of dancing, so didn't even notice them.

As they emerged from the bowels of the club, both took in deep, delicious breaths of the sweet, cool air, pulling it into their lungs with relish and joy.

Kimberly mopped her face with the bottom of her cotton shirt. "Man, I love the music, but what I wouldn't give for a giant fan above everyone."

"No kidding. They don't do ceiling fans here much. They don't seem to care for moving air. I have yet to see one in any of the rooms or B&Bs I've been in, much less the restaurants or hotels."

"Yeah, I noticed that. Or the closets they claim are bathrooms."

Julie gave her a conspiratorial smile. "Oh, I could tell you stories about the bathrooms." She thought about her time with Paul and didn't fall into instant despair. Was she healing already? Then she realized Kimberly asked her a question. "What? Oh, a story about a tryst with a guy in England. The bathroom was our only private space." She grinned at Kimberly's shocked expression.

"In these tiny things? How did you not break your neck trying?"

Julie smiled more deeply and shrugged. "This bathroom sported a fantastic, large Victorian bathtub."

"Wow. That's mad and rad!" Kimberly's eyes grew wide with wonder.

Perhaps she had begun to live again.

Julie woke with a moan and a clatter, knocking her clock off the tiny table next to her bed. The alarm didn't go off. She'd only dreamt it.

Her roommate, Charmaine, stirred and shifted, pulling her covers up over her head. Holly'd already left, since she liked walking the city as it woke up, saying it helped clear her head in the morning.

Julie twisted herself out of her tangle of blankets, sitting on the edge of the tiny cot. She rubbed the sleep out of her eyes, trying to remember what she'd done last night to leave her in such a terrible state. Then she stopped thinking and ran to the bathroom to worship the porcelain gods.

Please God, kill me now. She'd hadn't drunk that much the night before. She suspected her dodgy stomach might be related to the horrible Drambuie odor. They combatted it in the flat with sandalwood candles to mask the sickly sweet, but this morning, it didn't work. The liqueur aroma combined with the musky candle to produce a bizarre mixture of nauseating scents.

Julie rose from the bathroom floor and prepared for a wash. She preferred showers, but this apartment only had a bath. Baths meant she only stewed in her dirt before trying to wipe off the dirty water. Showers were much more to her liking, but not as common in the UK as in the States.

For once, she had a day off, and hadn't needed to get up so early. Since her stomach insisted on the morning rise, she might as well make the most of it.

Julie took a page from Holly's book, going out for a brisk, refreshing walk. The weather looked decent enough for now. She dressed in sturdy shoes and clothes, with a jacket. It might be late August, but the morning air remained fresh in the morning and evenings.

She made her way to the Royal Mile, then to Arthur's Seat. She didn't have a passion for hill climbing, but this hill had a set path. She stopped often and sat on the velvet green grass, gazing out at the panoramic city. By the time she made it to the top, two hours passed. She breathed deep of the clear and refreshing air.

Julie rested, having brought a sandwich and fruit, enjoying her picnic while she surveyed the city. The people in Edinburgh seemed nice enough, once you got past their gruff, stolid exteriors. They didn't act jovial until you got several pints in them. Their solemn manner often masked keen interest and intelligence, with fierce loyalty and gallantry.

Several nights before, she and Kimberly walked home from a pub, on the tipsy side. They stumbled against each other on the cobblestones. One man gave them a hard time, trying to take Kimberly's hand. Before they extracted themselves, another man came up, inserting himself between the girls and their accoster, shooing him away. He then bowed, walking off in another direction, not waiting for thanks or thought of reward. She glanced at Kimberly with raised eyebrows, then they both laughed in hysterics before moving on.

Julie pulled out her ever-present sketch pad, drafting her view of the city. She didn't care for cityscapes, but the architecture of Edinburgh just looked so incredible. So much gothic detail, she loved drawing it. Curlicues and flying buttresses everywhere she looked. It seemed organic, like the Gaudi buildings in Barcelona. She drew with pencils, no color, to capture the stark monochromatic city. From where she perched, she couldn't make out a lot of detail, as the hill rose high. However, she captured the general sense of the imposing castle, Holyrood, the Royal Mile, and the docks in the distance.

The wind picked up, and she needed to tack down the corners of her page. They fluttered as she drew, which proved distracting.

After fighting with the wind, Julie shivered and pulled her shawl around her shoulders. The descent became chancier in the steep bits then going up, and she slid more than once. She didn't hurt herself, but climbing hills on her own, with no one aware of her location, might not be the wisest thing.

Don't be silly. Lots of people walk up here. It's not like I'd be stranded for days. Look, there's someone now, walking his dog up the path. Nevertheless, she descended with care. She ought to let someone know the next time she went hiking.

The dog bounded up to her and, as dogs do, sniffed between her legs. Julie laughed and pet the dog, guiding his head away, but it made her think. She couldn't remember the last time she'd bled. She counted back as the man and his dog walked on.

More than a month? She plopped down, verifying the math, but knowing she didn't need to. The last time she'd bled must have been in East Grinstead in May. She'd been here in Scotland since the end of July. September loomed in a week. *Oh, no!* It must have been the bathtub. *Great,* that's *a fantastic story to tell my child someday.*

The baby might not be Paul's. George might be the father. At least Roger wasn't a candidate. Her later two lovers had been closer together.

What can I do? Adoption? Abortion? Keep it? Kill myself? She dismissed the last one right away. She'd never considered such a thing before, and she wasn't about to now. A child wasn't tragic, motherhood was beautiful. But how could she keep it?

Julie wouldn't have to kill herself. Her father would kill her.

She imagined herself telling Paul about the child, asking him to leave his wife for her and the baby, but shook it off. He had a wife. Julie had never been one to rock the boat. Seeing herself as one of those selfish women who broke up families made her gag. Paul might already have children with his wife. No, better if he never knew. If George was the father... but she remembered his free spirit. He wouldn't appreciate being trapped with a child.

Julie met girls in San Francisco who were single mothers, but they lived in a commune or in one case, a strange, open relationship with three men. Abortion wasn't legal or safe. Adoption? She'd still have to give birth. She understood now why the Drambuie sickened her.

Well, she wouldn't have to decide on adoption until after the birth. Julie breathed in the incongruous fresh air and grass smells, determined this would not destroy her life. She'd make plans, but why should it be such a problem? The Church would help her. She had friends, a community. *I can do this.*

While making her way back down to her flat, she decided she didn't like days off.

2000, Miami, Florida

Almost a year passed since Kirsten wrote that letter. She'd heard nothing in reply, not even an angry retort, saying she wrote to the wrong person, denouncing her as a charlatan and a liar. She might have welcomed that. At least she'd have gotten a reaction, which she could have worked with. Perhaps her mother had been right. Perhaps she shouldn't have tried to get hold of him.

"What's wrong, Kirsten?"

Cathy, one of the other CPAs in the office, burst into her office. When she started, she'd introduced herself as the original Chatty Cathy, and she hadn't exaggerated. The woman talked more than any of the other accountants combined. Kirsten felt hard pressed to get a word in edgewise. She peered at Kirsten with intent curiosity, her short gray hair swinging around her round face in a bob cut.

Kristen shrugged. "Just drifting, I suppose. I'm stuck on a… genealogical research problem, I guess. Nothing to do with work."

Cathy's face lit up. "I didn't know you liked genealogical research. Oh, I love the stuff. I have dozens of CDs from Family Tree Maker, and Everton's Genealogical Helper. Do you read Everton's? I've even got microfiches. Have you tried the Mormon Church files? They have lots of stuff on their computer database, even microfiche. If you find anything, you can ask for them to send it from Salt Lake City. It's where their headquarters are, you know. Largest genealogical library in the world! I've been there twice. It's a mecca for genealogists. Have you ever been?"

Kirsten mumbled out a quick "no" while Cathy stopped to take a breath, rambling on about her last trip to Salt Lake City. Kirsten tuned her out, as she learned to do, but held onto at least one nugget of information in the avalanche. Mormon Church? Everyone knew they kept files.

She waited for Cathy's next breath to stop the torrent. "Cathy? Is there a Mormon Church nearby? With a research center?"

"Of course, didn't I say? It's up on Roebuck Road. The family history center is to the right, the church is to the left. They close at five, but they stay open late Wednesday nights, until nine. That's the best

171

time to go. The weekends are busy. Just bring coins for photocopies, though, unless you like writing a lot. I hope you find lots of fascinating new clues!"

"Thanks, Cathy, I'll let you know how I do." Julie halted the conversation by leaving toward the bathroom. By the time she returned, Cathy had left, so Kirsten planned her visit for the following evening.

Wednesday, Kirsten escaped work by six, a short day for tax season. She found the church without too much wandering around, in a cleared area off a wooded road. The sign outside looked new and well maintained. She signed in and read the list of rules near the unattended front desk. Some paperwork was free to request from the main center in Utah, but others required payment. *Fair enough.* She hefted her book bag and walked in, looking for a terminal.

Six cubicles lined one wall, each with a huge computer monitor, green letters flashing on the screens. Only two of them had occupants, so she chose an empty one and pulled out her family tree sheets. She might as well make the most of her time here. She planned on checking on each of her "brick walls" to see what sort of information she might discover.

Lost in a maze of information and possibilities, Kirsten glanced up to notice several hours had passed. She'd only searched halfway through her list of projects. Julie found good nuggets of information, noting their sources to get copies of the relevant birth certificates, death notices, and marriage licenses. She had time for one more tonight, but would have to come back next week for the rest. With a deep breath, she pulled out the notes on her father's line.

Back when she received a copy of her father's birth certificate, Kirsten wrote to get copies of his parents' birth certificates. With those, she got information on her father, his parents, and both sets of their parents. They had nice, unusual names, a boon to any genealogical researcher. Kirsten searched for Fred B. Stein, Johanna Lembeck, Paul H. Ford and Josephine Moraveck. Sure, the men's names were more common, but those wonderful, unique women's names helped. They should be easy to find. Still, she prepped herself for disappointment, knowing women seldom made their way into historical records in the nineteenth century.

Sometime later, Kirsten sat back, staring at the screen. Fred Bernard Stein married Johanna Anna Lembeck, in 1908 in Minnesota. No doubt about it, the names matched those of her great-grandparents. She searched for the submitter information. These details came from of a family tree, so someone had compiled it and submitted it to the Mormon Church database. *Where was it? There.* Sharon Henderson, of Minneapolis, with an address. With shaking fingers, Kirsten jotted down the details.

At home, she wrote a lengthy letter to Ms. Henderson, detailing the account of her mother's adventures in England and her extensive search for her father. She spoke of discovering Ms. Henderson's family tree, begging her to send information, if she found any, on her father's branch of the family. She hoped the woman knew concrete data, not merely a snippet of stray information.

Kirsten held onto that hope. She'd been disappointed before. But she kept a hard grip on her optimism, her true strength.

For the next few days, Kirsten held onto that hope with tense fingers, gripped tight upon her heart. However, as they passed without word, Kirsten relaxed into disappointment. She'd gone through this before, with other dead ends. Like when she first contacted the researcher from Everton's. Though she got useful information from him, it never panned out.

Tax season swung into full fervor at work, so she had little energy to devote to worry. She worked long hours, not getting home until well after eight.

173

Kirsten flopped down, exhausted, watched television, or played a computer game to disengage her mind. She'd fall asleep, only to do it again the next day. She almost longed for the days she attended classes at night, as it gave her something to think about other than tax returns.

With practiced ease, she shoved the hope into a dark corner of her mind.

CHAPTER SEVEN

Escape

1968, Edinburgh, Scotland

Perhaps this hadn't been a marvelous idea.

Julie clung onto her purse as if it represented a lifeline, or at least an anchor. Why had she let Barry talk her into this? She didn't relish walking home on her own, in the dark. Not tonight. She vowed to strengthen her resolve and get a grip. What had she been thinking, going out to party while pregnant?

Crowds of young people spoke in hushed tones, huddled in groups around an ever-growing scrap pile of wood and broken furniture. Barry told her the bonfires happened all over the UK on Guy Fawkes Night. People all over the country burned an enormous bonfire in effigy, to celebrate the capture of a man who plotted to blow up the government four hundred years ago. The group here, on Broughton Road, comprised of teenagers and twenty-somethings, almost all locals. They seemed rougher than the folks Julie had met, on the threadbare side. They spoke a language she didn't understand, but she couldn't tell if they spoke accented English slang, or another language, like Scots or Gaelic. Whatever they said, they didn't sound like they spoke of rainbows and butterflies.

She turned to Barry, to ask they should leave, when movement caught her eye. A parade of sorts marched down the street, with the front man carrying a scarecrow. The stuffed figure wore pants and a shirt, and someone had mounted the form on a cross, stuffed with hay and rags. The figure had nothing resembling a head, only the top bit of the cross sticking out of the neck of the shirt. It looked like a sick parody of a Christ statue.

This must be the effigy they burn on the bonfire. She stepped back, giving the procession plenty of room as they marched. She glanced at Barry, her friend's eyes wide in anticipation. Judging by her grin, she enjoyed the show, spellbound by the drama and showmanship.

The effigy arrived at a bonfire built at the crossroads. Criminals were hanged at crossroads, to keep their ghosts from wandering. The leaders of the parade secured the scarecrow in the center of the pile of wood, then backed up, forming a solid ring around the area. Barry fumbled for Julie's hand and squeezed in excitement and anticipation.

This ceremony seemed so primal, so ancient, hearkening to a Celtic or Nordic primeval past. The crowd might be calling to the gods of fire, or the spirits of chaos. Even worship of the sun, asking it to return after winter was over. How could she say these beliefs were unworthy, or outdated? Fire spoke to something seminal in each person's soul. Controllable magic, and yet dangerous, man's most useful tool. Also, his greatest enemy, comforting and terrifying in turns.

"Remember, remember, the fifth of November." The crowd chanted, without music or song, but with strength and enthusiasm.

> *"The gunpowder treason and plot*
> *I know of no reason why the gunpowder treason*
> *Should ever be forgot."*

The leader who carried the effigy walked up to the pile of debris, lighting the wood with a torch.

They must have soaked the pile in pitch or gasoline, as it caught quickly, flames licking all around the straw man. The stink of pine and turpentine overwhelmed her. The stench made her choke, her gorge rising. She backed off, releasing Barry's hand, seeking clearer air behind the ring of watchers.

Barry came to check on her, but Julie waved her back to the festivities. The ring of people held hands now, swaying and walking around the fire, a gigantic game of Ring-Around-the-Rosy. A surreal children's game before a primal god of fire. *What a strange sight in modern Edinburgh. I suppose we are all still slaves to our primitive urges.*

Her stomach had enough of strange sounds and smells, ejecting its meager contents on the sidewalk. Julie hunched over, holding her own hair back, until the wave of nausea passed. She swished saliva around her mouth and spit, disgusted at the necessity, but her stomach calmed. She rejoined the chanters and partook in their primitive ceremony around the now raging bonfire, dizzy and light with wonder.

The next day at work, Julie regretted her late night. Her throat grew scratchy and raw from all the smoke and turpentine. She might even have the beginning of a nasty cold. She couldn't catch a break.

She planned on meeting Barry for lunch at a hole-in-the-wall café with a lunch counter, the Greasy Spoon Café. The sandwiches and soups would be cheap and filling, and the restaurant sat within walking distance of the offices. Most of the decent restaurants and pubs lay closer to the Royal Mile where the tourists thronged, about five blocks away. Tourist traps were fine for an evening out, but too far to walk on a meager half-hour lunch break, and much too expensive for regular use.

They walked to the café, which normally catered to sailors and dockworkers, so the crowd usually seemed on the rough side. However, most seats remained empty today as they ordered sandwiches with fizzy lemonade.

Barry rarely beat around the bush. She took a bite of her egg salad sandwich and lifted an eyebrow as she chewed. "Right, Julie. What's going on?"

Julie took a deep breath and stared at her own sandwich. "Well, I'm in a mess, you see. I need insight, maybe even advice."

"What sort of mess? Something at your job?"

"No, well, yes, related to my job, but that's not the primary problem."

"C'mon, Julie. Spit it out. What's wrong?" Barry may sound abrupt, but she cared. Julie's eyes burned, her throat closing with tears. She'd never been so prone to tears as in the last few months.

"I'm…" Julie lowered her voice to a whisper, "I'm pregnant." She glanced up at Barry to watch the reaction in her blue eyes.

Barry stood up, pulled Julie out of the chair, and looked her up and down. She placed her hand on Julie's stomach, and her eyes grew wide. Julie had never been thin and often wore baggy shirts and dresses. Barry wrapped her arms around Julie. She hugged tight, but when Julie moved to disengage, she hugged tighter. Julie hugged back and they embraced for several moments, until the waitress returned with their sodas.

She peered at both of them with concern. "Are ye girls grand, then?"

Julie sat on her stool, plunked her straw in her soda and took a long sip, enjoying the carbonated burn as it seared her throat. "We're fine, thank you." She kept hold of Barry's hand over the round, silver table. When Julie had control over herself, she took a smaller sip of her soda, relishing the lemony sweetness.

Barry took another bite of her sandwich. "What are you thinking of doing, Julie? Are you going to keep the baby?"

"I have to, at this point. I haven't decided yet if I want to put it up for adoption, but I don't think I could do... the other."

Barry shook her head. "I don't blame you, hon. Who's the father?"

Once again, Julie had the flash of an image, her telling Paul, him leaving his wife for her. "Someone I met in East Grinstead." Julie felt tears hammering behind her eyes, so she took a sip of her drink. *But am I really sure it's Paul's?*

"And? Have you told him?"

"No, and I never can. He's American. He went back... back to his wife." She got it all out in a rush, hoping she wouldn't have to say anymore.

"Oh. I see. Well." Barry took a deep breath, flung her hair, squeezing Julie's hand. "You'll be fine, Julie, you'll see. Lots of things are possible nowadays. You'll have me here to help, with Kimberly, and Tammy. We'll be your family."

Barry might have good intentions, but she didn't count on moving a couple weeks later. The Church sent Barry and her fiancé, Bruce, to work in the Copenhagen office, to help their group fall in line with the UK organization. Kimberly returned to California the month before, so only Tammy remained from the original group of Dangerous Ladies, as Barry labeled them.

Julie wished she could talk more to Barry or Bruce about her worries, but most of her questions were about having a baby. They'd been trying to have one of their own, so she didn't want to rub in their faces that she would, truth be told, be happier without a child.

She didn't get along as well with Tammy, who was far more interested in finding a new man, her flavor of the week, than in hanging out with a mere woman. She sowed her oats, wild or otherwise, with a vengeance. Julie didn't want to search for men, as she had about had her fill with the fickle beasts, so she didn't accompany Tammy on her conquests. They grew further apart each day.

Julie adopted the solitary existence she had first suffered in Edinburgh, before Barry had blown into her life, living to work, with the occasional break to go out and draw. Her efficiency at everything reduced as her belly grew. Just walking the few blocks from her flat to the offices grew difficult, especially in the rain or snow. She invested in good, sturdy boots with wide, corrugated soles, to keep her from slipping on slushy cobblestones or hidden potholes. She carried her sketchpad in a waterproof portfolio, eager to get away from the office in stolen bits and scraps, to feed her soul with art.

Since these chances came few and far between, Julie sketched gesture drawings, or quick rough drawings of people, while she sipped coffee at a café. She filled up several sketchpads this way over the months. The large pad became a shield for her. If she had a project while she ate alone, she felt less desolate. Working on a project kept her from looking desperate for eating alone. She treasured her artwork as a companion to keep her on track.

Julie tried hard not to look forward to the baby. She referred to the child as her little Angel. She might have a boy or a girl, and the name acknowledged its innocent state. If she didn't think about the baby much, they might be easier to give up for adoption. As her body grew and stretched in response, she caught herself stroking the mound, smiling to herself. As soon as noticed this, she stopped, scolding herself for unwanted sentimentality. *Don't get attached.*

Would her determination be strong enough?

Julie studied the numbers again, then a third and a fourth time. She used the adding machine to run a tape and check yet again. No, checking changed nothing. She'd screwed up, and screwed up big.

Despite her diligence, she overpaid every single person on the last payroll. Nobody would be happy about this. This meant, to fix her error, she must short everyone's payroll this paycheck. She didn't look forward to her conversation with Chas.

She'd been doing payroll for five months now but had no better grasp of the complex process than when the ledger books had been dropped on her desk in a puff of dust and ink. They left her to puzzle out what they'd done and what she needed to do. No one had checked her work, trusting her to figure it out.

Julie protested vociferously, many times, but her protests fell on deaf ears. Now she'd be in trouble for having botched everything. Well, she had no way to run and hide. Julie couldn't run anywhere, being eight months pregnant, as big as a house, and about as nimble as a whale with club feet.

She rose, put a hand to the small of her back to ease the pain, and waddled into Chas' office, damning paperwork in hand, into the lion's den.

After the first sentence, she barely got a word in edgewise. Chas screamed at her, shouting angry insults, and berated her for idiocy.

About a half hour of verbal abuse later, Julie gathered her things from her desk. She packed her belongings, nodded farewell to Barbara, and left. How much of her firing had been from her mistake, and how much from her condition? She would have to stop in a couple weeks, anyway, due to her baby.

Julie held the tears back until she got back to her flat. She had no other way to release her frustration. The firing had been inevitable. This realization hadn't made things any easier to take when Chas exploded in her face, called her an incompetent cow, and then told her to leave and never return.

Julie cried herself out, then washed her face. She poured herself cold, bitter coffee from the kitchenette carafe, picking up the phone to call Barry.

While Julie didn't relish living in a country which spoke a different language, she figured moving to Denmark with Barry might be her best option. Besides, her friend offered her a place in their home months back. Julie hadn't escaped work long enough to take a real trip. She had plenty of time now.

The phone ringed twice. She hoped Barry answered. It rang again and clicked. "Goomourn?"

What? Oh, that must be Danish. "May I speak to Barry?"

"This is Barry, who is this?"

She let out a sigh, her breath catching. "This is Julie. I am *so* glad it's you."

"Julie, what's wrong? Are you okay?"

"Chas fired me over a payroll error." Barry had gotten many tearful stories about how much she hated her payroll duties, so this wouldn't surprise her friend.

Julie wished she saw the smile she heard in Barry's voice. "Well, you can come and stay with us now! Have you enough money for a flight? Tell me when you've made arrangements, and I'll pick you up at the airport." Barry said all this rapid fire, in a tone which allowed for no argument.

Julie sniffed mightily, trying to hold back the tears that threatened to take over. "Barry, you are the best friend a girl can have. Thank you so much. Are you sure Bruce won't mind?"

"He won't mind in the slightest, but even if he did, I'd make him change his mind. Do you have much stuff to bring with you? I can arrange for shipping if you'd like."

"No, no, I pared my stuff down when I moved to Scotland. I've only got clothes and art supplies."

"Call when you know your details. Chin up, girl. I can't wait to see how big you've gotten."

Relief washed over her. "I will as soon as I do."

After she hung up, Julie gave in to the sobs again. She'd turned into an emotional wreck. When she recovered, she looked up the closest travel agent in the phone book. Using an agent would be easier than trying to buy a ticket on the phone, despite the difficulty in walking places. She also had the suspicion her pregnant state might be an issue, but she hoped the short flight wouldn't matter.

Julie found an inexpensive flight, and thankfully, her condition didn't make a difference. Her flight would go first down to London, then to Copenhagen. She gathered her belongings, packed up what she wanted and left the rest. Her roommates, whom she never saw anyhow, could keep the lot.

Like so many times before, she took a taxi to the airport for her flight, leaving the latest chapter of her life without so much as a backwards glance.

CHAPTER EIGHT

A Star is Born

1969, Copenhagen, Denmark

Julie stared at the dingy hotel room, reminiscent of the apartment she rented in Washington, D.C.

Barry and Bruce welcomed her into their lovely home with open arms. However, when Bruce's parents came for an unexpected week-long visit, they needed the spare room. So off Julie trundled to this hotel.

Julie had to keep reminding herself they didn't reject or dismiss her, but her mind kept returning to the idea.

The doctor told her she might get sad after giving birth. What about before? Her due date should be any day now, and every move she took made her feel unsightly and disgusting. Awkward as she felt, she'd made no new friends in the few weeks she'd been there.

Most people rode bikes to get around town. She could no sooner ride a bike than jump on a horse. Her back ached when she walked for too long. Julie drew and sketched everything around the tidy suburban house several times. She'd gone utterly stir-crazy.

Thinking back to that room in D.C., Julie took stock of herself. Had she gotten anywhere in two years? She'd enjoyed many adventures, but also experienced a lot of heartache. Thoughts of George, Paul, and Roger swam in her memory, but she veered away from that painful subject. She'd soon have her permanent souvenir from those dalliances. Julie still hadn't decided about adoption.

After pushing herself up from the bed with significant effort, she grunted, pressing her hands to the small of her back. She bundled herself up against the frigid February weather and scooped up a pad and her pencils. The elevator was always scary and bumpy. She wandered to the nearby park. At least the hotel offered a change of scenery. She had fresh subjects to draw and create.

The sun shone bright in a brilliant blue sky, which helped her mood. Stark snow sparkled in the sunlight as she picked her way to the park. Even in the blanket of winter, the place looked like a magical wonderland. It would be sublime in the spring, when flowers bloomed and trees offered shade. Now, even stark and monochromatic, the beauty took on a unique cast. A beauty well-suited to pencil work and charcoal.

While sitting on a bench, she drew skeletal trees reaching above her, creeping hands extended to tear the flesh from her bones. *My, how morbid.* She attempted to lighten the mood of her piece, but it remained haunting and sinister. *So be it.* She sketched the bones of the trees, the random patterns of branch and twig, against the faultless sky.

After several hours, her butt had frozen to the bench seat. With cautious movement, she extracted herself and headed back to the hotel. As she did so, she almost slipped on ice, but she caught the arm of the bench. It scared her, as no one else walked in the park. A fall now would not only be dangerous for her and the baby, she might be out here for hours until someone came. Humbled by her mortality, she waddled back to the hotel.

Most of the staff in the hotel spoke no English, but one young bellhop on the day staff had some. Sometimes she chatted with him, but he must be off today, as she didn't see him. Julie sat in the lobby café for hot chocolate. Perhaps soup would thaw her inside and out.

Julie relaxed in the warm seat, enjoying the strange fruit soup on offer, called *sødsuppe*, and her hot chocolate. She wished for little mini-marshmallows she would have gotten at home, but settled for thick whipped cream.

After she scraped the bowl for the last taste of her soup, Barry made an entrance, dressed in a long red wool jacket and red hat. Julie waved her over to the table, but didn't bother trying to stand up, as that process would have taken several minutes and considerable effort.

"Julie. How are you? I got out of work early, so I thought I'd drop in to see how you're doing. Are you enjoying the warmth?"

"Yeah, I went out to draw and got chilled. I needed some hot chocolate. Would you like some?"

"Oh, no, I can't stay long. I wanted to tell you Bruce's parents plan on going home on the seventeenth, so you can come back after. Will this work for you?"

The seventeenth? That meant three more days than she'd first thought. But she needed to accept the gift horse with a smile. "That's fine, Barry. Though I may be in hospital by then. I'm due any day now, according to the Royal Infirmary."

Barry raised an eyebrow. "Haven't you gone to the hospital here for an update?"

"Sure, but their English isn't great, and my Danish is nonexistent. The best information I have came from the Edinburgh staff." Julie made a rueful face. "I've made myself more or less understood. There's a lot more similarity between Danish and English, more than I'd believed. Those Germanic roots rear their ugly heads."

Barry grimaced with a half-smile. "Well, be careful. Tell me when you hear anything. And if nothing has happened yet, I'll come by on the seventeenth to help you with your stuff."

"Sounds good. Are you sure you won't stay for a cup of chocolate?"

"No, the parents are expecting me. Let me give you a hug. No, don't get up." Barry wrapped her arms around Julie in an awkward embrace, but her arms grew warm. Then her friend stood and left in a flurry of scarf and long jacket.

Julie's back ached, and her skin grew hot and flushed, despite cracking the window in the hotel room. She couldn't sleep on her side or her back with comfort. She sat up with a sigh, deciding to read her novel.

After she pulled on her robe, she rifled through her papers and books to find it. *Where was the bloody thing?* A *thunk* on the floor to her left made her turn, spying the paperback which fell from within a stack of sketchpads.

Great. The floor seemed miles away. With grunts and slow movements, she bent to pick it up, and stopped.

That's an unusual pain. Maybe she'd better sit.

Julie eased herself into the big armchair next to the bed, breathing hard, to push through the pain. It rose deep in her belly, like a horrible gas pain. Breathing didn't seem to help much, but she kept doing it. Then her belly rippled as the pain returned. That *had* to be a contraction. *Okay, Little Angel. It's show time.*

When the pain passed, Julie pushed herself up from the chair, and plunked right back down again. She took a couple breaths and tried again. This time she succeeded, and shuffled to the dresser, taking out some clothing. With great effort, she changed her pajamas into an acceptable outdoor outfit. She packed a bag, wrapped up in boots, coat, hat, and had just grabbed her sketchbook and novel when another contraction hit. Using the bed as a brace, she bent over double until the pain passed.

Once outside with her bag, she navigated to the lobby. While searching for her English-speaking bellhop friend, she walked to the front desk. With a wave, she got the attention of the tiny blond woman behind the counter. "Excuse me, do you speak English?"

The woman shook her head. "*Ingen Engelsk.*" This meant "no English."

"I need a taxi to the hospital, uh, the *hospitalet?*" Julie's mind fogged and drifted. Another contraction hit and she bent over, gripping the counter for balance. The blond woman shrieked to someone out of sight, picking up the telephone.

The contraction passed. Julie did her best to show, with sign language, that her baby was coming. The heavy coat she wore hid her condition, but she motioned with her hands downward, to demonstrate "coming out and down."

The desk clerk nodded, waving Julie to a bench near the door.

Two contractions later, a taxi pulled up. Julie pushed and shoved until she teetered on her feet, waddling outside. The driver hastened out to help her. He held her arm so she wouldn't slip on the icy pavement, making sure she got settled before he jumped into the driver's seat.

He sped off at what Julie considered a reckless and insane speed on the pre-dawn, icy February streets of Copenhagen.

Was he taking every corner in the city? Julie fell back and forth, side to side, as the taxi driver took hairpin turns at breakneck speed. Then she paid little attention as another contraction took her. She felt wet and slimy and disgusting. Her water must have broken.

This horrified her, but she forbad saying anything. The driver would discover soon enough.

Their taxi screeched into the emergency bay at the Copenhagen College Hospital, the *Rigshospitalet*. The driver came around to help her out. She handed her bag out first, then slid over the leather seat in her slimy state. As she emerged, looking down at her soaked clothing, she glanced in horror at the driver. He smiled, almost laughing, as he helped her out. This must not have been the first time someone had done this in his taxi.

Another pain shot through her before she reached the door, and she stopped to double over. The driver yelled at someone in Danish. An orderly rushed up with a wheelchair. She fumbled for her purse to pay the taxi driver, but he waved it away, smiling, saying goodbye. *Farvel*, one of the few phrases she had picked up.

Farvel. Farvel *to my old life.* Farvel *to being single. I would have a baby soon. Life will be different. Hello, Little Angel.*

Life merged into unreality, as they gave her an epidural. The situation grew fuzzy and unfocused. She floated but felt a tremendous pressure on her midsection. She pushed, bearing down until she knew nothing else. Over and over again, pushing and breathing, floating and dreaming. Julie must have succeeded, because the ring of strangers around her stopped telling her to push. A thin wail broke through her fog, then she drifted off to sleep, dreaming dreams she forgot.

When Julie woke, the nurse brought her beer to drink. She didn't care for beer and tried to refuse it. The nurse brought a doctor who spoke a little English.

"The beer, it is good for milk. You drink, then you nurse." The doctor mimed her drinking then holding a baby to her breast. With reluctance, Julie drank the beer, Carlsberg, a Danish brand, and tamped down on her gag reflex. She'd forgotten how bitter beer tasted. She let out a small burp. "The baby, are they well?"

"Ya, the baby is good. You wish to see?"

"Please."

The doctor motioned to a nurse, who brought a swaddled bundle. Julie wondered how long she'd been out, as the baby looked cleaned and asleep.

As she took it into her arms, the world felt right again. "Is it a boy or a girl?"

"A baby girl. What name would you like?"

Julie had tried not to think of a name, in case she decided to give the child up for adoption, but as she held her daughter in her arms, adoption no longer appealed.

Despite her determination not to think of a name, one from a childhood story came to mind. "Kristen, please."

The doctor furrowed his brow. "Christian? It is a boy's name. No good for girls."

"No, Kristen. It's a girl's name." Julie enunciated the word.

"Kirsten, ya, okay." The doctor scribbled on her chart, leaving with the nurse, leaving Julie to hold her precious bundle.

The baby's wrinkled face looked red and tiny and her eyes closed against the new, bright, scary world. Julie held her in her arms, knowing she'd never again be alone in the world. She had a daughter now.

2000, Miami, Florida

Kirsten enjoyed a long weekend off after tax season. Most CPA firms gave a "Tax Recovery Day" on the sixteenth of April, after they either filed or extended any remaining personal tax returns. This year, the sixteenth fell on a Saturday, so everyone took Monday off instead.

The first day back still had lots of work. Now they had to finish the first quarter payroll tax returns they'd shoved to the back burner during the first half of the month. Kirsten bent to her work as the day flew by.

Despite the workload, she left at a reasonable time, arriving home while it was still daylight. She savored and enjoyed this novel sensation, as tax season meant eighty-hour work weeks. She picked up the mail, walking into her house.

Almost as soon as she walked in, the phone rang. "Hello, this is Kirsten."

"Hello, Kirsten? This is Sharon Henderson."

Fuzzy with the last several weeks' worth of hard work, Kirsten scoured her memory for the name, but when the connection hit, she almost dropped the phone.

"Ms. Henderson? Then you got my letter? I wondered, as hadn't heard from you. I thought I'd gotten an old address." Old addresses had been the bane of her genealogical research.

The woman on the line laughed. "Oh, call me Sharon, please. No, I got it, you bet, but I had to track down information for you. My Uncle Fred Stein appears to be your Great-Uncle Fred Stein. He needed to find someone who had your dad's information. I have it all here."

Kirsten caught her breath. When she exhaled, it came out in a sob. Had she found him?

"Are you there, Kirsten?"

"I'm ... I'm here, Sharon. I'm, well this has been an extensive search, so I can't believe I've found anything."

Sharon's voice brightened. "You have found something! I've got your dad's address and phone number, he's in California. I also found your grandparents' phone number and address, both in Minnesota and in their winter place in Arizona. And Kirsten?"

Kirsten stumbled out a strangled noise which she hoped sounded like "uh-huh?"

"If, for whatever reason, your father cannot or will not acknowledge you, please understand you have cousins who welcome you into the family, my dear."

She burst out in tears now, trying without success to hide them. "Thank you, Sharon. Thank you so very, very much. For this, for everything." She put the phone down for a second, blowing her nose hard, trying to clear her eyes enough to see the paper. "Alright, I've got a pencil. What are the addresses?"

Kirsten cradled the phone for a long time. She stared at the addresses and phone numbers, taking several deep breaths. *Well, why not? Might as well go for it. I've got the data, use it.* It would be so much wasted effort if she stopped now, out of simple fear.

Perhaps she should tell her mom. Yeah, that might help calm her.

The line rang twice. "Hello, this is Julie."

Kirsten kept her voice even. "Hi, Mom, how are you?"

"Kirsten! I'm doing great, how about you? Recovering from tax season yet?"

"Pretty much, but I've another puzzle to occupy my mind. Have you got a minute to talk?"

Worry painted her mother's voice at this gambit. "Of course, my dear. For you, anytime. What's wrong?"

Kirsten shook her head. "No, nothing's wrong. I've got information, but I wanted to tell you before I used it."

"Well, nothing like ominous innuendo to begin your day. This might be anything from nuclear launch codes to proof of alien life. Can you be more specific?"

Kirsten took a deep breath. "I have my father's phone number. His address, too. And his parents', as well."

This quelled her mom's joking tone. "Oh. I see."

"I want to call him, but I wanted to tell you first."

Her mother cleared her throat. "Why?"

Kirsten swallowed. "What if ... what if he wants to get in touch with you? Would you mind if I gave him your phone number? He may want to, I don't know, verify things, perhaps?"

Several moments of silence preceded her mother's answer. "Well, if he asks for it, I don't mind if you share my number. But I doubt he will. You realize this may upset his family, perhaps derail his life, right? And you still want to go through with it?"

"I do, Mom. But I've got to ask. I have to find out what he's like. I wish you understood how essential this is to me."

"I don't understand, not in the way you mean, but I *do* understand why you might need to know. Tread carefully, will you? This affects other people's lives."

Kirsten's heartbeat slowed. "I'll do my best, Mom. Do you have any message for him?"

Her mom took in a deep breath and let it go with a big *whoosh*. "No, no message. I said all I needed to the last time we spoke. If he wants to talk to me, that's fine, but I won't initiate contact. Do let me know how it goes, will you?"

Kirsten grinned. "I will, Mom, I will. Wish me luck?"

"Good luck, my special child. Good luck with everything."

1969, Copenhagen, Denmark

Despite Julie's insistence at the hospital, the doctor had written the child's name as Kirsten, rather than Kristen, but it would be fine. Sometimes fate had its own way, despite her best efforts. She didn't care. She had this joyous creature to herself now.

When the hospital released her, she returned to Barry's guest room, a bright, cheerful space, painted white with red trim. Barry found a used crib. Julie fell into a routine of napping whenever she could, as the baby only slept a couple hours at a time, waking in furious anger, demanding to be fed. Julie didn't know if the beer helped, but at least she had no problem nursing the child. Her adequate cleavage burst into abundance over the last months of her pregnancy.

Barry brought artwork to Julie for the local branch of the Church, whose needs were much smaller than the large organization in the UK, so she might keep her mind busy as she cared for the baby. She still never got enough sleep, but nothing required much intense concentration, so she skated on.

On a bright March morning, the sun shone so bright on the snow, Julie decided she must get out. However, rather than walking out the door, leaving became a major expedition. She bundled up the baby until the poor thing couldn't move, putting her into the homemade sling Barry had fashioned for her, which let her carry the baby without using her arms. Julie bundled herself up, grabbed her sketching stuff, and went out for a walk.

Julie reveled in the sunlight, face up and eyes closed, absorbing the light and the bright, the scant daylight hours of winter being a precious resource. She strolled, rested on benches, and wandered. She didn't even stop to draw, so intent in catching the sun, like a spring blossom searching for the elusive summer.

She returned to the house just as Barry did. Barry stowed her bicycle in the shed, and they gathered in the kitchen for tea and coffee after disrobing their multiple layers.

"It is so glorious outside, I had to enjoy it." Julie felt like she needed to explain the outing, for some reason. She held her cold hands around the hot coffee mug while Barry steeped her tea bag.

"I don't blame you, my dear. Enjoy the bright days, there are few enough of them. God, how I miss California weather."

The short days and interminable nights left their impression on Julie. She commiserated with Barry. While summer would bring lengthy days and short nights, it seemed so far away, a mere dream and a promise.

Julie clenched her jaw and broached a subject that had been bothering her. "Barry, will there be any permanent work for me here, do you think? Or have I overstayed my welcome?"

Barry's sad eyes told her the truth. "To be honest, Julie, no. I mean, there will always be piece work, but full time, or permanent? This tiny place doesn't need it. But you, my dear, are the mother of our Goddaughter, so will always have a place here. Don't you worry about it." One of Barry's famous hair flings accompanied her words, with an extra dramatic flounce.

Julie giggled, "You know I'll worry about it, Barry. Besides, it isn't fair to keep my parents in the dark. I should return to them, introduce them to their grandchild. Their first grandchild." Julie smiled, thinking of her tiny girl. Then she frowned, thinking of her father's reaction to her bastard child.

"Hey, none of that. No frowning permitted."

"I need to go back, Barry, but I'm not looking forward to telling my father about this. Mom, no problem. She'll be shocked at first, but she'll love the baby, I'm certain. Dad? He's a right stubborn ass sometimes."

With a shrug, Barry finished off her cup. "Well, you can't travel overseas yet, anyhow. Doesn't Kirsten need to be eight weeks before a flight so long? You'll have time to decide how to play it, at any rate."

Julie got up then, running the tap into the tea pot. "I suppose so. Do you want more tea?"

"I think more would be fantastic. I never liked the stuff until I moved to Scotland. For them, tea is the answer to everything."

Someone shook her shoulder. "Julie? Julie, wake up, hon. There's a phone call for you. It's your mom." She opened her eyes to see Bruce's worried face hovering above her.

"Bruce? What's wrong?" He was a quiet, taciturn man, good-natured, but never talkative. Julie felt a rumbling in the distance and identified it as thunder, not a distant train. She shivered.

"I'm not sure, Julie, your mother didn't say, but she sounded strained."

Julie jumped up and pulled her robe on, thrusting her feet into the slippers. The house was still freezing cold in the morning, the hardwood floors retaining none of the day's heat. She shuffled into the kitchen, to the phone mounted on the wall near the door. "Mom? It's Julie."

Thunder boomed again in the distance. She waited for the delay as the signal bounced to the States and back.

Her mother's voice came hoarse and harsh. "Julie, is that you? Julie, there's been an accident. It's your sister. She's in the hospital. A train hit her car. How soon can you get home? We need you here, Julie."

Julie caught her breath. *Katy, in the hospital? Oh, God, Kirsten can't fly yet.* She couldn't tell her mother about that on the phone, either. "Mom, I can't, I can't come home right now. Do you have the number to the hospital? Can I call Katy?"

"She's not conscious, Julie. She hasn't been since the crash. What in the world is so important that you can't come home? Is it money? I can buy you the ticket, just come home."

"Mom, I *can't!* I wish I could, oh, dammit. I can't tell you why now, but I can't. Mom?"

Was the hesitation from the trans-Atlantic delay? Or something else? "Well, if that's your decision, then it is what it is. I hope you can live with it." A sob came through before a loud click. Julie stared at the phone, unable to place it on the cradle.

Bruce came up behind her, taking the phone gently from her hands. "Julie? Is everything okay?"

"No, and there isn't a damn thing I can do about it from here. Damn! Shit!" She glanced up at Bruce, not noticing the tears dripping down her cheeks. "My sister got hurt in a train crash. She's in the hospital, lying in a coma, and I can't fly yet." Julie pounded one fist on the wall in frustration, welcoming the pain which radiated up her arm. She cradled it, sobbing. A bright light flashed and the crash made them all jump. Julie let out a shriek.

Bruce pulled her into a hug and rocked her like a child, comforting her with soothing noises.

Julie pulled away and stomped into her room, looking down at the sweet, innocent baby, burbling in her sleep. "You! It's all your fault. If it wasn't for you, I'd be with Katy. *Damn* you!"

Kirsten woke up when she shouted, smiling with bright eyes into her mother's face.

Julie sobbed and snatched the baby up to cradle her, rocking. How could she stay mad at this tiny wonder? Her heart released her sudden rage. She comforted herself by swaying with the child back and forth, feeding her. She burped her and rocked her back to sleep once more, back and forth, back and forth. The thunder booms moved further away, as the constant sound of rain on the roof soothed her. In time, Morpheus came, and she slept in the rocking chair, runnels of dried tears still on her cheeks.

April 7th, 1969

Dear Julie:
Your sister Katy died yesterday. She recovered from her coma only briefly before she passed away, and told us what happened. The accident happened on her way to the airport to fly to London, to meet with her fiancé. She'd borrowed the Volkswagen from her friend, Karen. The car stalled on a train tracks near Monroe Avenue. The train came, and she panicked. She fumbled with the door lock and escaped from the car before the train hit it. However, the debris from the crash hit her. An ambulance took her to the hospital on March 15th. She died April 5th. The service is on April 12th.

We know you loved your sister dearly, so we don't understand why you didn't return to be with your sister on her last days. There is nothing to be done about it now.

Your mother,
Carol Jensen

Julie spent the afternoon crying. When Kirsten echoed her sobs, she rocked the baby against her breast. She cried for being unable to be with her sister, her best friend, her other half, her closest confidante. Julie cried until she got the hiccups, then cried more. She dozed in and out, but when she woke, more tears flooded her.

When Barry got home, Julie slept in the rocking chair, the baby in her arms, tear-stained cheeks and red eyes giving testament to her misery. She saw the crumpled letter on the floor where Julie had thrown it, and, suffering no guilt, read it. Barry wiped her own tears away by the time she finished.

Not wanting to wake Julie from any respite sleep might bring, Barry covered the two with an afghan, shutting the door behind her. Quietly, Barry made soup. When they awoke, they'd need nourishment. It wouldn't help much, but the warm liquid might ease her raw throat.

When Bruce arrived an hour later, Barry didn't reach the door in time to warn him to be quiet. He shut the door hard, rattling the house enough to wake the sleepers. Groggy from sleep and despair, Julie set the still-dozing infant in her crib and stumbled into the kitchen. Even if she didn't want food, her stomach had other ideas. It recognized the tantalizing odors coming from the kitchen.

As soon as Julie spied the sad expression on Barry's face, she realized her friend had read the letter. Julie's eyes prickled with tears again, but she fought the urge to give in. She sat at the table, after a silent Barry hugged her hard. Her friend then handed her a bowl of soup, which she ate after cradling the warmth of the bowl. The heat leeched into her frozen hands. Despite herself, her mood lifted after the meal.

Barry sat next to her, a cup of tea in her hand. "When will you be able to travel home?"

"The doctor said not until next week. I wish I went before ..." The tears threatened to return. The soup became a lump in her stomach. She swallowed several times.

Barry jumped up and brought her a glass of water. "Shh, shh. It'll be fine. You will go back, and your parents will understand why you didn't go. It's not news you can tell them on the phone, now, is it?" Barry peered at her, using one finger to pull her chin up to look into Julie's eyes.

Julie took a deep sigh, "Exactly. They have enough to deal with. I couldn't give them more bad news. They'll learn soon enough, I guess. And when they do, I have no idea what they'll do. Mom'll come around, I'm sure, but Dad?"

She didn't relish thinking of what her father's reaction would be. He'd raged so loudly when she'd quit college. To show up on his doorstep, unmarried, with a bastard child in her arms, might send him over the edge.

What would he do? Yell and curse at her. As a navy sergeant in World War II, he'd learned many colorful curses. She'd borne the brunt of them before, but she surely hadn't received the full spectrum yet.

Would he send her away? Disown her? She must try. As difficult as it would be, swallowing her pride and moving back to her parents' house was her only option. She'd thought of moving in with Katy before … before. But Katy was gone. The tears flooded back, so she swallowed more water, and choked on a chunk of ice.

Bruce swatted her back, dislodging it. Julie dabbed her eyes with a napkin and sniffed, looking at Barry. "Can you take me to the travel agent tomorrow? I need to make the arrangements. Time to face the music."

"Whatever you need. What else can we do to help?"

"Can you ship my boxes home? I'll have my hands full with baby stuff, so I have to send the art supplies and sketchbooks separately. I don't fancy carrying everything while moving through the airports and home."

Bruce gripped her shoulder. "Consider it done. And Julie? Good luck. Whatever we can do to help, call us. We cherish you, and our goddaughter, of course."

CHAPTER NINE

Origins

1969, Detroit, Michigan

*P**lease let it be Mom. Mom, not Dad, only Mom.*
Julie chanted this, almost like a meditation, most of the flight across the Atlantic. She hoped against hope her mother would pick her up from the airport, so she could explain first, before having to face her father. Having an ally would make things easier.

Her mother worked as an art teacher three days a week at Edsel Ford High School. Other days she worked as a substitute. She taught everything from Algebra to Spanish, History to Music. But her passion, her vocation, had always been art.

Both Julie and Katy inherited their talent and passion for art from their mother. Her mother's mother, Wilda, (but everyone called her Meema), had been an artist who taught oil painting in private classes. Meema never worked full time, not in her generation, but she enjoyed the classes.

Julie's father possessed no artistic sense. He lived in a world of mathematics, as an engineer, combining creativity with mathematics in a way which mystified her.

Much to her mother's chagrin, Julie never got the teaching bug. She enjoyed creating art, but not passing the knowledge to others. Her passion remained in the solitude of creativity, the sublime otherworld she transported herself to while in the throes of her muse. Julie might paint or draw for hours, paying no attention to the outside world, almost like a trance, an Eastern Yogi meditation. But a classroom of students terrified her.

Katy understood.

Julie took another sip of the miniature Coke can with the Delta logo, using the dying carbonation to fight her tears. She had no wish to let her seatmates witness her misery.

She sat sandwiched in the middle seat, between a large, sweaty man with shoulders broad enough for a football team and a young boy. The child belonged to a woman across the aisle, busy with two younger children, and she seldom checked on the boy. The man dozed most of the flight, though he kept leaning into her, his beefy shoulders pushing her into the child's space.

She'd eyed the boy when she boarded, Kirsten in her arms, but he'd remained angelic, busy coloring his activity books throughout the eight-hour flight. Kirsten remained surprisingly quiet, though Julie had to walk to the galley to feed her twice.

As she had many times in the last few months, she conjured up the scene of confronting her father with the baby, playing it in her mind like a stage production. Each time it played out differently, as she imagined the setting, the reactions, the words.

Every scenario ended with him kicking her out of his home and his life.

As the plane descended into Detroit, Kirsten woke and whimpered. Julie made popping sounds with her mouth, to distract her from the pain. It worked for a while, but the whimper became a whine. Soon, it turned into a full-blown wail.

Julie bounced the fretful child on her knee as the plane descended, praying it would be over soon.

Julie sent frantic, apologetic glances to those around her. She had little control over her baby's need to cry, but her overriding guilt kept her trying.

Once they landed, the man next to her retrieved her bags from the overhead bin, a process made impossible with Kirsten in her arms. He beamed at the baby, nodded to her, then walked down the aisle as Julie juggled the bags into place.

When Julie emerged onto the concourse, she peered around, hoping to see her mother's face among those gathered to meet the arrivals. She held Kirsten close, face into her chest, to mask identification to a casual look. She did not search for her father's face.

Finally, she spied a familiar smiling face, crowned with a halo of fuzzy, curly light brown hair. Her brother, Larry, waved like a clown, and next to him? Her mother's dark wavy hair, with a glimpse of her loud turquoise floral dress.

No father.

Julie let an enormous sigh of relief, waved at Larry so he'd stop his crazy gesticulations, then hefted her bags.

As she made her way around the ropes, Larry moved to hug her, but stopped when she put her hand on his chest. Her little brother, prone to unthinking enthusiasm, might hurt Kirsten. He wrinkled his brow. With a finger on her lips, she unfolded her arm, revealing the gurgling infant.

Larry stared at the baby, then at Julie, then back to the baby, his mouth open in an O, looking like nothing so much as a goldfish with an afro. Then he let out a whoop and shot his arm up in the air like a sports fan.

Julie shushed him and glanced at her mother.

Understanding and sympathy warred with disappointment on her mother's face, but the former won. "Julie, is this why you didn't come for Katy? Why didn't you tell me? Oh, my dear, sweet, special daughter." She enveloped Julie in her arms, loose in the front but tight around her shoulders. Larry joined the hug.

Julie blinked several times, determined not to let tears take over again. Did her tears stem from motherhood or Katy's death? "This isn't something I should tell you over the phone, Mom. You had so many other things to worry about. I didn't want Dad to know yet." Julie stuck her finger out for the child to grab onto.

Her mom smiled at the child, putting her finger out to caress the baby-soft cheek. "And what is my grandchild's name?"

"Her name is Kirsten. She arrived February 16th."

Larry, with awkward acuity, cut in. "Wait, sis, did you get married without telling us?"

Julie stared at him as she clenched her jaw, a look which had quelled him as a child, but worked less so now he was nineteen. "No, I'm not married." She willed him not to ask further embarrassing questions. She straightened her spine to look defiant.

Her mom and brother exchanged looks.

If they talked it out on neutral ground, things might become less awkward. "Well, shall we get ourselves out of this madhouse and to someplace quiet to eat, where we can talk?"

"That's an excellent idea, Julie. Larry, fetch her bags. Let's see if we can find the car."

They sat around a wooden table at New Hellas in Greek Town, one of Julie's favorites. They ordered saganaki and moussaka. Between mouthfuls of food, she told them the story of Paul, and why she didn't tell him about Kirsten. She explained the disaster of a job in Edinburgh, of her loneliness. Julie didn't mean to unload, not as soon as she returned. However, being with family she trusted, someone she could talk to, came as such an incredible relief. As helpful as Barry and Bruce had been, their own fertility issues kept her from confiding everything in them.

Julie's mom clapped her hands together. "Well, I'm delighted to meet my granddaughter, and welcome her into the family. I think we'll install you in the upstairs rooms. Your father built out the attic space, you know. It's now two rooms and a bathroom, perfect for you and Kirsten."

Larry piped up, a piece of moussaka on his fork. "Hey! I live in one of those rooms!"

"Shush, dear. Kirsten won't need her own room for months yet. You should be on your own by then."

Julie swallowed her own bite. "But what about Dad?"

Her mom, fussing with her short hair, paused before she answered. "Your father's changed since Katy passed on." Tears glistening her mother's eyes, and Julie offered her a glass of water. "He's much quieter, not given to his normal tempers. It's as if a section of his soul died. He read a poem at the funeral and cried as he read it."

Julie's own eyes burned, as she glanced at her brother to see his reddened eyes. They all stopped, in mutual agreement, eating to regain control.

Her mother took a shuddering breath. "I think he would welcome new life into the family, my dear. Truly, I do."

Other than a few clipped questions about the origins of the child, Julie's father accepted them without a fuss. No thunderstorm of shouts and tears, which she'd expected, dreaded, since she'd discovered her condition. Her father's lost fire frightened Julie, almost as if he'd given up on life.

Some days, when she remembered Katy, she didn't blame him. Then Julie glanced at her daughter, a fresh spark of joy in a saddened home.

Still, the dead time didn't last forever. Her father loved building things. He built a crib for the baby, and then a huge dollhouse. Next, he bought a play set and erected it in the backyard, even though she wouldn't use it for years. He played with the child, often while he thought no one watched. If anyone came in, or made a noise, he'd pretend he'd been checking up on the child, but Julie spied a few rare moments of tenderness.

Life settled into an uneasy routine. Her father left every day for Detroit, where he worked as an engineer for Chrysler. Her mother worked most days, though she accepted fewer substitute jobs to help take care of the baby. Julie missed Katy with an ache which settled into her bones. Everything in the house reminded her of her sister, flashes of memory which hit her at random times, like punches in the gut.

Julie and Kirsten settled into an upstairs room, while Larry, just as their mother had predicted, moved out to live with some friends. Her parents ran the house downstairs. The front door opened onto a landing, with the stairs to the right and the living room to the left, so she even had a bit of privacy.

Not that she entertained often. Julie harbored too much guilt to enjoy herself. She remained keenly aware she now lived on her parents' charity and goodwill.

Finding a job, especially one that paid enough money to afford a babysitter, proved an enormous challenge. Months marched by with no success. Though she found temporary gigs at Greenfield Village, demonstrating crafts on school trip days, she found nothing permanent.

Her life became a fencing match. Her father stood on one side, sullen and taciturn, going about his daily tasks without speaking to her, even at dinner. His silence became his reproach for her lack of a college degree, employment, and her fall from grace. Julie stood on the other side, torn between caring for her baby and trying to impress her father.

Katy had been the golden child, excelling at everything she tried. Julie showed as a poor shadow, the remnants of the goddess who had forever gone. Her mother sat torn in the middle, a referee trying to make everyone happy, and failing.

Her best escape became visits with her best friend. Gail had two children now, Ross and Kelly. She had her hands full with caring for them, with Ross aged six and Kelly, two. Julie enjoyed visits, letting the three children play together.

She made peace with Sandy, who, though fierce of temper and quick with criticism, could also forgive, given time and plenty of encouragement. Sandy had moved to an apartment in downtown Detroit, so Julie had to take two busses to visit, as she didn't drive. Sandy's apartment wasn't much bigger than her place in New York had been, though her neighbor had young children for Kirsten to play with.

Julie's room took a full third of the second floor. She set up the other room, just as large, for Kirsten. A half bathroom with no tub or shower filled out the area.

She loved deep reds and decorated with them. Julie haunted the thrift stores for curtains, bedspread, and rugs to fill this craving. She arranged trinkets she received as gifts on her travels, precious pieces Katy had made, with a light wind chime near the window made with round pieces of frosted glass. She'd finally learned to collect memories in things.

Kirsten's room became more of a mishmash, but for now it housed her crib and playpen. Julie's dad had crafted a huge wooden toy box, and it filled at an alarming rate. He still worked on the dollhouse, though it had grown larger than Kirsten already.

Julie studied her reflection in the full-length mirror, trying to pull in her stomach so the slacks didn't pouch in the middle. Then she let out her breath, watching her tummy pouf out again, grimacing. She hadn't been able to get rid of her pregnancy fat.

This morning, she had an interview at a local needlework shop. They needed a clerk and someone to paint patterns onto needlepoint canvas. It would only be part time, and three blocks away, so she could ride her bike. Julie abandoned the pants and tried on a long skirt instead.

The skirt bloused out and didn't show her belly and hips in relief. She fluffed her hair, now cut short for ease of care, touched up her make-up, and gathered Kirsten and the playpen to take them downstairs. Julie left Kirsten with a kiss on her sleepy cheek, thanking her mother for watching the child during the interview.

The sun shone bright and warm, downright sultry. If the store had been too much farther away, she'd have arrived in a sweaty mess. Julie rode down the block to the corner, where Pete's Grocery Store stood, turned right onto Monroe, and down two blocks to the shop. She stashed her bike next to the front door, checked her hair in the glass window, and entered.

The place looked like a magpie's nest, but a glorious one. Yarns of all descriptions sat in baskets, hung in skeins, and dripped from the ceiling. A huge rack along one wall held hundreds of painted needlepoint canvases. At a tiny counter near the back, an older lady read a novel. She glanced up as the front door chimed, giving Julie a nod.

Needlepoint wasn't Julie's passion, but her mother had always loved the craft. A huge needlepoint of the Blue Willow oriental pattern, all sewn by her mother, covered the valences above their large bay windows. It must have cost a fortune in time and materials, but her mom loved her Blue Willow.

Julie had arrived a few minutes early, so she took time to look around. Her father had always said if one wasn't ten minutes early to a business appointment, then it counted as late. She hadn't come here before and grew fascinated by the variety on offer behind the narrow storefront. The lady at the counter, her pointy-ended glasses covered in lavish rhinestones, returned to her novel. She'd pulled back her graying hair into a huge bun, and she looked about fifty.

When Julie wended her way to the back desk, the lady looked up with inquiry.

Julie tried to sound professional and calm. "Hello, I've an appointment with Shay at noon?"

The woman's grin widened. "I'm Shay. You must be Julie. How do you like our little store?" Shay managed to both shake Julie's hand and gesture with her other, encompassing her world with one wave.

Though nervous enough that her stomach roiled, she smiled. "It's overwhelming. I'd done needlework, but never realized the variety available."

Shay laughed, holding her belly. "It can be a bit much at first, I'm sure. We try to stuff as much into a tiny space as we can. So, you're Carol's daughter, then? I don't think we've met before."

Her mother must have mentioned it. "Yes, I am. I'd been away at Art School, then living abroad for several years." She'd chosen the most innocuous way to describe her adventures to the curious. Her adventures were on the wild side for suburban Dearborn.

"And what sort of art did you study?"

"Mostly two-dimensional design; painting and drawing. I did courses in sculpture, but I focused on the flat forms. I've dabbled in lots of areas."

"Excellent. And have you ever painted on canvas before, for needlepoint?"

Julie nodded. "I helped my mother with her Blue Willow canvas preparations. She painted one, then I helped her with the others. We completed the project together. Have you seen them?"

Shay grinned and clapped her hands, showing a missing eyetooth. "I have! She bought her supplies here. She's always been an excellent customer. I'd be happy to welcome her daughter to my fold. Can you begin tomorrow at ten? I'll show you the ropes, staying with you a couple days before I leave you on your own. The pay is $1.50 per hour."

Julie sucked in her breath. "Oh, that would be fantastic! Thank you." She pumped Shay's hand. Realizing how much the older lady jiggled, she gentled her handshake. After so many months, a job, any job, thrilled her. An artistic job would be icing on the cake.

"Carol also mentioned you have a young child? An infant?" Shay's question brought Julie back to earth with a thud, as her stomach fluttered again.

"Yes, Kirsten. She's five months old." Would Shay not want to hire her after all? A disgraced single mother?

As if she recognized Julie's anxiety, Shay smiled wide. "Well, you are welcome to bring her with you unless we've got a class scheduled. If you bring a playpen, she sounds young enough to not be too much bother. Does that help?"

Julie let out her held breath with a *whoosh,* giving Shay a look of sheer gratitude.

Shay placed a warm hand on Julie's arm. "I was once a single mother, my dear. Well, widowed, from the war, but with a young child, details don't matter. I *do* understand." Shay took Julie's hand in both of hers, holding it. She held Julie's eyes. "I try to help out others in your situation when I can."

While blinking back tears, Julie mumbled, "thank you," and dropped her gaze.

Shay wouldn't relinquish her hand yet. "Be strong, my dear. Plenty of people will assume the worst of you, but remember, you are *strong*. You are *woman*. You are *yourself*. The opinions of others are meaningless. Don't give them such power."

With a final squeeze of her hand, Shay let go. "I'll see you tomorrow, then. Is that your bicycle outside? If you bring it around the back tomorrow, we can place it inside the storage room, to keep it from being stolen or hit in the alleyway." She busied herself under the counter, and Julie made her escape.

Julie hadn't counted on such kindness and had to blink away tears of gratitude. Shay's support made her spirits soar as she flew home on the bike. Previous job interviews *had* met with the prejudice Shay mentioned. Women and men alike looked down on her with disdain. Dearborn remained a small city, and news of her situation had spread. Even those ignorant of her personal details saw that she'd never finished college. This gave them plenty of ammunition. When Julie asked about the hours, Kirsten usually came up. That ended the interview.

She looked forward to working at Needle Arts. At least she'd found a kindred spirit in Shay, someone who had an inkling into her struggles, both past and future.

1970, Dearborn, Michigan

Julie juggled her covered dish and the baby while attempting to get into the car, gave up, and placed the dish in the back seat before trying again.

She turned to her friend, Gail. "Can you hold Kirsten? I have to go back and get her playpen." She rushed back into the house, emerging laden with the collapsed playpen and a huge quilted bag of supplies and toys. While she walked to the car, Gail popped open the back of her woody station wagon to stash them.

Julie eyed her dish, City Chicken. It contained no chicken, but pork cooked on skewers, with onions and peppers, smothered in chicken gravy. A poor man's chicken shish-ka-bob, a family recipe. "How many people do you think we'll have?"

Gail shrugged. "I don't know, thirty? We invited the whole block, but a few left on vacation. Don't worry, there's always plenty of food. Jan's got the barbecue fired up in the front yard and will supply a constant stream of meat."

Jan and Gail threw block parties every summer. They erected barricades on either end of the block to keep the traffic out, taking over the street with games and tables, to drink chilled beer in the hot sunshine.

Kirsten would be ensconced in her playpen in Gail's house, with a couple other infants her age. Julie hung out in the dining room, with its gigantic bay window overlooking the street, in view of both the party and the babies. Jan would be out in the yard, playing the Barbecue King, drinking beer, being the loudest person on the block.
Julie grinned at his antics. He loved being the center of attention. He told fantastic stories, reveling in a party atmosphere. Gail would sit by his side, filling in the bits of story he forgot. Julie envied their relationship and partnership.

She very much looked forward to a day of relaxation, drinking, and socializing with people her own age. While she loved working at the shop, most of Shay's customers were women her mother's age. Even when she taught a class, with social interaction encouraged, a teacher/student relationship didn't come close to a friendship.

But this, with people of all ages in a party environment, the wholesome family atmosphere, she missed this since East Grinstead. This satisfied her craving for camaraderie and a sense of community.

Julie sipped her soda. She still hated the taste of beer. Jan gesticulated outside. The windows stood open, screens keeping the bugs at bay, so his dissertation drifted in, on the merits of his method of barbecue, complete with vinegar-based marinade in the sauce. She grinned at the rapt attention of his audience, a group of six younger men, all awaiting the first taste of chicken on the verge of bursting into flame. The buffet table creaked under a plethora of covered dishes. Most looked empty now, except Julie's offering, which remained barely touched. Julie harbored no illusions about her skills as a cook, but it still stung.

Kirsten gurgled, playing in her pen, though she'd crumpled the blanket into the corner. Her daughter had made it into a cave, hiding her toys inside, then pulling them out as if making a magnificent discovery. Julie beamed at her daughter, so happy to have her. When she didn't cry bloody murder, she smiled so sweetly. The child learned, though, crying or fussing around Grandpa wasn't acceptable. He'd made it clear he already raised his children, so wouldn't tolerate another screaming baby in his house. A firm look from him would quell any fussiness in the baby. At least Kirsten had a father figure of sorts. Julie veered away from the thought, glancing out at the party again.

Gail returned from bringing Jan a fresh Pabst Blue Ribbon beer from the huge cooler, settling into the chair between Julie and their friend, Helen. "God, it's great to relax today. The kids have run me off my feet. Jan is in fine fettle out there, isn't he?"

Julie grinned and held up her soda in a toast. "He's in his element. Jan must not get to socialize much at his job. He must remain stuck under an engine, covered in grease. It's hard to fascinate the multitude from under there."

Once again, Julie's mind strayed to the partnership with Paul she'd enjoyed, letting out a sigh.

Helen had always had the uncanny ability to follow her thoughts. "Do you miss him?"

Julie gave her friend a wry smile. "I do, of course I do. But I can't do anything about it, really."

"You might find someone else?"

After letting out an abrupt bark of laughter, Julie chugged her Coke to quell the threatening sadness. "I've tried, but who wants a woman with a child? Besides, no one measures up. I mean, Paul and I were completely natural. No pretense needed, no mask, no acting. We had the two of us. Who else could measure up to that?"

Helen raised an eyebrow. "At least you've a bit of him to keep with you in Kirsten?"

"Yes, at least I've got Kirsten. I hope she'll be enough to sustain me in my spinsterhood." She sounded bitter, old, and full of despair.

Gail waggled an admonishing finger at her. "Hey, none of that. You've a delightful daughter to fill your life with joy. It's a blessing, my friend. You keep that in mind."

Julie stuck her tongue out at her friend. "Yes, mother."

2000, Miami, Florida

Kirsten took in a long, shuddering breath, and let it out again. She stared at the number Sharon had given her, the one that should lead to her father on the other end. With sudden decision, she punched the numbers in.

The phone rang once. Kirsten's heart leapt to her throat. She swallowed hard to keep it down.

A second ring. She glanced at the clock. Six in Miami meant three in California. He probably had a job.

Three rings and a click. "Hello, you have reached the Starship Enterprise. The bridge crew is not here to receive your hail. Please leave your name, hailing frequency, and planet of origin, and a member of the bridge crew will get back to you as soon as possible. *Beep!*"

With a slightly hysterical giggle, Kirsten covered her mouth. *Well, at least he had a sense of humor. And a science fiction geek, which worked fine.*

Kirsten didn't want to appear to be a kook and scare him off, so she'd given her opening gambit some thought. "Hello, my name is Kirsten. I've been doing some family research, and I think we might be related. Can you please call me?" She gave her number, and hung up the phone, letting out a huge breath of relief. Then she waited.

He sounded fun. Not like a stiff or a like a redneck, but someone who appreciated a good laugh. Kirsten had grown up loving Star Trek, science fiction and fantasy books, movies, and films. She had little choice, as her mother loved them, too.

Kirsten grew up reading Tolkien, Asimov, Heinlein, and Anne McCaffrey. She loved dragons as a child, fantasizing about finding a dragon egg to hatch her personal dragon steed. She dreamt of going into space to colonize Mars. Kirsten even studied computer science so she might join the space program. A failure to pass Physics convinced her to switch to accounting instead. At least accounting still provided puzzles to solve, her true passion.

Nothing to do now but wait, no matter how hard. Kirsten had waited her whole life. At thirty years old, she had a career, a fiancé, and a purpose in life.

Had she held off until she found her father, before marrying? Waited until she'd found the last bit of her background? No fairy tale wedding would be complete without the father bringing his princess down the aisle.

She busied herself with computer work, so when the phone rang, it startled her. She dropped her mouse on the tile floor with a loud clatter and picked up the phone.

Her heart beat so fast, it would win the Kentucky Derby.

Her voice shook. "Hello, this is Kirsten."

"Hello, Kirsten. This is Paul Stein. You left a message on my machine about genealogical research?"

"I did, yes." She forced herself to modulate her voice, to keep it from being shrill. "Let me first ensure I have the right Paul Stein, okay?"

The man chuckled. "Sure. Which one are you looking for?"

"One who lived in East Grinstead, England during 1968, and worked at the Church there."

"Yes, sounds like me. Unless I have a twin running around, but I never caught sight of him."

Breathe. Just breathe. "And do you remember a young lady named Julie Jensen?"

Silence for a moment. *Breathe.*

"It *has* been thirty years. I don't remember the name, but perhaps you could describe her?"

Her heart skipped again. "She was about twenty-five years old, 5'4", thick, long brown hair, with gray eyes. Quiet, loved music. She did artwork for the Church."

Another pause which seemed a month long. "Oh! Yes, I do remember her, with great fondness."

Breathe again. C'mon, Kirsten, you can do this. "Well, she's my mother, and she says you're my father."

Kirsten waited through the lengthy pause, forgetting to breathe.

Finally, he responded. "Wow."

Her computer screen flashed to her screen saver. She stared at the mesmerizing pattern until he said something else.

"Wow. How come she never told me?"

Kirsten hadn't expected this to be the first question. She'd been expecting "How does she know" or "Can she prove it?" This instant acceptance of the fact came as a surprise. She didn't know how to answer. "She said you had a wife, and she didn't want to mess it up. Besides, she didn't know until you'd left, back to your wife."

Thunderous silence came from the other end of the line. Had he hung up the phone?

He let out a nervous laugh. "I suppose she acted wisely, at that. I wouldn't have been a decent father at that point. Shoot, I probably won't be a good one now."

Kirsten giggled, but tried to hide it. "So, I don't have any brothers or sisters?"

"No, well, none who I've heard from. I didn't know about you five minutes ago. Annie and I divorced about ten years past."

Her response came automatically. "Oh! I'm so sorry."

"Our break stayed amicable, and we're still close friends. We work better that way than as a couple. I'm pretty good at being friends with women. Your mother, too. How is she? I remember her to be pleasant company."

Kirsten got hold of both her breathing and her heartbeat. "She's fine. Mom lives in Miami. She didn't, I mean, she never got married. She raised me on her own."

He paused again. "Would she be amenable to, perhaps, hearing from me?"

Kirsten grinned. "I cleared that before I called you. She said she wouldn't mind."

Then they chatted about random things. They compared photographs via email, and Kirsten recognized her features in her father's photo, as if someone cut and pasted the eyes and mouth. Next, they compared favorite books and movies. Each loved travel and languages, puzzles and math, and both collected dragons. Father and daughter shared a joy in history, and even in puns. They laughed and cried, like she spoke to an old friend she hadn't seen for years.

After a few hours, exhausted with relief and effort, Kirsten said goodbye to this new man in her life.

At long last, she'd found her father.

1970, Dearborn, Michigan

Julie's father loomed over her, red-faced with clenched fists. "I told you to keep your screeching brat upstairs, Julie. I will not tolerate her running around, screaming like a fucking banshee through the dining room when I'm working on my designs. March yourself upstairs, take that hellion baby, and keep her quiet."

He had a tall frame and a barrel chest, so his deep voice carried far when he yelled. Julie imagined a hurricane blowing from his mouth, pushing her and Kirsten back against the wall. However, she'd had enough. "She didn't scream! She laughed, which *you* never learned to do. If you weren't such a gloomy sourpuss, you'd recognize joy when you heard it."

Her father grew even larger, inflating like a puffer fish with rage and vitriol.

Her mother held out her hands to placate them. "Now, Jerry, dear, I'm sure Julie will keep the child quiet. Julie, take her upstairs with you, won't you, darling? Jerry, let me brew you some coffee. I've fresh cookies baking now, those will be delicious."

She hustled the hulking form of Julie's father into the dining room while Julie made her escape to the landing. As she closed the landing door, her father spoke again, despite her mother's imprecations. "She's living under our roof, and she's got to live by our rules. She's a fucking charity case, and I won't have her disobeying me. Carol, stop trying to shove that cup into my hands."

Julie waited by the door, anxious to hear how her mother would answer.

"Dear, she's got a job, she's not mooching. Relax, your face is all red. Remember what the doctor said about your blood pressure. Now, drink your coffee." Her voice trailed off and Julie continued up the stairs. She brought Kirsten into her room, calming her. The child grew upset with all the noise and tempers. In calming Kirsten, Julie calmed herself. She played peek-a-boo until she coaxed a waterfall giggle from the child.

This wasn't the first argument she'd had with her father. It wouldn't be the last. She escaped most Saturdays when her dad worked on his engineering plans. However, today Gail left with friends in Ohio, and she couldn't get to Sandy's apartment in Detroit. A creeping despair grew on her, the fear of being trapped, but she tamped it down. She'd have to bear it until Kirsten was old enough to go to school. Perhaps then, she'd be able to move away, someplace where she might get a full-time job, when the child didn't take constant care. For now, though, she needed to escape this house.

She grabbed her purse, bundling Kirsten and her baby bag together. She extracted her bike from the garage. Today seemed like a perfect day for Angelo's Pizzeria, her escape place. Julie wanted lunch and respite.

As she bicycled along the suburban street, seeing houses and manicured lawns, she imagined what life might have been like without a child, able to live where she liked, as she had in San Francisco. *And where did that get me?* Involved with a married man and pregnant. Perhaps she hadn't been mature enough to control her own life.

Julie pulled up behind the restaurant, parking her bike. She pulled Kirsten out of the child seat, grabbed the bag, and walked into the rear entrance as she always did. She passed by the counter bar on the left, finding an empty booth on the right. The maroon vinyl and sparkling silver table-tops gleamed in the afternoon sun through the glass frontage.

Hal came up and asked her if she wanted her usual slice and a coke, so she said yes. Julie settled Kirsten into her seat, giving her a bottle to keep her occupied. Then she pulled out her book. She needed escape, even if only into a vicarious world. She had the latest book by Irwin Shaw, <u>Rich Man, Poor Man</u>. It spoke of Americans living abroad, escaping the McCarthyism she remembered from her youth. The narrative paralleled her own life.

A flash of memory came to her, a conversation she'd had with Katy, about the political machinations of the government. How they harmed the people in their attempt to protect them. The memory brought pride for her sister's intelligence and clarity, rage at her death, sadness at her absence. Her lunch came, but Hal knew better than to chat with her while she read, so he left her to her solitude.

The memory of Katy made it impossible to concentrate on reading, though.

Julie wished she'd brought sketching materials, but she found little time for art. The baby took up so much of her time, and her job had her working long hours. What free time she scraped out, she spent in her room, reading or listening to records. She withdrew into herself. The only things Julie had were herself and her daughter.

2000, Miami, Florida

Anxiety gripped Julie as she thought about what she'd say to Paul after all these years.

Kirsten had called her last night, to let her know she'd found him and talked to him. He expressed an interest in contacting Julie. Kirsten mentioned he'd gotten a divorce. Julie mopped the sweat from her cheeks. Would he sound the same? Would she be too silly?

Julie had plenty to do, but as she cleaned, she hovered near the phone. She caught herself sweeping the same part of the living room floor a third time before she made herself move on to the hallway.

When the phone did ring, she halted in rigid inaction. On the second ring, she dropped the broom with a loud clatter on the tile floor and ran to the phone. She waited to catch her breath. After the third ring, she picked up the handset. With a deliberate, even voice, forcing herself to sound as normal as possible, she answered. "Hello, this is Julie."

"Julie? This is Paul. Our daughter called me, saying you wouldn't mind a call from me."

He sounded so nonchalant, just like she remembered. Julie took a deep breath, trying to speak. It came out as an unintelligible grunt. Horrified, she cleared her throat and spoke again. "Hello, Paul. Yes, she mentioned she found you." She did her best to sound light-hearted rather than hysterical.

"She did indeed. It's quite a little detective you've raised. I thank you for her."

Julie's heart skipped a beat. She had no clue what to talk about. She'd imagined for years finding

223

him, speaking to him, but never on the phone. Her daydreams always formed in some random public place, running into him at the grocery store, or at the movies. A wild, chance encounter which might become romantic reunion and running away together. But this strange reunion remained an unknown, a scene she never considered.

"Julie? Are you still there?"

She cleared her throat. "I'm here, Paul. I'm at a loss as to what to say."

"Well, how about I talk, then? I've always been rather good at it, you might remember. Let me start by saying I'm sorry. I had no idea you were with child. I would have helped, I promise you. But you did well to keep me in ignorance. I wouldn't have been able to handle the responsibility then."

"That sounds about right." She sounded bitter. She didn't want to sound bitter, but it came out that way.

He let out a breath. "I don't blame you for being upset. How can I make this up to you?"

What did she want? What did Kirsten need? "Can you… would you like to be a part of her life? Fill in the void she grew up with? I know it's a lot to ask, but it would mean the world to her."

"The plans are already made. Her call shocked me, but also thrilled me. Annie and I discussed children, then decided we'd rather be the rich Aunt and Uncle than the poor parents. I had a vasectomy five years after I knew you."

Julie's breathing eased. "So, you have no other children?"

"No, only Kirsten. I'm so very glad she found me." The pride and joy shone in his voice, the smile in his words.

Her own grin matched his obvious delight. "I'm glad, too."

"It can't have been easy, raising her on your own. I'm proud of you, too." He paused for a moment. "May I be your friend again?"

Keeping her excitement out of her voice, Julie said, "I think we can try, for Kirsten's sake if no other reason."

"I seem to recall enjoying your company. I can't see why I wouldn't enjoy it now. Unless you've objections?"

Julie tried for a joke. "Well, it's not convenient to go out for a walk when we're three thousand miles apart."

Paul laughed, sounding nervous. "Fair enough, but we can at least get to know each other again, through phone calls and emails. I'm sure I'll be making a visit out there in the coming months, to meet my lovely daughter. I should like to meet you again."

Breathe, Julie. Breathe. "That would be a lovely plan."

They got past the fencing stage and chatted with more ease. They spoke of their missing thirty years, about how their hopes and dreams had turned into lives and careers. Julie told of her jobs as a secretary, occasional artist, and property manager, now doing art for an architect. How she never married nor had any other children. Paul described his career in electronics, then computers, teaching classes in Linux and Red Hat for Hewlett Packard. His job sent him to teach seminars all around the country, sometimes around the world. He needed to travel to Orlando in September for work. They made arrangements for him to come out a week earlier, so they had time together.

As she hung up the phone, Julie sat in a daze, trying to collect her feelings. She hadn't considered this curve ball, about the next step after the imagined chance meeting in the grocery store or at the movies. Would they fall into the easy friendship and affection they'd enjoyed before? Or would it be awkward and strange? Perhaps it would be both.

CHAPTER TEN

Full Circle

2000, San Francisco, California

Julie got off the plane in San Francisco, more nervous than she'd imagined. As a grown woman, almost fifty-five years old, she should be calm. Even knowing it to be futile, she considered turning around and getting back on the plane.

So many years had passed since she'd been in this city. So many years since Paul knew her. She'd grown heavier, older, more settled, and less attractive than at age twenty-five. That's how nature worked, and Paul will have aged, too. They exchanged recent pictures. Still, she felt terrified he wouldn't like her any longer.

Recognizing someone she hadn't seen in years could be a tricky business, even if she knew them well. She formed an image of them in her mind, even if she'd seen recent photos. That person remained in her mind as they appeared years ago, young and vital, trapped in their younger self by memories. When they met again, older and gray, the two images merge. This new, older stranger melded with the younger memory, so they became one in her mind. Sometimes this was instant, and sometimes it took longer.

Paul invited her for a two-week visit, for his friend's wedding. This would give them time to explore their relationship again. Julie glanced around the crowded airport, with masses of people drifting in and out, swirling like eddies in a stream filled with rapids. She took a deep breath, forcing her legs to move towards the exit.

Would she recognize him from his photos? With growing anxiety, she scanned the faces of the people waiting in the arrivals area. Then she saw a stocky man with wispy, thin grayish hair, holding up a sign which said, "Julie." She remembered his warm, brown eyes that smiled, and they hadn't changed a bit.

Julie released her doubts like a balloon in the breeze.

She walked up to him, and he dropped the sign. They hugged hard, holding on for an eternity. She trembled in his arms, so he squeezed her tight, murmuring comforting sounds in her hair, smoothing it with one hand.

After eons, they parted, and she stared into his eyes. He grinned wide. Her own face ached as she mirrored his. Paul lifted her bag and offered an arm, as they walked out of the raucous lounge.

Amidst her dismay, Paul took her to see his room, in the basement of a friend's house. While they both owned the house, he took the basement as his living quarters, as he owned a smaller share. Joy and her daughter, Christine, lived upstairs. His housemates welcomed them both, embracing her with open arms and tears. Paul told them the story and happiness shone in their smiles. Joy was marrying her fiancé, Stephan, next week. Julie offered to help, so Joy put her to work making wedding favors and table decorations.

During the days, Paul took her sightseeing, to the Japanese gardens, to Muir Woods. Julie remembered her time there with George, smiling at the memory. That seemed so long ago, a lifetime away, during a more innocent, adventurous time. While raising Kirsten took a lot of work, at least she enjoyed life first.

The iconic city seemed so different from the sixties. The buildings, the people, the vibe, all felt as if her previous time had been in a dreamland, a place out of an almost-forgotten book of fairy tales from her childhood, a half-remembered dream. Haight Ashbury transformed into the prosaic. Gone were the twisted jellybean fonts. A few shops that catered to the memory of days past, but most became new, glitzy, with ethnic restaurants, and clothing shops.

Evenings, she spent with Paul, Joy, Christine, and sometimes Stephan. They seemed determined to show her every interesting restaurant in Alameda. Indian food, Chinese, Japanese, Thai, she might try a different curry every night and still never repeat a meal. Julie enjoyed the flavors, but couldn't handle very much spice, so Paul had made a game of trying to find dishes that didn't burn her mouth.

Julie worried about Paul expecting too much right away but he agreed they should move slowly. Nights, she slept on the couch.

They took their time rekindling their friendship, holding hands. He stole a few kisses lakeside at the Japanese Gardens.

Over the days, though, the two lovers rediscovered their affection for each other, and their passion. She'd dated no one since him, and everything felt clumsy. But, like riding a bicycle, one never lost the skill.

After an exotic meal of Ethiopian food downtown, the group returned home, retiring to the dining room for board games. They played Monopoly for two hours, until, one by one, each player trundled off to bed. Soon, only Paul and Julie remained awake. By mutual agreement, they headed down into Paul's basement.

Once inside the room, he put on slow music, something Celtic. Perhaps Clannad? It sounded ethereal and slow, rhythmic and primal. They danced close, as she closed her eyes, enjoying the shape of the music, of his warm, firm hand around her waist. They danced closer as he nuzzled her neck, making her shiver. Julie bent her neck, to give him more room. She didn't want him to stop.

Paul kissed her shoulder, down her arm to the inside of her elbow. They stopped dancing, but her eyes remained closed. She gasped at butterfly kisses on her skin, sensitive with the night and the music.

He pulled her wrist up, kissing the soft skin inside and her palm. She put her hand up to his face, caressing the rough stubble of his short beard, shot with bits of gray and white. She opened her eyes to look at the wiry hair, as she touched it, exploring it with her fingers, stroking along his chin line.

Paul caught up both her hands, placing them around his waist. He then stroked her hair, bending her head back for a long, lingering kiss. Did the music still play? Time came to a halt. She'd waited for this kiss most of her life. For thirty years.

Julie stopped thinking and enjoyed the kiss.

He led her to the bed, reveling that they could, at long last, enjoy their affections in a real bed, and not a Victorian bathtub.

Julie didn't relish this confrontation one bit, but she must do it. Torn between telling Sandy right away, like ripping off a Band-Aid, or trying to build up to it, she hesitated. Julie possessed no talent for the slow approach, while Sandy never pussy-footed around anything. Sandy would realize something felt wrong and draw it out of her. That would be worse. *Very well, time to dive in.*

They ate lunch in a tiny café they liked in South Miami, called Swensen's. While they served sandwiches and soups, their fame came from their ice cream, complex sundaes you created at the counter. Stained glass windows in art nouveau patterns, let the dappled light shine on booths made of wood and red leather.

Julie stared, glum, into her hot fudge sundae with strawberries, while Sandy devoured frozen yogurt with single-minded intent. Julie took a deep breath. Just one simple phrase. Sandy had enough intelligence to know the whys and wherefores.

"I'm moving to California next month."

Sandy froze. Then she stared at Julie for a long moment. The heat of her anger hit Julie like a firestorm. "You are a prime-A bitch, you know that? We said we'd grow old together, best friends forever, but as soon as that jerk waves his hand, you leave me here to die alone."

Julie's face grew hot. "Like you're full of sweet and innocence? When you stole Jeffrey?"

Sandy rolled her eyes. "Why do you bring that up every time we fight, Julie? That happened decades ago. He's long gone. Get over it."

Julie gritted her teeth. They ached from the cold ice cream. "You still betrayed me. Far worse than what I'm doing."

Her friend threw her spoon down on the marble-top table. It made a loud clatter, which got everyone listening to Sandy's tirade. "Well, fuck you very much, Julie. You go run after your little man. I'll be fine on my own."

Sandy grabbed her purse, stomping off, heeled boots thumping on the tile floor. Julie took a deep breath, but what else should she have done? Sandy would have raged regardless.

They *had* planned to grow old together. While Sandy dated many men, neither of them ever got serious about marriage. They'd lived together ever since they moved down from Michigan, over twenty years earlier. Sandy helped raise Kirsten, acting as the father figure. Her tough, stern demeanor and psychology degree had been a god send in the teenage years. Sandy had been a staunch friend and useful partner.

After all those years, Julie abandoned her friend. But then again, she should stop putting someone else's happiness above her own. Julie postponed her own happiness most of her life. She deserved her long-awaited reward. Still, she regretted Sandy's rejection. Julie hoped her best friend would forgive her someday, relent, and understand.

Paul had asked her to come live with him in California a couple weeks earlier, and she told him yes. He sold his stake in the house he shared with Joy to Stephan and bought a huge trailer outright.

Julie finished her sundae in miserable silence, climbing on her bike to go back home. She might as well pack. Sandy wouldn't make this easy.

September 2000, West Palm Beach, Florida

Kirsten fidgeted, picking at her cuticle. She'd created an image of her father, from his photos, but seeing him for the first time would be different.

Most of her life, her mental image of her father stayed blurry, nebulous, and shifting. Dark hair and eyes, with a nice singing voice, according to her mother, but nothing else. Her mother, despite being an artist, never described him well. Kirsten came across an old photo at one point, thinking it may have been her father. The photo showed a handsome man with dark eyes and a thick mop of dark hair, in a black turtleneck shirt, perhaps a formal high school photo. She held it in a special box where she kept keepsakes.

However, her mother found it, recognizing her old friend, George, from San Francisco. Not her father.

Her mother traveled to San Francisco a couple months earlier, to visit her father. That must have been awkward, but it worked out well. Now, her father came to Florida on a business trip, so they'd arranged a meeting, with several days in EPCOT and Disneyworld. Her parents (that sounded so strange to say!) drove up from Miami to meet Kirsten and her fiancé, Jason. They'd travel to Orlando from there.

A car drove by. *Is that them?* Kirsten rushed to the window, watched a blue car back up and pull in, hearing the whoosh of the tires on the gravel driveway. Her mother emerged from the passenger seat. Kirsten forced herself to look at the driver's side.

He seemed shorter than she'd imagined. Fathers should be tall. His thin, gray, wispy hair ruffled in the wind as he walked to the front door. His heavy belly stuck out under a T-shirt with a Hewlett Packard logo, the company he worked for. He placed a baseball cap on as he climbed the porch steps. Kirsten backed away from the window, not wishing them to see her watching. She positioned herself near the door, poised to open it.

The knock startled her, despite all her preparation. She flung open the door to see her father for the first time.

They both stared for several long moments. Then, he drew her in for a long, solid hug. The tears burned her face. Her mother's eyes echoed her own. Kirsten swallowed to keep down the sobs, then gave up. Her father did the same.

They broke the hug, staring at each other again. "Hello, my daughter. I am thrilled to meet finally you."

"I've waited my entire life to hear that." The tears didn't stop. They both hugged again, as Julie joined them.

October 2001, West Palm Beach, Florida

Julie wore a medieval-style dress she'd made, with dark, floral velvet, and gold lace trim. Paul wore a purple and gold tunic with a crown. He needed to play the king.

They drove to the Friends of the Police Hall in Palm Beach. They'd bedecked the place with strands of silk ivy, dark green tablecloths, and centerpieces with dried flowers in purples and greens. A lunch buffet sat along one wall, with an enormous cake shaped like a three-tiered castle in the middle.

Kirsten wore her dark purple wedding dress, with long, drooping sleeves and a train, with purple grape trim along the edges. Jason stood next to her, resplendent in a medieval shirt of velvet, forest green and purple.

Guests trickled in, all in medieval garb. Well, all except for Julie's dad. "I've got an excuse. I'm old and cranky and I need a walker."

Julie's mother, however, decked herself out in a long, flowing dress reminiscent of the Lady of Shalot. Even her brother, Larry, wore a tunic that looked too small for him, while his wife, Pat, looked sweet in a light purple and gold dress, sleeves hanging to the floor.

Jason's young niece, Nokomis, fluttered around in a fairy outfit, complete with wings, her long, blond hair floating as she bounced around from table to table.

They held the service outdoors, in the pine forest behind the hall, candles and glamorous costumes everywhere. The October day remained overcast, cool enough for comfort. Julie beamed with pride to see her precious daughter walking down the aisle with her father, the king giving away the princess.

Her hair darkened from her childhood blond, but the mousy brown hair turned flyaway and thin, like her father's. She dyed it red, which suited her freckles, another legacy from Paul. They seemed so alike, standing next to each other. Julie felt the prickle of tears behind her eyes, seeing her family together at long last. She dug into her purse for tissues.

The ceremony proceeded, with a few giggles and hiccups here and there. She held Paul's hand tight as her daughter said her vows. Did Kirsten wait so long to get married to find her father first? Thirty was old for a first marriage. But she only met Jason two years ago. Perhaps the timing just worked, so her father gave her away the year after she found him.

Julie wished Sandy were here. Her parting words that day had been prophetic. Sandy couldn't have known at the time that she'd get uterine cancer. Nor could Julie have ever predicted that Sandy would ignore the diagnosis, spend all her money, and die alone before Julie even got word. She bore the guilt across her shoulders for leaving her best friend, leaving her to die alone. Julie failed Sandy, like she'd failed Katy. Julie sniffled, thinking Katy would have loved this ceremony.

Could either of them see this? But Katy never knew Kirsten. She recognized flashes of her sister in her daughter now and then, a style of drawing, or a glance with her eyes, when her hair was red, like Katy's. As if her sister's ghost came and touched her daughter once in a while.

December 23, 2004, Las Vegas, Nevada

Kirsten and Jason rustled about the posh hotel room in Las Vegas, pulling on their costumes. Kirsten's

235

red velvet shirt looked a reasonable facsimile of a uniform when paired with black slacks. Jason borrowed his Starfleet uniform shirt from Paul. He even found Captain's pips to attach to the sleeves.

Someone knocked at the door. "Are you two ready? They'll start soon."

Kirsten's Uncle Larry came in, leaping around in his uniform like a gazelle. "Look at me. Beam me up, Scotty!"

With a grin, Kirsten said, "Almost. Give us a minute." Uncle Larry was Kirsten's favorite, the fun one, the silly man who always made her laugh. He and Jason got along well, too. They'd done their best to drink each other under the table at the rehearsal party the night before, almost succeeding. "We're about set. Are Mom and Dad downstairs already?"

"They're talking to the Admiral as we speak. Pat's already down there, but I don't think all of your dad's friends have arrived."

Kirsten took Jason's arm, motioning for Larry to lead the way. "Okay, let's do this." They rode down to the Hilton's lobby. Turning to the right, they found the entrance to the Star Trek Experience Exhibition. Props from all the various Star Trek series had been gathered in one place. A replica of the Enterprise hung above them at the entrance, with doorways and walls from the inside of the ship in its various incarnations. The place reminded Kirsten of a mix between Disney and NASA.

No one stood outside the entrance, much less her mom and dad or anyone she recognized. "Do we go in? Or is there a special entrance we go through? I remember a lot of other stuff before we arrived at the Bridge when we did the tour."

At that moment, a tall woman dressed like a Klingon came out. "What are you humans doing in here? You're supposed to be inside already." She waved a dismissive hand at an unmarked door along one wall.

Kirsten glanced at Larry and he shrugged. They all walked through.

They came into an empty, dark hallway, a door on the other end streaming with golden light. As they moved toward the light and entered, the Bridge of the Enterprise surrounded them. The Admiral stood in front, with her mother and father, in costume, chatting and laughing. They glanced up as Kirsten, Jason, and Larry came in.

The bridge had been set up for *Star Trek: The Next Generation*. Jason marched straight to Mr. Worf's station, posing for a photo at his hero's spot.

Kirsten looked at both of them, searching their eyes for nervousness. "Are you both ready for this, Mom? Dad?"

Her dad took her mom's hands, peered into her eyes, saying, "I've been ready for years."

Her mom nodded, eyes glistening with tears. Kirsten had never seen her mom this happy before. She blinked back her own tears, taking her place as Matron of Honor, by her mother's side on the Bridge.

As odd as the setting seemed, with a Klingon and a Ferengi as witness, on the Bridge of the Starship Enterprise, the ceremony remained short and sweet. The emotions and the history ran strong, though. Even Larry teared up, seeing his big sister wed at long last.

The party afterwards, at Quark's Bar and Grill, ran raucous and genial. Klingons came in, knocking people's water glasses over, while her dad corrected their Klingon grammar, him being fluent in the made-up language. Jason and Larry once again tried to out-drink each other, while Pat and Kirsten laughed at their attempts.

It had been an epic journey, but her mom finally got the man she loved, The One, so to speak. She'd needed to create her own detective to do the job, but it happened. Her mom looked ecstatic, but no longer scared, nervous, or worried.

Epilogue

The next year, Julie surveyed the mess of boxes in the garage, despairing that they'd ever work their way through them all.

When Kirsten and Jason looked for their first house in Gainesville, Paul suggested retiring from his job and moving to Gainesville, to get to know his daughter. Jason proposed they might buy a bigger house if they all moved in together. As noble a gesture as that was, they searched hard to find a house the right size. This one had four bedrooms, including a mother-in-law suite in the back, with its own bathroom and kitchenette. Kirsten and Jason would take the back, while Paul and Julie occupied the front "wing," leaving one guest room.

Julie hoped it would work, four powerful personalities thrown together. She remembered Jason, a chef, got proprietary about his kitchen. They needed to go through all these boxes. Paul lived his entire life as a packrat, a trait he'd passed onto his daughter. Julie and Jason had grown into being acquisitive.

She squinted at a dot-matrix printer on top of a box. Yes, a dot-matrix printer. They owned no computers capable of interfacing with it. But Paul saved it.

After sighing with long-suffering, she opened the next box, calling out to Paul. "This one is full of Star Trek Books."

"Put that in the attic. We'll go through all those later."

Much later.

∞∞∞

The life she covets is imprinted onto her psyche. The world she crafts holds mysteries beyond understanding.

Past Storm and Fire is a whirlwind of a time travel romance novel. If you like steamy passion, stunning twists, and lush historical backdrops, then you'll love Emeline Rhys's gale-force inferno.

Buy ***Past Storm and Fire*** to rewrite the follies of fate today!

www.GreenDragonArtist.com/Books

∞ ∞ ∞

Thank You!

Thank you so much for enjoying ***Better To Have Loved***. If you've enjoyed the story, please consider leaving a review to help others discover the love of Julie and Paul.

If you would like to get updates, sneak previews, sales, and FREE STUFF, please sign up for my newsletter.

www.greendragonartist.com

∞∞∞

Other Books by This Author

**See all the books available through
Green Dragon Publishing at
http://www.greendragonartist.com/books**

Read Now

Historical Note

Dear Readers:

 This was the first novel I ever wrote. It had been building and bubbling inside of me for years, and finally burst out after I'd written my first two books. They were travel guides, but I finally felt ready to tackle this project.

 I based this novel on my parents' genuine love story, and my journey in finding my father. It's a novelization of the true story of my parents; how they loved each other, lost each other, and then found each other after thirty years. It was serendipity that my parents fell back in love after my discovery.

 While the basic details are true, I had to make up a lot of individuals and scenes to flesh out the full story, as three to four decades is a long time to hold on to minute detailed memories. Oddly enough, some things I had made up and my mother, upon reading the manuscript, said they were truer than she had ever told me.

 A part of my life became complete when I found my father, a part I always knew, subconsciously, was missing. Only after I found him did I realize what a large hole he had left.

To anyone who has had a child, please do your best to be part of that child's life. Even if only a little. Allow your child to know you, the person you are, your faults and virtues. It helps the child map their own soul, and to see what parts they inherit from each parent. It is a kindness and a beautiful duty.

Some wouldn't consider this a 'historical' novel. However, it was set mostly in the 1960s, and this being the 2020s, that's vaguely historical.

In order to research the details, I had to do a deep dive into the operations of a certain very powerful church that I don't feel comfortable naming outright. Their world headquarters are now in Clearwater, Florida.

But at the time my parents were involved, the headquarters of this church called East Grinstead its home, and had taken over a huge manor house, Saint Hill Manor. A lot of the details I used were from searching the construction of the house, the floor plan, and the history. I even added details from a place called The Monkey Room in one of the scenes.

Edinburgh in the 1960s is very different from what it is now, according to my mother. A lot less tourist oriented, certainly! I made sure to include details I got straight from my mom, such as the underground club that was so hot and stifling, the Guy Fawkes Day bonfire, and the smell of Drambuie on the air.

Haight-Ashbury was another research rabbit hole, and I did my best to get the right bands, the right shops, the right mood throughout that whole section. Again, Mom filled in a lot of the general information, but I had to make up a lot of details because 40-year-old memories, especially during a time like the 60s, are definitely suspect.

Of course, the details on my genealogical research were easy. Not only was I the one who did that research, but the results were rather spectacular, so they stuck in my mind.

About the Author

Christy Nicholas writes under several pen names, including Rowan Dillon, CN Jackson, and Emeline Rhys. She's an author, artist,and accountant. After she failed to become an airline pilot, she quit her ceaseless pursuit of careers that began with the letter 'A' and decided to concentrate on her writing. Since she has Project Completion Compulsion, she is one of the few authors with no unfinished novels.

Christy has her hands in many crafts, including digital art, beaded jewelry, writing, and photography. In real life, she's a CPA, but having grown up with art all around her (her mother, grandmother, and great-grandmother are/were all artists), it sort of infected her, as it were.

She wants to expose the incredible beauty in this world, hidden beneath the everyday grime of familiarity and habit, and share it with others. She uses characters out of time and places infused with magic and myth, writing magical realism stories in both historical fantasy and time travel flavors.

Combine this love of beauty with a bit of financial sense and you get an art business. She does local art and craft shows, as well as sending her art to various science fiction conventions throughout the country and abroad.

Social Media Links:
Blog: www.GreenDragonArtist.net
Website: www.GreenDragonArtist.com

Facebook: www.facebook.com/greendragonauthor
Instagram: www.instagram.com/greendragonartist9
TikTok: www.tiktok.com/@greendragonauthor